Tempting THE BIKER

ROYAL BASTARDS MC

20 19

CHARLESTON, WV

GLENNA MAYNARD

Tempting The Biker Glenna Maynard © 2020 all rights reserved

ISBN: 9798690497880

Dedication

To second chances and a love that never dies.

ROYAL BASTARDS CODE

PROTECT: The club and your brothers come before anything else and must be protected at all costs. CLUB is FAMILY.

RESPECT: Earn it & Give it. Respect club law. Respect the patch. Respect your brothers. Disrespect a member and there will be hell to pay.

HONOR: Being patched in is an honor, not a right. Your colors are sacred, not to be left alone, and NEVER let them touch the ground.

OL' LADIES: Never disrespect a member's or brother's Ol'Lady. PERIOD.

CHURCH is MANDATORY.

LOYALTY: Takes precedence over all, including well-being.

HONESTY: Never LIE, CHEAT, or STEAL from another member or the club.

TERRITORY: You are to respect your brother's property and follow their Chapter's club rules.

TRUST: Years to earn it...seconds to lose it.

NEVER RIDE OFF: Brothers do not abandon their family.

Tempting The Biker

He's married and twice my age, but I can't walk away.

Murder-

We were never supposed to happen. Alexa's my daughter's best friend. I'm a married man. I'm too old for her, but stolen glances turn into more than either of us are prepared for. I've made promises I can't keep. I'm the Prez of Royal Bastards MC. I'm not supposed to be tempted by her innocence. My head swears that I don't love her, but my heart won't let go.

Alexa-

Murder's married. Off Limits. But I want him. He's a powerful man. Untouchable and unbreakable. I'll be his dirty little secret. No one has to know. We're playing a dangerous game. A deadly one that will leave me with a broken heart or worse, but I'll do anything to prove to him that what we share is a ride or die love. And for Murder, I'm willing to risk it all.

Tempting The Biker is part of the Royal Bastards MC world.

Recommended reading order for best enjoyment within the Charleston, WV Chapter:

The Biker's Kiss

Lady & The Biker

Tempting The Biker

Dear Reader,

For best reading enjoyment it is recommended that you read Lady & The Biker prior to starting Tempting The Biker.

Enjoy the ride.

Glenna

Part One

Chapter One

MURDER

The Past

"I knew it. I knew you were cheating on me," Ruthie screeches at me for the millionth time.

I toss my hands up. "I'm done fuckin' arguin' with you. I've never stepped out on you but right now you make me wish I'd fucked every whore from West Virginia to California I've ever come into contact with. God damn."

"I want you out of my house. Just pack your shit and go." Her hand flies toward my face, but I grab her wrist before she makes contact. Ruthie draws her arm back, glaring at me. "I hate you."

I snort and stroke my beard. "You get the fuck gone if you don't want to be around me. This is my house. I pay the bills." I take another hard pull of my bottle of

Budweiser and drop onto the couch. I'm sick and tired of her shit. All the damn time she's flapping her jaws to bitch at me. I'm over it. I don't need it.

Her hand moves to her hip. "Why, so you can bring your whores here and fuck them in my bed too? You'd like that."

"You fucking caught me."

"I'll leave, James, and I'll never come back."

I shake my head. "Then what the fuck you still standing here for?"

"I hate you. I wish you'd die." her chest heaves as she stomps down the hall toward the master bedroom.

"Join the damn club. No one fuckin' likes me," I call out as the bedroom door slams shut. Closing my eyes, I scrub a palm over my face. Fuck me. If I'd known now what I knew when I was just a damn kid, I'd never stuck my dick in Ruthie Gibson. Was fifteen years old when I knocked the cunt up. When I drop my hand, Rochelle is standing in front of me with a hand on her hip mimicking her mother. "What?" I bark, and she flinches staring back at me with her big brown eyes, bottom lip jutting out trembling on the verge of tears.

"Mom said for me to pack a bag. That we're going to Nan's for the weekend."

"What of it?"

"I don't want to go with her. I want to stay home. I hate going there. It smells like muscle rub and peppermints. Nan is mean and hateful. She isn't like my Gigi." Nan is Ruthie's grandmother. Gigi is her mother, but Nan practically raised her.

"Mind your mother. You know how she gets when I come back from a run. She'll cool her shit, and by next week she'll be back to herself. You'll see."

"I guess, but—"

"No but. Just pack light and go on. Nan is old and set in her ways, but the crazy old bat means well enough."

"Dad," she whines, stomping a foot. "I have plans."

"Yeah well now you have new ones. Don't give me no attitude. Listen to your mother."

"Whatever." she huffs, flipping her dark brown hair over her shoulder. Kid is the only thing good that ever came out of my marrying Ruthie. But fuck she acts fifteen going on twenty. Hard to believe she's the same age her mother and I were when Ruthie told me she was pregnant.

Ruthie comes out of the bedroom with a suitcase in one hand, keys to her car in the other. She pulls this shit every damn time I've gone on the road. "Fuck you,

James," she spits her venom at me on her way to the front door.

"Don't let the door hit you where the good lord split you," I mutter.

"Bye, Daddy."

"Be good, kid. See you next week."

Rochelle gives me a weak smile and follows her cunt mother out the door. I don't relax until I hear the car back out the driveway and the tires squeal as Ruthie peels out in her red Corvette. She always has driven the damn thing too fuckin' fast.

I glance at the clock. Not even seven. I should grab a shower and head to the clubhouse. Only came home to see Rochelle anyway, and she ain't gonna be here. Not that she wants to hang with me much these days. Being a teenager means her life revolves around school, her friends, and boys. She's too cool for her old man.

A car door slams, and I get up off the couch. Ruthie must've forgot something or came back to yell some more. My head is pounding after all her damn screeching. A fist raps against the front door. I swing the door open and find Alexa, one of my kid's friends in tears as a car speeds away.

"Where's, Ro?" she peers up at me, another tear sliding down her cheek as she hiccups.

"Gone." I go to shut the door. I'm not in the mood to deal with her problems on top of mine, but she shoves past me with her black nylon sports bag slung over her shoulder.

"Well, I'll just wait for her then." She starts down the hall toward Rochelle's room. Her cheerleading skirt swishing as her hips sway, showing hints of her ass cheeks. Fucking hell. The sight is one that's etched into my brain. Alexa loves skirts that show her ass, and I'm a filthy bastard who loves getting his eyes full of the sinful sight.

"Not gonna happen. She's gone to her Nan's for the weekend or longer. Go call your mom to come pick you up."

"I can't. They aren't home. Todd dropped me here. Ro said I could stay over. Ruthie said it was okay."

"Like I said, Alexa, Rochelle isn't home and won't be. You can't stay. Wouldn't be right."

"You won't even know I'm here. I swear it. Please. I don't have anywhere else." She wipes at her cheek with the sleeve of her hoodie.

"Call whoever in the fuck Todd is then."

5

"He dumped me." Alexa sniffles.

"Hell, stop your crying."

"You don't even know what kind of day I've had. My mom threatened to throw me out because she found an ounce of weed in my room, but it wasn't mine. It was Todd's. Mom flushed it and he got mad at me. Said he still owed money for it."

"I'll take you to another friend."

"I don't have anyone but Ro."

I scrub a palm along my jaw. "Fine. But not a peep. You don't have anyone over. I'm going out for the night. I'll order you a pizza before I go and leave money on the counter for you. No boys. No dumb shit."

"Thank you, Mr.—"

"None of that Mr. shit. Told you before to call me James."

"James." She smiles, throwing her arms around my neck, squishing her tits against my arm. Her soft pink lips meet my cheek, and I pull back.

"Whatever." I shove her away and go to grab that shower. I feel weird having Alexa here with Ruthie and Rochelle gone. Makes me feel dirty as fuck. Alexa doesn't look like no damn high school girl. She's a few years older than Rochelle and I told my wife letting them be friends was a bad idea. Older friends means older boys. But they cheer together and are always attached at the damn hip.

Alexa is one of them girls you know is pure trouble just by looking at her. Big tits, thick hips, and ass for days. Long blonde hair, pretty green eyes. The kind of girl who'd get a man thrown in jail if he wasn't careful. I know I shouldn't look at her the way I do. I know it and she knows it. She loves the attention and I'm sorry enough of a bastard to give it to her.

Alexa's daddy never took her over his knee and busted her ass for misbehaving. Maybe if he had she wouldn't constantly be in trouble. I keep tabs on her because her and Rochelle are close. Can't have her dragging my kid into her shit. Alexa hangs with a bad crowd. Shit for brains like Todd who hand their weed off to a teenager to keep from getting caught with it.

Stripping down I get in the shower, trying to erase the past hour. Trying to drown out the sound of Ruthie nagging in my ear. Trying to forget that my cock twitched at the sight of Alexa's ass cheeks under that skirt.

I've always been faithful since I put a ring on Ruthie's finger. I made a promise to her old man that I'd do right by her. Keith "Lion" Gibson is a mean ass prick.

He'd rather put a bullet between your eyes than deal with any bullshit. I know better than to wet my dick anywhere but between his daughter's thighs and he made damn sure everyone else knows it too. I put up with the asshole and pray for the day he takes his dying breaths. Even now I still remember him rolling up my parents' driveway when he found out I'd knocked up his youngest daughter. Nearly pissed my pants.

He didn't knock. A man like him doesn't. Barged right in and stuck the barrel of his handgun between my eyes and dared me to breathe.

I shake off the memory and scrub my body. Scrubbing away everything but my memory of the first time I saw Alexa.

She wore a red bikini, running through the sprinklers of my front yard. I rolled up on my dark cherry Road King. Her gaze met mine, soft pink lips tipping into a big smile, flashing her pearly whites at me as she pranced around barefoot. Thrusting a dandelion toward me dusted with gold glitter she said, "Make a wish." I closed my eyes and wished for strength because I knew somehow the devil had sent her to tempt me.

I step out the shower and towel off quickly, needing out of this house. Needing far away from her.

Music belts from somewhere in the house. I shake my head and snag a t-shirt off the hanger and grab a clean pair of jeans off the top of the laundry basket at the foot of the bed.

I get dressed and walk toward the living room fingering through my wallet for pizza money. The smell of weed permeates the house. I follow the scent to the kitchen and find Alexa perched on the counter, bobbing her head, joint snug between her fingers as she takes a hit.

Stepping between her legs, I snatch the doobie from her and put it out in the ashtray sitting next to her ass. "The fuck you doing?"

"What's it look like?" She smirks her tempting lips at me, flipping her long blonde hair over her shoulder. "It's been a shitty day, Murder." Her brow arches as her finger rubs over the patch on my cut.

Knocking her hand away, I take a step back.

"Why do they call you Murder anyway? You kill someone?"

"None of your fuckin' business."

"Don't be a party pooper." Her smile droops into a frown. Her eyes glazed.

"Don't test my limits, pretty girl. I'll do what your daddy never did and bend you over my knee. Bust that ass till it's glowing red." The thought of it makes me hard, and I know I need to put some distance between us. Shit ain't right. The thoughts I have about Alexa aren't fatherly.

Alexa slides off the counter, stepping into my personal space. "You gonna use your hand or that big wooden spoon hanging on the wall over there." She nods to the decorative giant wooden spoon and fork Ruthie hung up over the sink.

I breathe in and out. Her sassy assed mouth makes my blood boil. "Mess with me and I'll shove it right up your ass," I growl. Alexa loves to push my buttons. Testing the limits of how far I'll let these games she plays go.

Her face colors crimson. Licking her lips, she cocks her head sideways. "At least get me good and wet first."

Steam nearly blows out my ears. "Shut that filthy mouth before I stick a bar of soap in it."

"You're no fun."

"I mean it. Behave." I slap a couple twenties in her palm. "Order a pizza. Keep the doors locked. I'll have eyes on the house," I warn. "Don't be bringing any of them fuckboys around here."

"Yes, Daddy," she mocks. "I'll be a good girl."

"If I were your daddy you wouldn't be pressing my buttons. You sure as fuck wouldn't be staying over at an outlaw's house."

"Pity. I was looking forward to you taking me over your knee."

My cock twitches again at the thought, pressing against the seam of my zipper. "Order the pizza for fuck's sake and put on some clothes. Try to stay out of trouble." I stomp through the door that leads into the garage. Climbing on my bike, I back down the driveway and roar off toward The Devil's Playground, my clubhouse.

**

"What are you doing here?" Nickel, the club VP, squeezes his whore's tit and bites her neck. She squirms in his lap.

I take up the empty seat at his table and nod to the prospect behind the bar to get me a beer. "Banks around?"

"Cleaning the shitters."

I shake my head. "What did he fuck up now?"

"Nothing. Bathroom is just nasty as fuck."

"Where's Lion?"

"Prez took off about an hour ago mad as hell about something. What's up with you?"

Shit. I hope Ruthie didn't go flapping her damn jaws again.

"Same shit different day."

"Ruthie," he mutters with a shake of his head.

It's always fucking Ruthie. "You." I look to the whore.

"Yeah." She leans forward, titty hanging out the top of her tank top. Mascara smudged under her blue eyes. Diamond pendant dangling around her neck.

"Go take over for Banks. Tell him Murder wants to see him."

"Wh-what? You want me to clean the bathrooms? I could you know…" she makes the motion of jerking her arm up and down with her fist clenched, pressing her tongue against her cheek.

"If I wanted my dick sucked, you'd already be on your fuckin' knees. Bathrooms now," I bark, slapping my palm against the table and the bitch visibly jerks.

Her gaze flicks to Nickel.

"You heard the man." He pushes her up from his lap.

The dumb cunt moves off toward the bathrooms. Someone slides my bottle of Bud in front of me.

I snort. "Where'd you find that one?"

"Poker game." He grins slicking his dark hair back into a ponytail.

"Fuck. I think you were cheated."

"Nah. Her daddy's big money. Fancy plastic surgeon or some shit."

"You getting your pecker enlarged?" I chuckle.

"Fuck you. My dick's plenty big enough. Just ask your Old Lady."

"Watch it." I take a hard drink of my beer. "On second thought, you want her? Bout' sick of her shit."

"Trouble in paradise?"

"More like the pits of hell. Started her same shit again. Took Ro to her Nan's for the weekend."

"She'll be back in a day or two. I don't know how you do it, man. One bitch since fuckin' high school. You know any woman in here would be happy to oblige. Most of them take offense you won't take them to your bed."

"Shit. Ruthie's got eyes and ears all over. One wrong step and she'd take Rochelle and turn her further against me."

"You're fuckin' paranoid. What she got on you anyway?"

"Now why would I tell you? Then you'd want something too." Her father's our club Prez that's what she

13

has over me. Nickel knows that but he won't say shit all against Lion. Not to mention the secret we share. The one the cunt likes to hold over my head and keep me in line.

"Well fuck you too, brother." He flips me off.

"You wanted to see me?" Banks pulls up a chair, flipping it backwards before taking a seat.

"Yeah. Need your eyes on my house. You see any cars that shouldn't be there, or any foot traffic let me know. Got a houseguest."

"On it." he jumps up.

"And Banks."

"Yeah?"

"Don't go in the house, just call me if there's anything to report."

"Will do, Murder." He struts out the door. Fucker better not go near Alexa.

"Who you got at the house?"

"Ro's friend showed up. Folks kicked her out."

"You expectin' trouble?"

"Nothing I can't handle."

"It ain't that pretty blonde with the big tits is it?"

"What would you know about Ro's friends?"

"Shit. I got eyes, man. Better lock Rochelle up soon. Won't be long before brothers start lookin' at her too."

"Not if they want to keep their eyes."

"I hear you. But is it the blonde?"

"You're a real sick bastard. You know that."

"Hell. Don't even try to tell me you ain't looked at her and thought about it even for a second."

I shake my head and finish my beer, signaling for another.

"You have." Nickel punches me.

I stay quiet because we both know he's right. *Asshole.*

"You sure Banks is the guy you want to put on her?"

"Something I should know about him?"

"Just saying if I had a pretty little thing like that at my place all alone for the weekend, I wouldn't be here. I'm sure Banks will keep it in his pants."

"Fuck."

I pull my cell out and dial Banks. "Never mind, man. False alarm."

The jukebox starts up and one of the hangarounds gets on the pole. Her tight body gyrating against the cool metal. Myla is gorgeous like an exotic flower in her bright orange bikini glowing against her tan skin.

15

"Hey, Murder," a voice like velvet purrs in my ear, as a beer appears in my hand. I look up and see Kristen, another muffler bunny.

"Thanks, darlin'."

"Anything for you, handsome." Her fingers caress mine.

"Fuck off with that shit. You know better," I grit.

"I just…you look tense."

"She ain't wrong," Nickel tacks on.

I rub the back of my neck feeling another headache coming on. Fuckin' Ruthie. Shit is her fault. If she didn't give me Rochelle, I'd killed her ass years ago.

Patting my pockets, I pull out the joint I confiscated from Alexa and Nickel gives me a light.

I sit back and smoke my joint, drinking my beer, watching the girls on stage but only thing on my mind is Alexa in that damn cheerleader uniform. Fuck me. I'm fucking fucked in the head. I must be crazy, and sex deprived. I keep telling myself to make things work with Ruthie and I've tried. I've given her and Rochelle everything they ever wanted since I got out of prison.

How is it I'm on the outside and still feel locked up. Gave everything to this club. Gave up my daughter for seven years. Went in when she was five. Got out when she was twelve. Came home to a wife who hated me and a kid who didn't know me.

Been trying since the day I was released to make it up to them. Both of them, but no matter what I do, I make shit worse.

Chapter Two

I'm dancing around the living room waiting on my pizza to arrive. *Sweet Emotion* by *Aerosmith*, belts through the speaker. It feels weird being at Rochelle's with everyone gone but there's no way in hell I was staying home with my bitch of a mom in that prison. I can't breathe in that house. My parents expect perfection. Not a hair out of place. Everything neat and perfect. My father is a psycho who thinks allowing me to use a tampon makes me a whore. If I stayed there another second, I'd suffocate.

I take another drink of my hotter than piss beer. I hate the stuff but right now I need an escape from my shitty life crushing me down. Rochelle has no idea how lucky she has it. Her parents are cool as hell. Her mom is a bit uptight but still she's cooler than mine. Her father is a different story. I don't know how I feel about him, but sometimes I think I catch him looking at me. Not in a creepy way. The man is way hot. He doesn't even look old enough to be her dad, but he was like sixteen or something when she was born.

Headlights flash through the living room window. I go to the kitchen and grab the money James gave me. I'm freaking starving. I've not ate since dinner yesterday. I was five minutes late to breakfast this morning and my father refused me my plate. Said I should be on time if I want to eat and dared my mom to give me any lunch money. I was too embarrassed to ask my friends if they could loan me five bucks. I lied and said I was on a new diet. I know Ro would have gave it to me no questions asked, but we don't have the same lunch period because I'm two grades above her. Flicking the porch light on I open the front door.

"You here alone?" Todd mumbles like he has rocks in his mouth, sweeping his hair back from his forehead, revealing his busted-up face.

"Jesus. What happened?"

"Fuckin' told you I needed that weed. This is all your fault, cunt." He shoves me and kicks the door shut as he enters the house.

"I'll get you your money. I promise. I'll make it up to you. I'm sorry. Okay?"

"You'll do more than that." His fingers dig into my arm.

"Stop. You're hurting me."

Todd laughs. "Hurting you? Look at my face," he snarls, bloody spit flying at me.

"Do you want some ice?" I try to jerk out of his hold, but this only serves to piss him off. His hand flies back. *Thwack.* His palm connects with my cheek. I bite my tongue as my skin burns and stings from the slap. "Please, Todd. I swear. I'll make it up to you."

His fist connects with my eye and I scream. "You can start now." His hand slides up my arm, squeezing my shoulder, and pressing me to my knees so that I'm kneeling at his feet.

I swallow the bile that creeps up the back of my throat. My stomach clenches and I grind my teeth. Jerking his belt, he undoes the button and zipper of his dark blue jeans. Tears gather in the creases of my eyes as he looms over me. Todd's always been a bit of a dickhead, but I never expected this from him. Grabbing me by the back of my hair, he yanks hard, forcing me to glance up at him.

21

Lips puffy, eyes swollen and bruises forming, Todd glares at me as though he wishes I were dead.

"Always a cock tease. Not anymore. Tonight you're gonna pay up."

"No. Please don't. I'll get you the money."

"Shut up, bitch," he growls in my face and knocks me on my ass. I roll to my stomach and try to crawl toward the kitchen. There's a set of butcher knives on the counter if I could get to them, I'd stab his eyes out and cut off his dick. Todd grabs hold of my hips and drags me across the carpet, the friction rubbing the exposed skin of my belly. Jerking the bottoms of my uniform down he bears down on me, his weight pinning me in place.

I choke out a sob. "Oh, God. Please no." I feel the heat of his skin poking against my back side. "Stop it, Todd. You don't want to do this. Not like this." Fear bubbles in my chest as he continues to ignore me, forcing me to spread my legs for him.

"Shut up. You've been teasing my cock for months, you fuckin' slut. Tonight you're gonna give me what I've been waiting for. You owe me."

Trembling beneath him I stare at the end table next to the couch. Beside the lamp is a picture of Rochelle's dad and her mom in a pretty white frame. It's

22

their wedding day. Both baby faced and not much older than I am now. James wearing this beautiful smile on his face and probably one of the only times the man has been in a suit. He's holding Rochelle on his hip. I imagine him gazing at me like that. Full of love, adoration, and hope for a brighter tomorrow.

As Todd's body slams against mine, I pretend I'm in that photo in place of Ruthie, and I get lost in the fantasy. Pretending I'm somewhere else. That I'm someone else with each brutal thrust as my stomach slides over the carpet. "That's it. Take it, you whore." The heat of his breath fans along my neck. Bile churns, in the pit of my belly, clawing its way up my throat.

Todd bites and nips at me like a savage animal. His teeth digging deep enough to draw blood.

I hear the front door open and pray its Murder.

"What do we have here?" A gritty voice growls.

I hear the bones in Todd's nose crunch, and he cries out.

I try to see who my savior is, but one eye is swollen, and my vision is hazy. "This the little bitch who got off with the product?"

"You broke my nose," Todd whines.

"Make yourself useful and tie her up."

I try to crawl away from them but it's no use. I'm no match for the two of them.

Chapter Three

MURDER

Two Weeks Later

"What are you looking at?" I step up behind Grudge who is staring hard at the gate to our compound. The Devil's Playground.

"That's the third time she's walked past the gate in the last ten minutes."

I move to stand next to him to see who *she* is.

One look at her blonde braids and the way her skirt swishes when she walks, hinting at the curve of her ass cheeks, and I know exactly who she is. Alexa. My daughter Rochelle's friend. "I got this."

"You know her?"

"Yup." I leave off the unfortunately. Fucking Alexa showed up at house two weeks ago in need of a place to stay and then she vanished. No one has seen her since. Her folks and the police been leaning on me for information, but I didn't know what the fuck to tell them. I pointed them in the direction of that stupid fuck she was dating. Little prick Todd but he's been missing too. I figured she skipped town with him.

"Looks like jailbait, brother."

"She is." I climb on my motorcycle wondering why she's wearing her cheerleading uniform still and Grudge opens the gate. I roar onto the main road and her red and black skirt flies up exposing her black lace thong and tanned ass cheeks. *Jesus*. I look away. I idle and wait for her to approach me. When I see her face, my blood runs cold. "What the fuck happened?" I glare at the black and blue bruise circling her left eye.

Alexa wraps her arms around her middle and shakes her head. "Nothing. I just…I don't want to be alone…I'm sorry. I shouldn't have come here." Her pearly whites graze her plump cherry stained lips. Her thick black lashes flutter as she blinks away her tears. She swipes them away quickly, sniffling. "I should go. I'm not your problem."

"Well you've made it mine by showing up here," I snarl at her. "Who gave you the shiner? You didn't have that shit las time I saw you."

"It's fine. I'll be fine."

26

"Asked you a question. I expect an answer."

"I'm sorry. I wasn't thinking. Just don't ask me any questions. Please."

"Get on."

"Umm."

"Now," I bark, and she startles, but climbs on. Her arms go around my middle, holding on for dear life. Her tits smash against my back, and I speed away hoping no one other than Grudge saw me putting another woman on the back of my Road King who isn't my wife. Politics within our club are fragile. Shit is split down the middle. I don't need any trouble with Lion right now.

As they say between the legs is between the legs and the only bitch who rides bitch should be your Old Lady, but this is an emergency.

Banks better not have had shit all to do with this. I'll deal with him later. Right now, finding out what in the hell happened to Alexa is my priority. She was under my roof when she disappeared. *Motherfucker*.

I drive to a safehouse the club owns but rarely uses. Alexa can sleep here for the night, and I can get her story before I turn her back over to her folks. I cut my bike off and Alexa climbs off. I push the kickstand down and lead her to the porch.

27

The spare key is in the black metal letterbox that hangs next to the front door. "Shouldn't be anyone here," I tell her as I unlock it. I flick the light switch just inside the door, but nothing happens. Shit. Bulb must've blown. The house is in a bad neighborhood, but everyone knows it belongs to the club, so no one bothers it.

Alexa stays close to my side, pressing into me, a hand wrapped around the sleeve of my leather jacket. Guiding her further into the house, I kick some empty beer bottles out the way and find the switch to the kitchen light. Luckily, it still works.

"What is this place?" Her gaze moves around the bare room. There's the usual appliances and a small table with one chair. The others are stacked in the corner, broken.

"Safehouse. You should be fine for the night. There's a bed or a couch. You got a way to get home in the morning?"

Her right shoulder lifts slightly. "Don't worry about me. No one else does."

I wince at her words. Someone should give a damn about her, but it can't be me. I've got enough on my plate.

"Where the fuck you been the past two weeks?"

"I don't want to talk about it. Please don't make me."

"Police been breathing down my neck for two weeks sticking their noses in my business. I need to know where the fuck you were. Don't pull no shit with me. Rochelle thinks you're dead. Hell, your folks too. Do you have any idea how worried sick we've all been?"

"You were worried about me?"

"You ready to tell me where you were?"

"I can't. I need time to think of what to say to my parents. You don't understand. If I talk, I'm dead."

"Right. Sure." I call bullshit." Bet she went off with that fucker and he beat her. She's trying to protect him. If she wants to go down that road its none of my business. "If you need a ride home, I can swing by in the morning. No big deal." *Fuck*. What am I doing? I shouldn't have even brought her here.

"Okay. Thanks." She shoots me a smile so big and bright that the hell I catch might be worth it.

"You need anything before I go?"

Alexa chews on her thumbnail. "Don't guess so. But could you stay until I fall asleep?"

"No can do. Got my own shit to deal with."

"Your wife?" she quirks a brow at me.

I grunt in response. What the hell would she know about my wife?

29

"It's just Ro told me her mom is kind of a bitch and that you guys fight a lot."

"Rochelle should keep her mouth shut."

"Calm down. Don't be hard on her. She worries about you. Says you deserve better. Says you and her mom are all wrong for each other." Her gaze catches mine. Pretty green eyes sparkling with something I can't get a read on. But one thing I do know is I need to get on home. And yet my feet stay planted where they are. "So, do you…" Alexa opens the fridge, peering inside.

"Do I what?"

She smirks over her shoulder. "Deserve better?" Closing the fridge, she holds up two bottles of Budweiser.

"Not discussing my marriage with you." I accept one of the bottles. I shouldn't let her have the other but fuck if she doesn't look like she couldn't use an escape. I know all about that. "I don't think I should need to say this, but you don't tell Rochelle shit all about your ridin' on my bike or me bringing you here tonight. Or anyone for that matter. You need to get your story straight whatever the fuck it is before you go home."

Alexa pops the cap off the bottle on the edge of the counter. The cap clinks on the dirty floor. "I can keep a secret."

I touch the puffy knot on the side of her temple. "I don't doubt that, sweetheart, but still I need your word."

Her lips wrap around the bottle, those green eyes burning through me as she takes a hard pull. "You can count on me. Don't worry."

"Right." I grab her beer. "That's enough. Take your ass to bed. I'll sleep on the couch." I know the last thing I should do is stay, but I'm afraid if I leave, she'll disappear again.

"Thanks, Murder."

"Yeah. Yeah. First door to the left down the hall. It's not the Ritz but it'll do for the night." I don't wait for a response. I find my way to the old worn-down couch and collapse with both beers after shedding my jacket. I bring the one Alexa was drinking to my lips, tasting her cherry lip gloss. Fucking sweet and pure trouble.

I hear the bedroom door close, and I let out a sigh. I should drive home and send a prospect for her in the morning, but if anything else happened to her, I'd feel responsible. She's not my responsibility but for some damn reason I can't walk away. If it were Rochelle, I'd want someone to look out for her. That's the excuse I tell myself, but I know it's a lie.

31

I pull out my cell and try Banks. If he had something to do with this, I'll rip him a new asshole. Fucker sends me to voicemail.

**

"No. Stop. Don't," pleas from down the hall awaken me. Rolling off the couch I hear a whimper and more begging. I shake off the grogginess of being asleep and shuffle toward the bedroom I put Alexa up in for the night. She must be having a nightmare. No one else is here.

I would have heard someone come in. I'm quiet as I open the door being careful not to scare her. The light is still on and the image before me nearly cuts a hard ass like me in two. Alexa is curled up under the bed in a protective ball sobbing. Fuck me what the hell happened to her? I drop to my knees and gently tap her arm. "Alexa?"

Her whole body trembles as another moan wracks through her small frame.

"Pretty girl, talk to me." I tug on her wrist and attempt to bring her out from under the bed.

"No one would believe me." She wipes her nose, smearing snot across her cheek.

Fucking hell.

I pull a bandanna I sometimes use when ridin' from my back pocket and hand it to her once she's sitting up with her back against the bed. "Try me," I press, though I shouldn't give a damn what's going on with her. She's not my problem.

But in a sense, she is because whatever went down happened when she was supposed to be under my roof. Guilt is eating at my insides. I don't like it.

"Who hurt you?"

Alexa stays quiet, other than a small hiccup as she sniffles.

I move to Alexa's left and put an arm around her, hugging her to me. Wishing I could shield this troubled girl from the pain tearing her apart right now.

She's fucking broken. I search her lost eyes missing the spark that's usually burning so damn bright it'd set the world on fire.

"You gotta promise you won't tell."

"You have my word. Whatever you say in this room…it's just you and me."

"Todd came back the other night to your house. I—I thought it was the pizza, so I didn't look. I opened the door and he barged in."

"He hit you?"

One nod. Her bottom lip trembles. More tears fall.

I grip her knee, my knuckles turning white. I'll kill that little prick.

"He do anything else?"

Turning away from me she cries harder.

I grab her by the chin with more force than I mean to and jerk her face to mine. "He rape you?"

Alexa stares at me for seems like forever, and I wait for her to give me the words.

"What will you do if I say yes?"

"I think you know what the fuck I'm gonna do. Don't fucking protect that piece of shit. You let me worry about it."

Another nod.

"Need you to be honest with me. This isn't something to fuck around about."

Alexa stands up. I don't know what she's doing, but I sense she needs me to stay put so I don't make any sudden movements. With her back to me she lets those braids out and lifts the cheer top over her head.

"Lex…" I start but she turns to face me as she arranges her wavy blonde locks over her breasts.

Fucking scrapes, bruises, and bite marks stain her skin like a painting. My veins burn, and I taste the rage bubbling within on my tongue. When she drops her skirt, I have to look away. Fingerprints bruise her inner thighs.

My face is the last thing he'll see before he leaves this world.

I stand up and wrap my arms around her, pulling her into me. I kiss the top of her forehead. "He'll pay. I swear to you I'll send him straight to hell."

Alexa swallows hard. "Make it painful."

"Promise you, pretty girl."

I'll make this right for her. Letting Alexa go, I place my cut on the bed and remove my tee then hand it over to her. "Put this on."

Alexa doesn't move so I shrug the shirt over her head and push her arms through the sleeves. Flashes of her bruises and scars paint my mind red. I'm going to drain that fucker. I'm gonna watch him bleed out in a slow and painful death.

"You need to get some sleep."

I've got a body to collect.

My cell phone vibrates, and I grab my cut off the bed. Fuck. It's the ball and chain.

Ruthie's gonna pitch a bitch fit if she finds out I spent the night with Alexa. You'd think she'd be used to this shit by now—club business but it never fails. Woman nags over anything and everything.

Ruthie: *I'm home and what a surprise you aren't. Don't bother to come home.*

I can't catch a motherfuckin' break.

James: *Don't start your shit.*

I shove my phone in my back pocket. "Was he the only one?"

Alexa hugs her arms to her stomach and shakes her head.

"Who else?"

"If I tell you I'm dead."

I get a sinking feeling I know exactly who the other one was.

"They keep you this whole time?"

She shakes her head. "After...I was kept in a dark room...I'm not sure how long I was there."

"Do you know where it was?"

"No. I woke up this morning at the park near my house. I didn't want to go home, but I didn't know where else to go so I came to the club and waited for you."

Chapter Four

"No one is gonna hurt you. Not on my watch. Never again."

I sit on the edge of the worn bed and suck in a breath, the scent of his earthy cologne hits my nose. James's words sound pretty but all they are is a beautiful lie. "You can't promise me something you can't guarantee. I was raped in your house. And it's not your fault it's mine."

Going to his knees, he kneels before me. "Lex, sweetheart. It's not your fault. Don't you dare fucking blame yourself for what happened to you. I said I'm gonna handle it."

I nod. I don't have the strength to argue with him. I wish I could believe him, but I played with fire and I got burned. I paid the price for being stupid. One mistake. One loser. Now look at me. "I actually thought Todd liked me at first. That he was gonna save me from the prison I live in at home."

"Are things really that bad at home with your folks?"

"You have no idea. I'd rather live in a box than go back there. What do you think my father will do if he finds out his perfect little angel went and got herself raped by not one but two drug dealing losers? He'll never let me back home. I might as well jump off a bridge. My life is over now. I fucked everything up. I ruin everything. Everyone thinks I have it all. I'm popular at school. I make good grades. But no matter what I do I'm never good enough for my parents. Even Rochelle is only my friend because she feels sorry for me. She knows I'm no good. You see it. You know I've got bad in me. Who's gonna want me now?"

"Shut the fuck up."

"What?"

"Lex, look at me." I meet his gaze. His chocolate eyes burning with such intensity I could melt into the bed. "You know you're beautiful. Got a mouth on you but one day…" he trails off, his gaze fixated on my lips. Trailing his fingers along my jaw he stops suddenly and gets to his feet. "Go to sleep. When you wake up, I want that other name."

"Sleep?" I laugh. "You think I can sleep. Whenever I close my eyes, I see them. I smell them. I hear them grunting. I feel their heavy weight pressing me down on the floor. I can still feel the carpet burning my stomach." I swipe a finger under my eye and lick my lips. "I'll never sleep again."

He shifts from foot to foot then sighs before settling on the bed. Laying back on the thin pillow he holds an arm out. "C'mere."

I stare at the skulls and roses covering his chest, getting hypnotized by the tattooed pattern.

"C'mere. I'll keep you safe. You can trust me, Alexa. I know you have no reason to because I've already let you down once, but I swear to you I won't fail you now."

I fall into his hold. My head to his chest, listening to the steady beat of his heart. Concentrating on the way his touch doesn't scare me. Centering on the fact that I've never felt safer than I do right now in this man's arms. I want to fade into nothing. Roll back time and disappear before all the bad. I thought I'd be safe at Rochelle's because her father is a man with the road name Murder. I mean no one would fuck with someone with ties to a man like that. Not if they were smart.

I was wrong.

"You breathe a word of this and you're dead." The man who came in while Todd was assaulting me taunted me repeatedly as he joined in on the torture. I passed out somewhere along the way, and when I woke up blood was crusted to my thighs and everything hurt. The other man had left but Todd was still there, waiting for me. *"You're lucky you aren't dead."*

Tense and wound up my body aches at the memory. I feel dead inside.

James strokes his rough fingers along the length of my arm. "Close your eyes and take a deep breath. I want you to imagine your happy place."

"I don't have one of those."

"Everyone has one."

"What's yours?"

"My happy place is the open road. Me and my motorcycle, leaving the rest of the world behind."

"That sounds good to me. Can I borrow your happy place?"

"All right then. Picture that you're riding on my motorcycle with me. Your arms are tight around me. The wind blowing through your hair. It's a bright and sunny day. Not a cloud for miles. Just you, me, and the open road. The fresh air burns through your lungs. The vibration of the ride hums through your veins."

I stare up at him as he continues to vividly paint my escape. His words becoming lost on me. I only see him and hear the steady rhythm of his heart pulsing between us replacing the sound of his motorcycle. The warmth of his body pressing into mine replacing the sunshine. The safety of those strong arms shielding me from every bad thing that's ever happened to me. We exist in a world that only we know. There's only us, and no one can hurt me now.

As long as I have James, I don't need anyone else.

"Better?" he glances down at me once he's realized I'm no longer crying.

"A little."

"You should think about talking to someone and getting looked over by a doctor."

"No." I jerk away from him. "You promised. No one will know."

"You on birth control?"

I shake my head and the tears return. I know where this conversation is going. "My father won't allow it. Says I'll just go around spreading my legs. He doesn't even believe in tampons." I shrug.

"I can get you a morning after pill, but I don't know how effective it'd be."

I gulp and cradle my stomach. "Do you think I'm pregnant?"

"Can't say for sure, but you should be concerned about it."

"What am I gonna do?"

"I can't tell you what to do, but I'll do what I can to help you. What about your mother?"

"She goes along with whatever my father wants. In their eye's abortion is a sin. If I told them they'd say I've gotten what girls like me get. I can't go back there."

"Gotta be smart. They'll call you a runaway, and if they think I'm involved—Fuck."

"I could get a job and pay rent. I can take care of myself."

"You gotta go home."

"Didn't you hear anything I said." I shove his chest and he wraps those big arms around me. The scent of his cologne hits me, and my insides go all gooey like the center of a fresh baked cookie.

"I heard every damn word. Now hear me. You don't know if you're pregnant, but there's other shit you gotta think about. Like STDs. Did they use protection?"

"I don't...I don't know. I think so. I remember seeing a wrapper on the floor."

"That's good, but darlin', you gotta get checked out. I'll drive you myself if you promise me, you'll go back to your folks for a little while. They need to know you're okay."

Chill bumps fan up and down my arms. I know he's right. Oh God. What if I'm pregnant and diseased? My life is over. I'm ruined.

"Get out of that dark headspace."

"My life is over."

"No. It's not."

"You don't know that. You know how it is around here. Once everyone knows...it's all anyone will think about when they look at me."

"People will believe what you want them to believe."

"You think so?"

"Know it."

"Okay. What do you see when you look at me?"

James studies me closely, staring so intently I'm certain he sees straight to my soul. "You're scared. A bit lost, but you're also resilient." A shiver passes through me.

"How'd you get the name Murder?"

"It's a secret."

I roll my eyes and the corners of his mouth twitches. "There's that fire."

"What?"

"Nuttin'. You really want to know how I earned my name?"

"Tell me," I demand, snuggling deeper into his side.

"Fuck. I tell you this it stays between us. Yeah? I know your secret and you'll know mine."

I yawn. "Sounds fair enough."

"Right." He chuckles and the sound warms me to the core. He has this deep raspy laugh. One that sounds like he's smoked too many cigarettes or like a cowboy in one of the old westerns my father watches all the time.

"I killed a man."

"Okay...and?"

"And what?"

"Where's the rest of the story?"

His cell phone goes off, and he slides his arm from around me. "Another time. Get some sleep. In the morning we're going for a ride." James rolls over me and off the bed, going to his feet as he answers the call. "Lo. Where the fuck have you been?"

I stare at his back taking in the Royal Bastards MC insignia covering most of his skin. He's a beautiful man. Ruthie doesn't deserve him. I don't either, but I want him.

Chapter Five

MURDER

I peek in at Alexa one more time. She finally conked out a few hours ago. I haven't slept a fuckin' wink. Got feelers out for that spineless piece of shit. He touched the wrong girl. Alexa doesn't have anyone to stand up for her so it's up to me. Shit I shouldn't be involved in but here I am. There's something about her since the moment I first laid eyes on her. Something inside her called out to me. I keep trying to deny and fight this pull I have, but our paths have crossed and tangled. This girl has rooted herself deep in me.

For what purpose, that remains to be seen, but I can't let this one go. If I'm being honest with myself, I need her as much as she needs me if not more. Been a long time since I've felt a connection with anyone. When I look at Ruthie all I see is regret and old wounds that I'm not sure can ever heal. Maybe if I help Alexa, I'll right some of my wrongs. Be the man she needs in her life to get her out of this town. She stays here she'll drown.

Three knocks in rapid succession tap on the front door. I peer out the blinds and see Slick on the porch with the shit I asked for. I open the front door and take the bags. "Anyone see you or ask any questions?"

"Nope. Got everything you asked for."

"Ruthie and Ro?"

"Didn't know I was there."

"Good. Good. You find that weasel yet?"

"No, but I'm looking and being discreet just like you asked me to."

"Appreciate it. Minute you tag his ass, I wanna know. Bring him to the basement."

"You got it, brother." He fishes the keys to his cage out of his pocket and trades me for the key to my bike.

"Call me soon as you got something."

Slick nods and takes off. I close the door and sit the food and drinks on the worn coffee table and lay the envelope with her new life to the side. Trudging to the bedroom where she sleeps my stomach rumbles at the scent of bacon, cheese, and egg biscuits. When I open the door she's just waking up.

"Hey," she whispers.

48

"Got you breakfast. Get dressed and meet me in the living room." I drop her bag on the edge of the bed.

"Okay. Thanks for last night. For listening. For just being here." Her wavy blonde hair hugs her shoulders as she slips out of bed in my tee looking too damn good in it. Too damn grown and fucking broken.

I grunt and clear the tickle from the back of my throat. "Don't mention it."

Alexa's gaze flitters over my chest. Her lips tip into a smirk that shakes me deep in my bones. She doesn't need to be looking at me, flashing me that fire in her eyes that threatens to burn me. To scorch me to the ends of the earth. "Guess you'll be wanting this." My shirt flies over her head and whips across the room. Her bruised and defiled body put on full display.

I close my eyes and grip my shirt in my fist. Turning my back to the sight, I call out, "Get a move on. Got shit to do today." *Like find that bastard and end his life.*

"Okay," she croaks, and I shut the door.

In the hallway I pause and lean against the wall. Sucking in a breath I shake my head and laugh. Who'd ever think Alexa Neville would be able to bring me to my knees, but here we are. That girl will be my undoing. I know it and so does she. I shove off and go to the living room and grab my biscuit, ripping into it with my teeth and tearing off a big chunk of egg. I crumple the wrapper and put my shirt back on. My shirt smells of Alexa. Fuck me.

The heat of her stare penetrates me minutes later. I glance up and gone is the broken girl. Alexa stands across from me a woman wearing too tight jeans and a black top with a deep V showing off her cleavage. Her hair hangs in a loose braid over her right shoulder. Makeup done up, pretty red lips. Gazing at her right now you wouldn't know she'd been raped, but I know. I can't forget. That bastard won't forget it either the short time he has left.

"Hungry?" I receive a nod in response.

Alexa plops down on the couch next to me, her thigh pressed to mine. The sweet yet faint smell of her perfume washes over me and hums through my veins. Sweet as candy. Sweet as that red lip gloss she's started wearing lately. She used to wear a shade of bubblegum pink. What's that say about me that I know when she changes shit up. I'm a filthy fucking bastard, and yet I don't give a fuck. The damage has been done. Her fate is wrapped up with mine. I knew it when I first saw her. I wanted her. I still do, but I can never act on those desires.

I'm not a good man, but I try to be for Rochelle. If it wasn't for my daughter, I'd left Ruthie a long time ago. My wife is a bitch, and I know she'd make damn sure I never have contact with Ro. Ruthie knows too much. Bitch could put my ass back in prison. Loves to hold shit from the past over my head. And yet I still stay loyal and faithful like a fucking dog.

Alexa twists the cap off her orange juice and takes a long drink. "What's the plan?"

"Taking you to get checked over. Don't give me no lip or fight me on this. I know someone who will be discreet. Bit of a drive though."

"All right. I won't."

"Good."

Her hand reaches out for mine, and I let her take it though I shouldn't. One touch could spark a fucking wildfire. "Thank you for doing this. For everything. If I didn't have you…I don't know what I'd do."

"Don't mention it. Finish that off we gotta head out." I drop her hand and stand up. Pulling my cigarettes out of my cut I light one up and peek outside through the blinds. A couple kids are walking toward the bus stop. They are about the same age as Alexa, but she's not like them. She is unlike anyone I've ever met.

51

I take a long draw off my Marlboro and dig Slick's keys out of my pocket.

"All set."

I look over at Alexa and she has her bag strung over her shoulder. "You got everything?"

"Yeah."

"Let's roll." I open the front door and glance around once more for prying eyes then shuffle Alexa toward the cage. Slick has a black Ford F-150 with tinted windows. Not something I'd choose myself, but it'll do for what I need it for. People see a pretty blonde in Slick's cage they won't think twice about it. They see her on the back of my motorcycle there'll be talk. Whisperings I don't need. Don't need the fucking 5-O getting in my business again.

"Buckle up," I growl, as I climb into the driver's seat and adjust the mirrors.

Alexa fiddles with the radio, and I ignore her for most of the drive. She tries to talk, but I shut her out. I need to get my head straight. Whenever she's near me I can't even breathe right. The AC blows, giving me whiffs of her sweetness. I steal a glance her way, and when I see her tears, I fucking break. I gotta fix this. Fix her. I just don't know how. We're an hour outside of Charleston now. I turn down the radio and catch her gaze as I pull off at a gas station.

"Want something?" She shakes her head. "I'll be back." I don't wait for a response. I get out needing a break from being so close to her and yet so far away. The smell of gasoline assaults my senses, and I head inside for a coffee. I grab what I need and at the counter is these big square red cinnamon flavored suckers Rochelle loves so I grab a handful of them. I think Alexa likes them too. I pay and get back in the truck. Alexa's resting her head against the window. Her eyes are closed. The weight of the world balanced on her shoulders.

"Hey." I tip her chin up. "You good?"

"No. I'm terrified. What if I'm pregnant? Then what?"

"Then you ask yourself what you want."

"To turn back time and to have never met Todd."

"Can't go back. We can only move forward. It's going to be fine."

"You can't know that."

"Rochelle tell you I did time?"

"Yeah."

"Circumstances can always change. I got out. Came home to my family."

Alexa snorts. "To a wife who despises you."

"To a daughter I love who has a pain in my ass best friend." That earns me a smile. "Here." I dump the suckers in her lap and situate my cup in the holder in the middle of the console.

"Thanks."

"Don't mention it."

Alexa tears the plastic wrapping off one and thrusts it between her sweet lips. My mind flashes to thoughts of those red lips wrapping around something else, and I hate myself a little more, but not nearly enough. We get back on the road and head North to Pennsylvania. I've got another two hours of this torture might as well fill the time with conversation.

"What's the deal with your old man?"

Her shoulder lifts. "He's an asshole. Wants everything perfect."

"What happens when you disappoint him?"

"Depends on what I did. Some things will get me grounded from the basics. No Tv. No going out. Other things will lose me a meal. Get me locked in my room. Make me acquainted with his newest belt. But I'm almost out of there."

"He beat you or just whip you?"

"Is there a difference?"

"Yeah there is."

"Tell that to him." She twiddles the end of her braid between her fingers. "He subjects me to a drug test once a month, and I have to take it in front of him."

"What do you mean you have to take it in front of him?"

"He stands in the doorway to the bathroom while I pee in the cup."

"Fucking hell."

"Oh, it gets worse. I don't know if you know this but my father's a gynecologist. He um makes me do these exams to check that I'm a virgin. So you see he'll know. But he'll blame me. I can't go back. You can't make me go back there. If he finds out I don't know what he'll do."

"You let me worry about it."

"No. You don't know him. He'll come after you and the club. You can't."

"I'm not afraid of him, Lex. You don't have to be either."

"Why?"

"Why what?"

"Why do you care? I'm not your problem."

"Because if it were Rochelle and she couldn't come to me, I'd want someone to step up and do the same. I swear to you, I'll fix this. I'll fix..." I stop.

"I'm damaged goods. I have been since the day I was born. My mother hates me because having me gave her stretchmarks. They hate me yet they love to control me."

God damn these pieces of shit have done a number on her.

"You're not damaged, pretty girl. Maybe a little bruised but don't let anyone ever make you think differently."

"You're just trying to make me feel better. That's such a thing a good dad would say, but you aren't my father. I don't look at you that way."

Don't I fucking know it.

I let the conversation end there.

Chapter Six

The truck rolls to a stop outside of a quaint white sided house. "Wait here," James tells me, so I stay put.

An older woman exits the front door and meets him on the cement steppingstones leading to the porch. She looks like a grandmother type. Silver hair styled in curls tight to her scalp. He greets her with a kiss to each cheek, and she pats him on the shoulder as she glances toward the truck at me.

James turns around and motions me to get out. I don't want to, but I trust him. He's the only person I can trust.

"Lex, this is an old family friend."

She gives him a pointed look. "Who you calling old? Call me Anna."

"Nice to meet you," I lie through my teeth. She may be the nicest lady in the world, but right now I don't want to be around anyone other than James. He makes me feel safe.

"Lily is out at the barn."

"You go with Anna. She'll take good care of you. I'll catch up in a bit." He stalks off before I can ask who Lily is.

"I understand you've been through an ordeal."

"I'm sorry, but I don't think I'm comfortable discussing this with you."

"Of course not." She wraps an arm around my shoulders and leads me into her house. I follow the woman into the living room. The décor is far from what I expected. I guess I expected the inside to look like my grandma's house. Old lace doilies, pictures, and knickknacks. Big fluffy pillows and fuzzy blankets are thrown over bean bag type chairs that form a circle. Some are occupied by other young women. Some don't acknowledge me at all while others stare at me as though they know every dirty detail and it hits me. The pain in their eyes and worn on their long faces. Chill bumps fan up and down my arms. They know because my story is their story. I suck in a breath and fight back the tears threatening to spill.

"In here." Her hand moves to the small of my back and she guides me into a private exam room. "Have a seat up here." She pats the table. "I'm gonna take a sample of your blood and urine to run some simple tests."

I sit quietly as she sterilizes her hands and puts some gloves on to take a few vials of blood. I look away. The sight of my own blood conjures images I don't want to remember.

"I'm gonna ask you to step into the bathroom and pee in this cup."

I nod, slide off the table, and accept the cup.

The bathroom is small and serves its purpose. I hurry to get the whole thing over with. The sooner I can leave the better. I finish up and place the cap on the cup and leave it on the tray that sits on the back of the toilet.

I return to the exam room and fold my arms over my chest. "What is this place?"

"Lily's Hope. We're a private center for women who've been the victim of abuse. You don't have to share your story if you aren't ready, but I need you to fill out this form and be as honest as you can so I know how best to serve you." Anna opens a drawer and takes out a clipboard that already has the form and a pen attached to it.

"How do you know James?"

"Lily is his sister. She founded this place years ago."

This piece of information surprises me. I've never heard Rochelle mention having an Aunt Lily before. I take the clipboard and a seat on the exam table. I stare frozenly at the questionnaire. The first question is a punch to the gut.

Are you pregnant? Yes No Not sure

My hand trembles as I grip the pen and circle not sure. On to question two. When was the last time you were sexually active?

My thoughts go to that nightmarish night. The night I was attacked and brutally raped on the floor of my best friend's living room. The back of my throat burns, growing tight. Tears gather in the creases of my eyes. I can't breathe. I drop the clipboard and run out of the room. Out of that house full of knowing stares. It's all too much. I can't do it. I run not caring where I'm running to. I just need air. I run through the garden until I nearly go face first into a tree. I brace my palms on the bark and slide down to the grass, wrapping my arms around my knees. Hard sobs shake my chest and bubble in my throat.

I was raped. I let the words settle in and take root. They violated my body. I had trusted Todd. When he lashed out I had him drop me off at Rochelle's thinking I'd be safe there. I never in a million years thought it could happen to me. I thought I was in control. I was stupid. I swipe at my tears. I hate him. The man, that sick man. A shiver courses up my spine. He was much older. That much I know. A tattoo flashes in my memory. A lion's head on his hand.

I didn't even see his face, but I remember his voice and his breath hot on my neck.

"Hey." James touches my shoulder.

I shrug him away. I can't stand to be touched right now not even by him. I cry harder. "What's wrong with me? Why did they do that to me?"

"Lex, honey," he speaks softly and squats in front of me. "Come back to the house. Anna can help you. She has experience with this."

"They all know. You didn't see how they looked at me. I'm so dirty."

"No, you're not."

"I can feel their touch. My skin crawls with their fingerprints. Their breath clings to my skin. I just want it to stop. Make it go away. Please?" I glance up at him, but

I can't see him through my tears. Gently he urges me to my feet and lifts me into his arms, cradling me like a child. I curl into his neck and breathe him in as he carries me toward his truck.

I close my eyes as he maneuvers to get me back in the seat. I feel the seat belt slide over my chest and relief floods me. The door closes, and I hear murmured voices, but I can't look or make out what is said. The driver's side door opens, and I lay my head back as the truck starts.

Tears continue to slide down my cheeks. My body itches all over. Like billions of tiny insects are attacking me and injecting me with venom. *"You're lucky you aren't dead,"* Todd's warning echoes through my thoughts like a broken record or one of those annoying radio advertising jingles that get stuck in your head for hours.

I'm not sure how much time passes or how far James drives until the truck eventually stops.

"I'll be back in a second," I hear him tell me, but I don't acknowledge him. It's hard to even breathe right now. Minutes pass, and he's back in the truck, but he doesn't drive far before he's climbing back out and coming to my side. The passenger door opens, the seat belt clicks and slides off my chest. "Pretty girl, need you to open those eyes and look at me and listen." He pinches my chin. "Lex. Gimme' them eyes, babe."

As dead and numb I feel hearing him call me babe has me opening my eyes to look at him. His face softens, and he loosens his hold but doesn't drop his hand away.

"I will never understand the hurt you feel. But I need you to trust me when I say I went through this with my sister. It's why I went to prison. I killed the fucker who beat and raped her. You didn't meet her today because I didn't think you were ready to see her. She's got permanent scars, babe. They run deep, but she survived, and I bled that piece of shit out. Got no regrets about it even though it cost me a lot of time with my baby girl. I'd do it again. You feel dirty but you're breathing. You're still here, and I promise you they won't be walking on this earth much longer. I'll give you that peace of mind."

I don't say anything, but I hold his gaze. I see the conviction in his eyes. He means every word. It's not bullshit he's feeding me. James is the only person who doesn't lie to me or treat me as though I'm stupid.

"You aren't ready to face this shit. I get that. I don't want to force you, but I got you a room. You can shower or take a nap, get yourself together. I'll get us some food and we can talk when you're ready." His lips press to my forehead.

I pull away. "You shouldn't want to touch me. I'm ruined."

"Stop that shit. There's not a damn thing spoiled or sour about you, Alexa. God damn, sweetheart. You're the prettiest girl I've ever seen. I mean that. The day I first laid eyes on you I knew you'd been sent here to torture me."

"What?"

"I have thoughts and feelings. Fuck." He drops his hand and I miss his touch. "Shouldn't be saying this shit right now or at all." He shakes his head and steps back. "Come on. Let me take care of you."

I nod and get out of the truck. He takes me into a motel room and goes straight to the bathroom sink and gets a cup of water. Tucking two pills in the palm of my hand he says, "Take these. It's antibiotics just in case."

I take one look at the pills and toss them down my throat and gulp the water to chase it down.

"Good girl. Go on and get in the shower I'll bring your bag in and leave it outside the bathroom then I'll go down a few blocks and grab some food. Sound good?"

"Okay." James goes out to get my bag and I go to the bathroom, closing the door behind me. The room isn't all that great or clean, but neither am I for that matter. I twist the knobs turning the water as hot as it will go. I strip out of my clothes as steam fills the small room. I don't know if James has brought my bag in or not. Standing in my bra and panties I stare at my reflection in the mirror. I want to cry at the girl I see looking back at me. Bruised and battered but like he said I'm still breathing. The mirror fogs up and my reflection disappears.

Bile rises up the back of my throat, and I drop to my knees throwing up violently. My chest heaves as I choke on my snot, tears, and vomit.

A light knock taps against the bathroom door.

"Lex, you decent?"

"It's unlocked," I tell him.

The door opens. "Oh shit. Sorry. Thought to you said it was cool." He holds a hand over his face.

"It's fine. No different than a bathing suit, right?" I shrug.

"Guess not. I was just gonna ask what you want to eat."

"I can't eat. I can't even find the energy to step into the shower."

65

He moves behind me and fiddles with the water temperature. "You got it hot enough to peel your damn skin off."

"That's kind of the point."

I glance at what he's doing and see him changing the flow from the shower to the tub and putting the plug in. "C'mon. Get in."

I nod and start sliding my bra straps down my arms. James stops me. "Leave that on."

"What for?"

"Because I decided you don't need to be alone right now, sweetheart. Let me take care of you."

"You don't have to."

"I want to."

I slide down into the tub. The warm water covers my legs, and I lay my head back on the tiles. James unwraps the complimentary soap and a washcloth. He wets both then lathers the soap on the cloth. Touching me light as a feather he takes his time washing my sins away, but I'll never be fully clean.

I'll never be free of the memories that haunt me.

"You can't see it now, but you're gonna be okay."

"I'm not your sister."

"I know that, Lex. There's nothing brotherly about the way I feel about you."

"What, you see me like Rochelle?"

"Cut the shit out. We both know what's growing between us even if it can never happen."

"James." I grab his arm.

"What?" he drops the washcloth and pulls away.

"Thank you."

"Don't mention it."

He leaves me alone with so many thoughts swirling in my head. I'm trying to push away the bad and hold on to the hope he just gave me.

"We both know what's growing between us." Yeah, I do. He doesn't see me as dirty. He wants me still even after...

Faith in him blooms in my chest. I sink down into the water and wet my hair.

Chapter Seven

I arrive back at the room with the food and find Alexa sitting on the edge of the bed wrapped in a thin towel with the air conditioner blowing. *Jesus.* "It's freezing in here. What the hell are you doing?" I sit the food and drinks on the table then proceed to turn off the AC.

"If I can't burn their touch away maybe I can freeze it."

I go to my knees and take her trembling hands in mine. "I'd take it away. Make you numb to it if I could."

"There's one way you can make it go away." Her teeth chatter as she speaks.

"And how's that? I'll do my best to do whatever it takes."

Alexa holds my gaze. "Make me forget. Show me that not all men are bad and hurt. That sex doesn't equal pain."

My throat bobs as I swallow hard. "Can't do that, Lex. One day when you're older and wiser you'll find a man who will treat you the way he ought to. Sex doesn't equal pain, but it should come from a place of love and not just need. You're hurting now, but in time you'll fall in love."

She jerks from my hold. "Don't feed me that love bullshit. You don't love your wife, but you still fuck her."

"Shut the fuck up. You don't know what you're talking about. If I touched you right now, I'd be just as bad if not worse than the scum who hurt you. I'm not that man. I won't be that guy."

"I'm giving you permission."

"You're hurting. You don't know what you want right now. You're lost."

"You said you'd do whatever it takes. So I'm begging you." Alexa grabs my hand, bringing it to her chest, flattening the palm over her heart. "Do whatever it takes. Make it go away. Fix me. I don't want to feel this way forever. Please. I don't want to remember. Give me something to replace those thoughts."

I drop my forehead against hers. "I can't."

"You mean you won't."

"Yeah," I whisper the words against her lips, getting a taste of heaven and hell before I pull away. "You need to get some food in you."

"I'm not hungry."

I go over to the table and start putting the food out. Greasy burgers and fries. "You like chocolate milkshakes?"

"Sure."

"Get some clothes on. I got one with your name on it with whip cream and a cherry on top." I don't wait for her to do as she's told. I pull out a chair and start eating. At some point the bathroom door closes and opens again. I glance up from my food and see Alexa sitting across from me picking at her fries in her same clothes from earlier. "When we get back, I'm gonna drop you at the house with Rochelle. It's up to you if you want to tell her anything or not about what happened to you, but I'm paying a visit to your old man and setting some shit straight."

"No offense but you can't expect me to want to go back to the scene of the crime."

Fuck. She's right. I didn't even think about that. "Well I'll take you back to the safehouse or get you another room until I figure out our next move. Shit is complicated."

"Do we have to go back today? Can't we just stay here?"

"Make you a deal. You give me that other name, and I'll wait till morning before we go back."

"I don't know his name, but I do remember something about him."

"What?"

"A tattoo. Um...on his hand. A lion's head in color with a big fancy crown like one a king would wear."

My stomach drops. "Anything else?"

She nods her head and takes a sip of her milkshake. "I know the sound of his voice and he smelled like um tobacco and a cough drop."

"Menthol," I growl.

"I guess. So, can we stay here for the night? A deal is a deal, right?"

"Gave you my word. Stay here, I need to make a call." I push my chair back and step outside. I call Ruthie. I need to check in. And I need to remind myself why I can't go off the rails. "I know you're pissed, but I'm gonna be out another night. We got a lot to talk about."

"I want a divorce, James."

"Now isn't the time for this shit."

"I met someone."

I grip the phone tighter. "You been stepping out on me? The fuck, Ruthie?"

"Neither of us are happy."

She's got that right. "How long has this shit been going on behind my back?" I snarl. Some things with this bitch never change.

"We'll talk when you get back. We'll figure out custody of Rochelle."

"You're not taking her any-damn-where."

"I don't want to fight. The right thing for you to do is give me the house."

"Not having this conversation right now. But this is totally fucked. You know it, and I know it. You saying you're done with me?"

"Yeah. We tried. It didn't work. I want out."

"Then you're out. And so am I." I hang up on her and shut my phone off. God damn her. Fucking cunt. I kick the side of the vending machine and fucking pop can falls out the slot. I go back to the room and sit the can of pop on the table. Alexa is eating the rest of her food and as pissed as I am it brings a smile to my face.

72

"When you're done with that, you need to take this."
I slide the pregnancy test out the bag that Anna gave me.

"I don't want to know."

"Gotta take the test so you can figure out what you want, Lex."

She gulps. "Fine. I'll do it now."

I hand the test over as she slides out her chair. Her fingers brush against mine, and I feel her touch so deeply it takes my breath away.

Alexa goes into the bathroom, and I wait impatiently as the minutes tick by.

Fucking hell I hope she isn't pregnant. A baby is the last thing she needs in her life.

The bathroom door opens and Alexa smiles at me big and wide holding up the test. "Negative."

"I got something I gotta do. Lock the door behind me. Don't open the door to anyone and don't leave this room. Got me?"

"I got you."

"Good." I hold her gaze and see she will be okay while I step out for a bit to let off some steam. I climb in the truck and throw my head back. Fuck. I punch the steering wheel. Ruthie met someone. I shake my head. Been faithful since we got together. Sure, I thought about it a few times, but I always put the needs of my family—of my club first. What's it gotten me? A cheating wife. A knife twisted in my heart. Gave her everything. Stuck with her for the sake of her reputation and for my kid. Stupid cunt. Fucking Ruthie. Story of my life. The bitch has been nothing but a thorn in my side since the day we met.

I'm so fucking done with all this shit. Living a life I don't even recognize anymore. Ruthie has the power to destroy me and take away my freedom if she chooses to do so. I've done shit I'm not proud of. I fucked up big when I got released from prison. I don't know what game Ruthie is playing, but I know she'll never stop holding the past over my head. I don't give a fuck what she says. Divorce or not she'll use what I did to get her way no matter what.

The fucked up thing is I should take her out, but she swears if anything happens to her then she has insurance in place to make sure everyone finds out what I did.

I drive to the nearest liquor store and buy a bottle of whiskey. Back in the truck I open the bottle and chug. Every argument Ruthie and I've had lately plays in my head on an endless loop.

Anna gives me a ring. The tests she did for Alexa came back negative too. Some of the STD panels will take a few days, but she thinks she will be fine with the antibiotics I gave her.

I drive around aimlessly, the liquor burning the back of my throat until I can no longer think straight. I shouldn't be driving. I should be home worrying about my daughter, but the last place I want to be is anywhere near my cunt wife. I try to be quiet when I return to the room, nearly tripping over my own feet. Alexa is curled up on top of the covers in the fetal position.

"She sleeps," I mutter to myself and drop to the floor after nabbing the remote control for the Tv off the nightstand. I flip through the channels and stop on some old slasher film.

"You're back," Alexa whispers in my ear, her warm breath fanning along my neck.

"Yup. Didn't mean to wake you."

"I wasn't asleep."

I take a hard pull off the bottle of Jack and light up a cigarette.

"You okay?"

I laugh at her question. "Nope."

"Anything I can do?"

"Put a bullet in my head."

"Don't say shit like that. It's not funny."

"You're right. I'm sorry. I'm an asshole."

"I don't think you're an asshole. You're one of the best people I know."

I snort. "Must not get out much then. You should meet new people."

"Can I have a drink of that?"

I glance up at her as she kneels at the end of the bed staring down at me, her tits practically spilling out of her top but what gets me is the longing in her eyes. "Yeah. Sure. Why not? Have at it."

Alexa takes the bottle from my hand, her fingers sliding over mine, an electric current passing between us. I move from the floor and go to the bathroom to put my cigarette out. I'm fucking beat. Exhaustion both mental and physical of the past day is wearing on me. I kick off my boots and shrug off my cut then my shirt. I lock the door and take a quick shower hoping it'll make me feel better, but it doesn't. After I start to go crawl in bed but remember I'm not alone. I pull my jeans back on and open the door.

Alexa is sitting in the same spot nursing the rest of my bottle of Jack looking beautifully broken. An avenging angel. My personal hell is being here in this room with her. Wanting her and unable to have her.

"Don't make yourself sick," I tell her as I flop onto the bed and curl an arm around one of the pillows. I know us being here is a bad idea, but I'm in no shape to drive. I need sleep. I close my eyes and feel her shifting on the bed, her sweet scent moving closer.

"Did something happen?" her liquor stained breath washes over my face. Intoxicating and tempting. "Did I do something wrong?"

"Nothing for you to concern yourself about."

"You're upset."

"Doesn't matter."

Her soft lips brush against mine. "It matters to me."

"Don't," I breathe out the word, her lips still touching mine but unmoving. Fuck me. I'm going to hell because there's never been anything sweeter than her in this moment. How can she be hurting the way that she is and still have it in her to care about a sorry fuck like me? "I don't deserve your sweetness."

"Says who?" Those torturous lips move against mine, and I don't stop it. I should, but I'm tired of doing the right thing and getting kicked in the teeth for it. "Let me take it away. Whatever is eating you. You'll take my pain, and I'll take yours, yeah?"

If I were a better man, I'd push her away. I'd drive her straight home and never look back, but I'm not a good man. I'm a fuckin' bastard, and I'm taking what I want. Why should I deny myself of this one guilty pleasure? Alexa parts her lips, opening to me, and I delve my tongue inside, tasting her passion but most of all her pain. The sweetest and deadliest sin. I stroke my fingers along her jaw and through her hair, getting swept away, consumed by one broken girl who can heal me and destroy me with one kiss.

Pulse pounding in my ears, I roll over top her, taking everything she's willing to give not caring that I've crossed a line neither of us will ever come back from. Threading our fingers together I hold Alexa's hands over her head, peppering kisses down the slender column of her throat.

"Nothing good will come of this."

"I don't need good or love, James. Not tonight. I just want to forget even if it's only for a little while."

"Me too," I rasp, getting lost in the sensation building up inside me and between us, feeling the flames of hell ready to welcome me home because the temptation of her is far too great to resist.

Chapter Eight

I know he's only gonna break my heart. But I don't care. Fevered with desire I give my all to him, whatever is left of me, it's his. I'm his. If only for this night. I'll hold him in my heart forever. My royal bastard.

"Fuck." he groans. His erection presses between my thighs as I wrap my legs around him.

"Show me pleasure." I nip at his neck, trailing my fingers down his back. "Show me what you feel for me."

"I shouldn't." He kisses me hard, deep, and wet. Heavy breaths pass between us fueled by liquor. I taste his last cigarette. "But fuck doing what's right. I want you, Lex. I can't deny it. I can't fight it. Baby, I don't want to. You have me, pretty girl. Fuck do you have me." James lifts my shirt over my head and smiles down at me. Gazing at me as though I'm truly beautiful and not damaged goods. He makes me feel whole. Like there's nothing wrong with what he sees when he looks at me.

His rough hands glide over my body, touching me anywhere and everywhere followed by his mouth. Sucking a nipple between his lips, he licks and kisses the taut skin until my back bows off the bed. James handles me with care but doesn't treat me as though I may break.

Rolling to his back, he brings me with him, positioning me on top, giving me control. I take my time enjoying tracing every line of ink marking his chest with my fingers and tongue memorizing every detail. "You're beautiful," I tell him.

"Been called a lot of things but beautiful was never on the list."

"There's a first time for everything." I go for his zipper, and he grabs my hips.

"Slow down. We've got the night."

"I don't want you changing your mind."

"You sure?"

"I want this. With you. No one else." Leaning forward I press my lips to his, tasting his tobacco and liquor deciding it's my new favorite thing.

My bad ass biker squeezes my backside. "Then take these off, lover."

I shimmy my jeans off my hips and down my thighs. With a little help from him, my denim goes sailing through the air, followed by his own. "Boxer briefs," I note and straddle his crotch. Big and thick his cock grows harder when I grind against him. I should be nervous and maybe a little scared, but I'm not. I trust him. Whether he's good or he's bad, I know he's meant to be mine. I don't care what the consequences are. Life is a bitch and then you die. I'd rather have one night with him, one moment of happiness where I belong to James than be left with nothing at all. To be left with brutal memories and what ifs.

He cups me between my thighs. "Jesus, Lex. You're fucking soaked."

Rolling my hips, I press my body closer to his, wanting him to touch me there. Needing him to give me this one piece of him. To color my world with more than pain. To show me that when a man takes a woman it can be beautiful. That what we share, whatever our connection is...that he feels something for me.

"Gonna make you forget anyone ever touched you, but me." Maybe it's the liquor talking for him, but I don't care. I'm getting my way. I know we're being reckless and being with a man like him is dangerous for more than my heart. He's a biker with the road name Murder, and he told me himself he's used his hands to kill. The same fingers wrapped around my throat have taken a life, but he won't hurt me.

Squeezing my throat, he gazes at me with such intensity. "So damn beautiful," he whispers, his dark voice and lethal touch consuming me.

I suck two of his fingers into my mouth earning me a deep throaty growl.

"Gonna be the death of me, pretty girl. Fuckin' ruining me." He shoves me to my back and looms over me, spreading my legs wide, hooking those strong hands of a killer around the skimpy waistline of my panties. With little effort James rips the fabric clean off. Dipping his head, he presses his nose to my pussy and inhales my scent. Giving me a kiss there my filthy biker grins up at me from between my thighs. "Never tasted anything sweeter."

My cheeks redden but its dark enough he can't see or doesn't notice. Eyes rolled to the ceiling, I grip the sheets and enjoy the ride. The wiry hairs of his beard tickling my thighs. The sweeping of his tongue against my sensitive skin. The firm hold of those rough hands on my hips. I take it all in. Taking the good he's gifting me.

I need it.

I need him.

Ravishing my body with affection like I've never felt before, James doesn't miss a beat, devouring me like his favorite dessert. The man has a way with his fingers and tongue. I can only imagine what else he can do.

I want it all.

I want him.

Under his touch, I unravel experiencing the greatest high as an orgasm rocks through me in heavy waves. Just when I think he's going to stop he comes at me again, sucking my clit, and thrusting his fingers in and out me like a piston.

Trembling beneath him, I'm about to shatter into a million pieces. Back arching up, I tug on his dark hair, forcing his head up. "Take me, James. Make me yours."

"You've been mine since the day I saw you in that little red bikini." He slides up my body, planting kisses along the way, covering every bruise and bite with his own mark. Branding my body as his until he reaches my mouth and plunges his tongue between my lips tasting of my desire. One hand on my throat and the other on his cock, James holds my gaze. "So God damn pretty it hurts to look at you, Lex." The head of thick erection kisses my pussy lips. Rubbing it back and forth he coats himself in my juices then lines up where I crave him the most.

I surge my hips up to meet his, forcing him deep inside as my body stretches to accommodate and accept the welcomed intrusion. "Fuck, baby." His forehead drops to mine. His hot liquor and smoke tainted breath fanning over me. "So damn greedy and eager." Lips crashing against mine, cock rooted in me, James makes love to me. I feel it and he does too. We're tethered together for life. Us against the world. A world that will never understand the way I feel for him. How deep this love I'm feeling goes.

We're one in the same him and I.

Misunderstood.

Unwanted.

We don't belong anywhere but here.

His hard body melded to mine.

My damaged soul mating with his.

Two halves of one whole.

My motorcycle man.

His broken girl.

Slick with sweat our bodies rock moving together as though we've been through the motions a million times. Three small but powerful words hang on the tip of my tongue and die there. I know better. He can't give me my unspoken prayer, but I want it anyway. That pretty fantasy where I'm his Old Lady and he's my man. But outside of these walls it will never come to fruition. So for now I take what I can. A drunken mistake on his part, and a promise to love him forever tattooed on my heart.

We go at each other like savage beasts. Rolling around in the sheets, the headboard beating the wall, like it's knocking on Heaven's door or maybe the gates of Hell. There is nothing holy about our union. I know we are a million shades of fucked up and wrong, but it feels right. I've never felt more alive than I do here with him.

James thrusts harder and deeper, hitting me in all the right spots. My body hums like a live wire. I come alive for him, giving as good as I'm receiving.

Back on top I hold his palm to my heart showing him what my words can't express. He owns me. I ride him fast then slow, repeating the rhythm until my body quakes, another orgasm rips through me. My lover knifes his hips up, cock jerking inside me, painting the walls of my pussy with his release.

When it's over, he hugs me to his chest. Our bodies still connected. My pulse racing. His heartbeat thumping in my ear. Lips to my forehead he whispers, "I'm sorry, Lex. I should've been stronger."

"Don't do that. Don't ruin this. I've never felt more alive than when you look at me, James. The little things you do. The brush of your fingertips on my cheek. The rhythm of your heart beating against mine. The way our bodies fit together perfectly. All the tiny fragments that add up and blend into the whole picture of you. I love you. I don't care if that makes me a horrible person. No one has ever given a shit about me. Not until you. Tomorrow you can be sorry. You can hate me if you want, but not tonight. It belongs to me. You belong to me."

"What if I don't want it to end?"

I quirk a brow at him. "That you or the liquor talking?"

"Both." His large hand cradles the back of my head and brings me in for a kiss so raw and beautiful my heart nearly beats out of my chest. He goes hard again inside me. Thumb pressed to my lips to silence me he has one request. "Get on your knees for me."

I do what he wants even though it's breaking me to do so. Being with him any other way I can do, but this…the position I was assaulted in has those flashes of torment I keep trying to bury rearing their ugly heads and vile threats. *"You're lucky to be alive."*

Dropping my head, I close my eyes as tears begin to fall. The bed shifts with his weight as he moves behind me. Biting my lip, I cry out when James presses down on me. I know he won't hurt me. He's not them. I shake my head. "I can't."

"This how they took you? Hold you down. Make you beg?"

"Shut up."

"Got to face it, baby. Don't give them that power over you. Take it back."

"You weren't there. You don't understand."

"I know I wasn't. If I were, they'd already be dead." Lips pressed to my spine, he traces the curve, dragging his lips slowly across my skin, rubbing me with his facial hair. "Never hurt you." An arm goes around my middle, holding me up. I lay my head back on James's shoulder, dropping my ass against his crotch and he slides right in. "This body is mine to take. You gave it to me, pretty girl." Pulling both arms behind my back he binds them with his bandanna then shoves me forward again down on my knees, face and chest pressed into the mattress.

I draw in a sharp breath and focus on him and him alone.

"I know you think they broke you, but I'm putting you back together again." His palm slaps my ass cheek, curving to hold me there as he thrusts deeper in. "Give it all to me. Your pain. Your beauty. Let go for me." Teeth dragging across my shoulder he bites me. Not hard or rough but in a playful nip. Body slapping against mine he takes that horrible memory and turns it into dust. Giving me something good in its place.

Giving me all his beauty and sparks of color in a darkened and fucked up world that will never accept the way he makes me feel. I know I'll love him forever. People will say I'm too young. They won't understand. He sees the real me. The girl who hides behind the idea of who people expect me to be.

When others tell you who you are enough eventually you become that version of yourself even when it feels wrong.

But this isn't wrong. This is who we are. Two wandering souls connecting in the only way we know how to. Skin to skin. Mouth to mouth. He ravishes my body, taking and taking until I have nothing left but my aching soul. With one final thrust he shudders and quakes, his cock jerking inside me, filling me completely.

Pulling out he rolls off the bed, unbinds my wrists, and brings me with him. In the bathroom, this man handles me with care, wiping away the remnants of his passion that's running down my thighs. Neither of us speak. We don't need to. We both know that I'd be happy if tomorrow never comes. After I fall onto the bed and he holds me close. Nothing passes between us except shallow breaths and unspoken promises of what can never be.

I lay with him, stroking my fingers along his skulls and roses that are inked over his chest. My bad man. My lover. My protector. He doesn't know it, but I do…James—Murder…he's gonna be my world.

Grabbing my hand, he threads his fingers with mine and kisses my knuckles. "Get some sleep."

I wish I could but I'm afraid that once I close my eyes this…him…we'll disappear. He'll be gone, and all it will have been is a fantasy that felt all too real.

I close my eyes and fall asleep quicker than I wanted to.

Morning comes too soon, returning us to reality. To a world where we can't exist. But for one night I had everything I ever wanted, and it was all I dreamed it would be and more. I awaken with his heavy body curled around mine. Our legs tangled together. My cheek pressed to his tattooed chest. His heartbeat drumming a soothing melody in my ear. The only sound I want to hear forever.

The ringing of his cell phone interrupts our bliss. James curses under his breath, and I go to move away, but he holds me tighter. It's unexpected but welcome. Part of me was afraid that we'd wake up and he'd be chock-full of liquid regret.

The ringing continues, sounding like a warning that our minutes together are fleeting.

"Should you get that?"

He grunts and slides away, tagging his phone from his jeans as he goes to the bathroom. I stay where I lay and pray that this isn't all there is for us. If I lose him, I don't know if I can survive. I'm not strong enough. I need him to save me from the monsters out there waiting to hurt me, but no one can hurt me more than I hurt myself but him.

Chapter Nine

MURDER

"Yeah. I'm still out of town."

"I found what you've been searching for."

"You've crated the dog?"

"Yup. Scrappy pup."

"I'll be there to start the training as soon as possible."
Ending the call with Slick, I knew he wouldn't let me
down. I glance at Alexa. She's curled up under the covers
staring at me all wide and starry-eyed. Fuck. Last night
shouldn't have happened, but I'm not sorry. I should be,
but I'm not. Best night of my damn life. How fucked up
is that. Yeah, I was drunk. It's no excuse. I knew what I
was doing and who I was doing it with. I know what that
says about me, only I can't find it in me to care.

"Get dressed. We need to talk."

"Yeah. Sure." Her lips turn down, and I don't want
to hurt her, but we both know that when we leave this
room whatever this is and was is all it can ever be. I get

my jeans on and dig the other pill that was tucked in with the antibiotics.

Alexa slips from the bed with the sheet wrapped around her. Blonde hair all mussed up, looking like a goddess. Swollen lips and flushed cheeks. I grab her arm as she goes to pass me by. "I don't regret last night." She stares up at me with unshed tears glittering in her eyes. "Don't cry."

"Let me go."

"You need to take this." I shove the pill between her lips and don't offer an explanation. It's a morning after pill. I shouldn't have fucked her, but I did. My stomach churns as she sticks her tongue out to show me she swallowed it down. "Good girl." I hold her gaze for a minute then let her go. Alexa disappears into the bathroom, and I go out to the truck and grab the envelope Slick gave me. Helping her disappear is the best thing I can do for her. Alexa needs away from West Virginia. Away from me because if she stays, I know I'll only ruin her.

Back in the motel room, Alexa is sitting at the table. Her bag is on the bed zipped and ready. I drop the envelope on the table and pull out the other chair. "If you could go anywhere in the world and start over where would you go?"

Her shoulder lifts. The left corner of her mouth twitches. "I don't know. I've never really thought about it."

"Bullshit. Everyone thinks about it. What's the first place that comes to your mind?"

"I don't want to play this game."

"I don't play games, Lex. Not with this. Not with you. Best thing I can do for you is make Alexa Neville disappear for good. So, tell me, pretty girl. Where do you want to go? What do you want?"

"You want rid of me." She stares blankly out the window at the parking lot.

"I can't be the man you want me to be. Last night shouldn't have happened. I'm not sorry, but this has to end before it goes any further."

"Right. Just like the rest of them. You don't really want me. I'm too much of a problem. I get it, but don't sugarcoat it and treat me like I'm stupid. You want me gone so your wife doesn't find out. So Rochelle doesn't find out you fucked her best friend."

"It's not like that. Don't cheapen last night to that."

"No. Then what's it like? Enlighten me."

"I don't know what I can say except that I'm keeping my promise to make it right for you. Got something to take care of, and I gotta leave you somewhere safe while I do that. You don't have to decide now, but I need you to think about what you really want."

"Where are you taking me?"

"To the one person I trust most in this world."

"Your sister?"

"Yeah. Let's go. Put that in your bag and keep it safe. Everything you need to start over is in there. Access to a bank account. Identification."

"Got it." She jumps up quickly and the hurt in those pretty green orbs cuts me deeper than it ought to. Alexa stuffs the envelope in her bag, and I tell her to wait in the truck while I go check out.

When I'm done, the truck is empty. Fucking hell. She couldn't have gotten far. I look across the street and down both sides of the sidewalk and that's when I see her getting into the back of a cab. If I were smart, I'd let her go, but I got to see this through and make sure she knows once she's gone, she can't come back.

The cab starts down the road and I step into its path. The driver blows his horn at me, but I don't budge. "What the fuck, man?" He hangs out the window shouting at me.

"Get out of the car, Lex." I practically growl the words. The driver takes one good look at me and my leather cut then shuts the car off. Smart choice. I fling the back-passenger door open and jerk her out the car. "Don't be a stupid brat."

She says nothing, coming with me willingly.

We get on the road and she's giving me the silent treatment. It's for the best. She should hate me. I need her to make the choice because I don't know that I'm strong enough to let her go on my own. I must be fucking crazy. My life is falling apart and yet all I can think about is her. Keeping her safe. But to do that I gotta let her go. Send her out into the world to live a better life than I can give her if she stays here. I don't know what the hell she's done to me. Put me under some sort of fucking spell or what because for her I'm feeling ready to burn the world down.

"You want breakfast?"

No response.

"You thirsty?"

She continues to gaze at the scenery out the passenger window. Eventually I hear her messing with the wrapper of one them cinnamon suckers. I steal a glance out the corner of my eye, but she never looks my way.

I shut the radio off. "I'm fuckin' talking to you."

I'm met with more silence. Then she cranks the radio up as loud as it'll go. Stubborn fucking brat. I swerve off the road and turn down a dirt road, stopping only when we get out of view from passing traffic. I shut the truck off and go to the passenger side. When I put my hand on the handle, I hear the lock engage.

"Open the door."

Alexa shakes her head.

"We don't have time for your petty ass bullshit. Alexa." I slap the door and she flinches. "Open the God damned door now." She continues to defy me, shooting me this prissy assed expression that has me wanting to bend her over my damn knee and spank that attitude right out of her. I remember I have the damn keys in my hand, and I get the door unlocked easily enough. When I open her side, she scrambles to crawl across the seat, but I'm faster, and when I get hold of her, she goes rigid like a damn statue.

"We're settling this shit right now." I grab her throat and press her back in the seat. "You think this is easy. For the first time in years I've found something I want, and I gotta give it up. Because I'm not right for you."

We both know this won't lead anywhere good. Her gaze meets mine, and it's so damn cold I'd swear she's dead if it weren't for the erratic breaths leaving her parted lips. Her tongue darts out to wet her mouth and I lose it. "When I look into your eyes and see that fire gone, Lexi…fuck, baby. Damn near kills me." I bring my mouth down on hers, thrusting my tongue deep between those sweet cinnamon flavored lips needing her to know I care more than she knows.

Alexa moans into my mouth and the sound travels to my dick. Her hand goes to the back of my neck and she kisses me like it's goodbye and maybe it is. Even though I need to be back in West Virginia, I take my time, savoring this moment. This last piece of heaven I'll ever taste.

Sliding my hand from her throat to her jaw, I break away and hold her gaze. "I see you, pretty girl, but I can't keep you as bad as I want to."

Her forehead drops to mine. Her cinnamon breath fanning over my lips. "I hear you."

"Yeah?"

"Yeah," she whispers with a slight nod.

"Would give you the world if I could." I kiss her once more, having a hard time doing what I know I gotta.

Alexa breaks away. "I don't want the world. I only wanna live in yours." Her words punch me straight in the damn gut and suck all the wind right outta me.

"Would if I could. Give you it all." I drop my hand and peer into her eyes seeing the flecks of color brighter than before. "You gonna stop being a brat?"

"I think we both know that'll never happen."

"Right. You good?"

"No, but I will be."

"Most girls your age don't even know who they are, but not you. You're a cut above the rest."

"I'm no one special. No one at all, but you treat me like I'm somebody."

I climb back in the driver's seat and drive back to Lily's Hope.

"I'm glad you came back." Anna welcomes Alexa with open arms. "We're about to start on lunch, you can give us a hand in the kitchen."

"Later, pretty girl." I shoot her a wink as Anna steers her inside with her bag slung over her shoulder. It's better this way.

The second the door shuts behind them Lily is up in my face. "What are you doing with this girl, James? How old is she?"

"Don't worry about it. I got it handled."

"That's what you said when I got into trouble and look where it got you."

"Shit is different now. Don't worry."

"What about Ruthie and Ro?"

"Let me worry about it. Just look after Alexa for me. She doesn't leave and no one is to know she's here."

"I don't like this. The way she looks at you…you're fucking her."

"You don't know what you're talking about."

"Just promise me that you won't do anything stupid."

"Promise," I lie. It's too little too late. I've already fucked up more times than I can't count. I'm already going to hell, and I'll gladly burn for the night I shared with Alexa. I know I'm a dirty bastard for what I've done, but I've only just begun. The body count is about to get a lot higher. I made a promise to Alexa, and I won't let her down. Todd is going to pay.

"Love you, James." Lily wraps an arm around me, and I kiss her temple.

"You worry too damn much." I run my finger along the scar on her left cheek. Yeah, I'd kill that fuck and serve my time all over again for the shit he did to my sister. You wouldn't know the shit she's been through just by looking at her. The sick fuck nearly killed her. Beat her so damn bad it's a miracle she's here today.

Took three reconstructive surgeries to repair the bones he broke in her face. I killed him for it, but he still got off easy. Todd won't get that same courtesy. His death will be slow and painful. I was sloppy the last time. I won't make that mistake this time around.

**

I lift the punk motherfucker's head up as blood seeps between his lips. "How long you been working for Lion?"

Mustering a weak smile, he spits a mouthful of blood at me. "What's it matter? I'm dead anyway. Did she tell you how she screamed out your name when I fucked her?" A gurgled laugh erupts in his throat.

"No but I'll be sure to tell her how you cried like a bitch when I cut your balls off. Get him up," I tell Slick. This isn't usually his thing, but right now I don't trust anyone else. Not when I know Lion, my club Prez played a key part in assaulting Alexa. He'll pay, but I gotta do it right. I've wanted the prick gone for years. It's time to take him out and turn this club back around. Too many brothers are hooked on Cloud Nine and dying. Lion can't see what he's doing or he's too damn greedy to care. I won't sit back and watch him dig our graves. A man like him there's only one way to take him out—by surprise and under everyone's noses. It has to appear natural. Gotta beat him at his own damn game.

I rear my fist back and nail Todd in the nose with my spiked brass knuckles hearing his bones crunch.

Chapter Ten

MURDER

"I tell you I've met someone and that I want a divorce and all you can do is say okay? When did you stop loving me? When did you stop caring about our family?"

I shake my head. "I'm not in the mood for more of your shit. Enough with the fucking games, Ruthie. If you met someone who makes you happy then fucking go be with him."

"You don't mean that."

"I do. You want a divorce then I'll give you one."

"So that's it."

"What the hell do you want from me?"

"I want you to fight for me. To show me you give a damn. To tell me you'll kill him or me. That you'll never let me go."

"I can't do that."

"Why?"

"Because I'm not in love with you."

"You've met someone else. That's all there is to it."

"No," I lie. My mind flashes to Alexa. Someone I can't have. Someone I shouldn't want but crave. If Rochelle found out I don't know how she'd react. Ruthie would take her far away and Lion would put a bullet between my eyes. That's not going to happen though I can't and won't let it. Everything inside me screams in protest as I take a step toward Ruthie. "You want me to fight?" I grab her by the back of the head and tighten my grip, forcing her head to tilt.

"You loved me once," she whispers.

"Is there another man or not? You know what I did the last time you fucked around on me." I slit that fucker's throat and Ruthie helped me dispose of the body.

She licks her lips. "I just wanted to make you mad. Wanted you to come home and pretend that you give a damn about me."

"Is that blood on your shirt?"

"What?"

"What did you do?"

"Nothing for you to concern yourself with." I let her go. "I gotta get a shower then head to the clubhouse."

104

"You're leaving already?"

"I'll be back, and we can talk then."

"I don't want to wait till later we need to talk about this now."

"Well wish in one hand and shit in the other and see which fills faster."

"You're an asshole."

"But I'm the asshole you married for better or worse. Guess neither of us knew that the worst part would last us till death do us part, huh, sweetheart."

"I hate you. I hate you." She cries, punching at me as she sinks to her knees.

Black streaks of mascara trickle down her face. "What did I ever do to you to deserve this? Why are you so heartless?"

"You moved another man into my house. Had him play daddy to my kid. You tell me how I shoulda felt about that?"

"I said I was sorry. You can't hold it against me forever."

"Play stupid games, babe, you win stupid prizes. Yeah?"

"What's that mean?"

"It means you ever think for a minute that it was you who should be fighting for me?"

"You're right. I'm selfish and terrible. But I do love you, James. You're Rochelle's father."

"Is that all I am to you?"

"I don't know."

"Well when you figure it out you let me know."

"I want things to go back to the way they were before all the bad," she calls out as I close the bathroom door.

My life's been nothing but bad since the first time I kissed her.

I hurry through my shower, I'm eager to personally deliver the news to Alexa that Todd is no longer breathing the same air as the rest of us. I exit the bathroom to find Ruthie in the bedroom. Candles lit, lined up on the dresser top. Soft music plays. She's laying across the bed in a purple nightie. I take one look at her and feel nothing at all. She no longer resembles the girl I thought I loved when I was a stupid kid. Young, dumb, and full of come. Her dark hair rests on her shoulder, stick straight with a few highlights. Heavy makeup that makes her look old and worn. She never used to wear too much makeup. Back then she didn't need it. Would look better now if she washed all that shit off her face. Still has a banging body though. I'll give her that much. Hell, I paid for her to have a tummy tuck and get her tits done.

Bitch doesn't do it for me. Looks like a damn plastic doll now, but it's what she wanted to make herself feel good, and I didn't want to deny her.

"You shouldn't have gone to the trouble."

"James...don't you want to try? Rochelle needs us together. Before you know it, she'll be off to college, and then it'll be the two of us. We can get back to good."

I should cross the room and go to her. She's my wife. But I don't love her. "Smells like desperation in here. Told you, I'm not playing your games. You can't control me with sex. I'm not fifteen anymore. You sure as shit aren't either."

"Who is she?"

"None of your fuckin' business."

"James...please." Ruthie hops up off the bed, her fake titties popping out the see-through purple lace. "Let me show you that I do care. That we're worth saving." Bitch drops to her knees and wraps her arms around my leg. "Don't leave."

I breathe out heavily through my nostrils. "I don't have time for this. I got somewhere to be." I bend down to pull her arms off me. "Stop embarrassing yourself."

"You told me to fight." She cries. And scratches my jaw, digging her nails in so damn deep it burns.

I grab her up by the hair, sling her on the bed, and undo my belt. "This how you want me? Rough and unfeeling, babe. Want me to act like a monster for you?"

"I want you to take your pants off and make love to me."

"I can fuck you but there's no love between us. Roll over. I don't want to see your face."

Ruthie rolls to her stomach and sticks her ass in the air. I'm not even hard, but I unzip and start stroking my length, thinking about Alexa and her pretty red lips. The way she gazes at me as though I'm her white knight instead of a demon from the pits of hell. I'm no hero. No saint, but when she stares at me with them pretty green eyes I feel as though I could be saved.

My cock grows erect, and I part Ruthie's thighs. I don't want her body or her heart. I slide inside her wishing she were someone else and hating myself for wanting what I can't have.

"Yes," Ruthie hisses.

I jerk her head back and clamp a palm to her lips. "Shut the fuck up. Don't want to hear you either." She nods, and I grip her shoulder, driving into her harder and harder, closing my eyes and remembering how good Alexa felt when she gave herself to me.

The sweet part of her lips and thighs so ready to be owned by me. The taste of her on my tongue. Fuck. I pull out and beat the head of my dick against the crack of Ruthie's ass, to finish getting off.

"That's it?" she seethes as I tuck back into my jeans.

I shrug and she flies at me like a crazy bearcat. Scratching and hitting anywhere she can connect with me. I wrap my arms around her, caging her in. her body sags against mine. "You gonna stop," I murmur in her ear.

"I swear to you, James, if I find out who you're fucking I'll tell my father, and he'll cut out her heart and make you eat it while I watch."

"Don't threaten me with a good time, sweetheart. I'm a heartless bastard. Bitches I stick my dick in to get it wet don't matter to me. No more than you do." I let her go. "Don't wait up."

"If you leave, I'll tell my father you hit me."

"Think I'm scared of your old man? One day he won't be around to protect you. Then what will you do?"

Ruthie flings herself onto the bed and punches the mattress like a damn toddler pitching a fit. I leave her to wallow in her own misery. I slam the door and see

Rochelle's light is on. I pray she didn't hear. I stop at her doorway and peer in at her to see her asleep with her headphones in. Probably to drown out her mother and me. I flick her light off.

"Sleep tight, princess." I shut her door and go out to climb on my Road King, roaring off into the night toward Alexa.

Chapter Eleven

It's late that much I know when my door creaks and he enters the room I've been staying in at Lily's. She's been great to me. Letting me share what I want to at my own pace and never forcing me into any uncomfortable situations or conversations. I've been here three or four days and have gotten to know some of the other women and their heartbreaking stories. One thing I have taken away from them is I'm not alone and there is hope for all of us.

"Hey, pretty girl. Did I wake you?" he leans against the wall looking like a biker dream, but there's a sadness in his eyes.

"No. I couldn't sleep anyway." I sit up against the headboard and fiddle with the strap of my tank top that keeps sliding down my arm. "Wasn't sure I'd see you again."

"Made you a promise. You'll never have to worry about Todd ever again."

I suck in a breath. Chills tingle up and down my spine. The hair on my arms stands. I know Todd's dead. Part of me is relieved. The rest of me is worried about James. He committed murder for me. "I see. Is that all?" my chin wobbles and tears burn in the creases of my eyes. I don't want to cry but can't seem to stop myself. My body trembles, my stomach twists in knots.

In three strides he comes to me. Knuckles brushing along my jaw he smiles. "I'm not good at goodbyes."

"Does it have to be?"

"Seeing you again was a risk. Got a lot of shit going on. Shit I don't want you dragged into."

I wrap my fingers around his wrist. "Don't go. Not yet."

"Lex," he winces, saying my name as if it pains him.

"Please, James. I know you have to go but can't you just hold me for a minute."

"It's not a good idea, babe." His lips brush over my forehead, and the tears I've been holding back fall freely. "Don't cry."

"I'll be okay. You have to go." I hiccup on a sob, turning my head away, unable to watch him walk out the door for good.

"Look at me." He jerks my head toward him. "Wish it didn't have to be this way."

"I know. Will you….can I kiss you goodbye?"

James sucks in a breath then exhales. "Wish I was strong enough to resist the temptation of you." His mouth comes down hard on mine, tongue prodding at the seam of my lips. I open to him and taste the saltiness of my own tears.

I grab the collar of his shirt and yank him toward me, catching him off guard. My sexy savior falls onto the bed with me. Fevered by desire he doesn't break away. He continues to kiss me deep and with lots of tongue, fingers yanking at my clothes. My tank top gets tossed to the floor, and I return the favor, removing his tee, needing to feel him skin to skin one last time. A wave of perfume hits me, and I jerk away.

"You've been with someone else." Scrubbing a palm over his beard he doesn't deny it. I know he isn't mine. I wish he were. The realization that I'm not the only woman in his life sucker punches me in the gut.

"You know I'm a married man."

"I wish you were mine," I confess. "I hate her. I shouldn't, but I do. I wish terrible horrible things on her. I know that makes me a bad person."

"If things were different, I'd make you mine." He brings my hand to his lips, kisses my knuckles, and slides me to his side, hugging me tight. "I need to go. You deserve better. A fresh start somewhere new. Leave the mistakes you've made and the pain you endured behind."

"Come with me. We can go anywhere. No one would ever find us."

"We both know I can't." he nabs his shirt off the floor, but I stop him from putting it back on. I straddle his thighs. James wraps an arm around my back, and I cup his face between my hands, rubbing his beard.

"I don't care that you're married. You were meant to be with me. I know it, and you feel it, don't you?" I press his palm to my heart over my bare breast. "It can be our secret. Just you and me. No one else. We can make it work. I'll be with you any way I can be."

I roll my hips and kiss his lips softly.

"Wouldn't be fair. Wouldn't be right."

"You're an outlaw. Since when do you care about doing the right thing? Do you love her?"

I hold his gaze refusing to back down from my question.

"Not talking about this with you."

"I can handle the truth. I may be young, but I'm a good listener."

"Last thing I wanna do is talk about my marital problems."

"Then. What. Do. You. Want. To. Do."

"Bury myself so deep inside you I disappear." He holds me tighter.

"I wish we could stay like this right here forever." I breathe him in and hate that I can smell his wife on him. Doing my best to block it out, I cradle my arms around his neck, pressing my breasts against his chest. "Stay with me. For the night."

His hands rest on my wrists. "I'm no good for you."

"I can't unlove you and I don't want to. You'll never belong to me in the way that I belong to you. It kills me. But I'd rather take what pieces I can and hold on tight for as long as you'll let me."

"Don't you want better, Lex. Better than this. Better than me."

"How could there ever be better for me than you? No one has ever made me feel the way I do when you look at

115

me. When you touch me, I think I could die because you showed me what true love is. You'll say I'm young and don't know what love is, but I know what hate is. I've seen ugly. I've tasted it. You killed for me. If that isn't love, then what is? Who else would go that far for me? No one."

"I'm no hero. Far from a saint." Running his hand through my hair he smiles. "You've changed. Been forced to grow up a lot faster than you should've. You're going to be just fine without me." Hand sliding down my back, his fingers trace the ridges of my spine. "I've gotta let you go. I can't keep you, babe. I've made a lot of mistakes, but you aren't one of them."

I rock against him as our lips meet. James kisses me slow and methodical. He does this switch move, flipping me to my back. He gazes down at me, and I swear I can see his soul blazing behind his eyes. Burning for me. I'll never forget this moment. I've committed the memory to my heart. The flames of his kisses dance across my skin. Dragging my shorts down my legs, he continues to taste every inch of my skin along the way until he meets my pelvic bone.

Heart thumping out of my chest I anticipate his next move.

He buries his head between my legs and shows me just how much he adores me with his fingers and tongue.

Teeth sinking into my lip, I bite it to keep from crying out. No one can know about us. They wouldn't understand that he took the broken fragments holding me together, filled the gaps, and made me whole. Head thrown back on the bed I close my eyes as every stroke of his tongue is killing me slowly. I've never been more turned on.

The man doesn't stop till my knees shakes and my stomach drops as though I've just gone down the big dip on a roller coaster.

"Look at me, Lex."

I go up on my elbows.

"Can't make you no promises. Can't give you a damn thing but this. Understand?"

I nod. "You're not mine. I know that. But it doesn't mean I can't be yours." He snakes up my body and looms over me with intimidation masked over his features. "Shh." I press my finger to his mouth. "Don't argue. If this is goodbye let's make it count. Make love to me."

His forehead drops to mine, and I'm afraid he's going to leave. I grab him between the legs, he's hard as steel.

"I need you."

A groan leaves his lips. "I fucked my wife before I came here tonight."

I squeeze him harder. "It doesn't matter. She's not here now, but we are. You don't love her."

"No." he tries to jerk away.

"So that's it. You're going to pretend that you don't want me? That you feel nothing. That you don't want to give me one last piece of you before you go. You gonna go home and kiss your wife after you ate me all night?"

"Watch it," he growls the words at me.

"You want me."

"Doesn't mean I can have you."

"C'mere." I crook a finger at him.

"Fuck me," he mutters and leans toward me.

I wrap a hand around the back of his neck. "Can you really walk away from what you feel for me?"

He pulls away and my heart shatters. My breath hitches in my throat. This is it. I've lost him.

"No." I never knew one word could mean so much till now. He comes at me hot and fast. I go for his zipper, and he makes quick work of getting his jeans off. James lays me down, and slides inside me in one hard thrust that makes my body jolt. "When I'm inside you, feels like home," he whispers into my neck. "But, baby, tonight I'm going to fuck you till you cry."

His body moves against mine violently. Our skin slaps together, hips rubbing and rocking as though we can't get close enough. Hard and deep his strokes are vicious. Sweat drips down his body and clings to me.

"Fuck. So wet. So tight." He grunts and his cock jerks inside me, his warmth washing over me. Short of breath he kisses me, stroking my cheek. "Perfect, Lex."

I hug him to me not ready to let go but knowing I have to.

Chapter Twelve

"Where you off to?" I glance at Rochelle, noticing my daughter is growing up too damn fast. I swear she keeps getting taller.

"I'm going out with Colter."

I raise my brow at her. "Papa's boy?"

"Yes." She smiles, batting her lashes.

"Is this a date?"

"Maybe. I don't know. I think so. I really like him."

"You know the rule."

"You already know him, so I didn't think it's a big deal. You like Colter and Papa is one of your best buds or whatever."

"Whether or not I like him ain't got shit do with him taking my daughter out."

Ruthie comes out of the kitchen licking chocolate frosting off her fingers. "You leaving?"

"You knew about this?" Of course she did.

"I didn't think it'd be that big a deal."

Ignoring her, I turn my attention back to Rochelle. "He picking you up?"

"Yeah, then we're grabbing Alexa and going out to eat."

Hearing Alexa's name freezes my blood.

I walked away from her. Our last conversation sounds inside my head.

"Why you gotta make shit so damn hard for me, pretty girl?"

A tear slid down her cheek. *"Because I wish you'd choose me. That you'd show me I'm worth the fight. That somewhere buried deep in that black heart a part of you loves me."*

I cupped her jaw, my heart split in two. I'm living a double life. Caught between heaven and hell. *"I care about you, baby. You're the only woman I go on my knees for."* I went to my knees and practically begged her to understand. I never asked for any of this. Hell, she didn't either. I never expected to fall for her.

"Hello." A hand waves over my face. "Earth to, Dad."

"What?" I grumble.

"So can I go?"

"Yeah whatever, but I want a word with him first."

"Thanks. You're the best dad ever." She comes in for a hug.

Ruthie mutters, "That's debatable."

Fucking cunt. I've been trying my damnedest to appease her. Keeping my enemy close, working her for information on her bastard father. He's at the top of my list. He's not an easy man to get to. He started asking too many questions when Alexa turned back up a few days after I dropped her at the train station and Todd didn't. Called up Lily's old man, Bronson. Sticking his nose where it doesn't belong. Pressing for answers asking if there had been any new girls brought in.

Only person who knew about Alexa other than Slick was Grudge. I trust Slick. He wouldn't have turned on me nor Lily, now Grudge that's debatable. The fucker has a temper and when you piss him off forgiveness doesn't come easy hence the name. I don't think I've gotten on his bad side, though he did feel slighted when Lily turned him down, but hell that was years ago.

No. Lion's got eyes on me. And if anything, he knows about Alexa, but the bastard has kept quiet. I know his secret and he knows mine.

"Is it okay if Alexa spends the night?"

"I don't know if you hanging out with her is such a good idea."

"She's my best friend, and I have barely seen her since she got back."

"Don't her folks want her at home?"

"They kicked her out."

"Where is she living then?" Ruthie questions, looking concerned.

Rochelle shrugs. "She's been staying with Carla, but she can't live there. I was hoping she could stay here."

"Here?" I nearly choke the word out.

"She can stay tonight, but your father and I will need to talk about it. Her folks won't let her come back?"

"I mean, you know how strict her dad is. He's pretty pissed about her running off with Todd. He dumped her at some motel and left her stranded."

Fuck me. My fist curls around my beer. She made up a story about that piece of shit. I know she probably did it thinking she was helping to protect me for what I did, but I don't want her involved. Alexa never should've returned.

A knock sounds at the front door. "That's Colter," Rochelle says with a squeal. "And, Dad, be nice please."

I grunt in response as she flies toward the door practically floating. Jesus. I'm not ready for this shit.

"Hey, Colter. Um…can you come in for a sec. My dad wants to talk to you."

Colter breezes in every bit his father's son. Dark hair swept back in a ponytail, showing off the shaved sides of his head. Tattooed and dangerous. He looks too damn old to be taking out my princess.

"Murder." He extends his right hand, and I spy a Tasmanian Devil tattooed on his forearm. I give him a firm shake and it pleases me that he's not nervous. I respect that he had the balls to show up and face me like a man.

"Colter. Rochelle tells me you're taking her out tonight."

"That's the plan." He grins at my daughter and my first instinct is to wrap my hand around his throat and toss him out on his ass, but I won't. Papa's a good man, and I know Colter is a good kid. If Rochelle is going to date anyone, I'd rather it be him. I know he'll treat her right or answer to me and his old man.

"Where you taking her?"

"Dinner and a movie."

"All right. Want her home by ten."

"Dad," Rochelle wines and Colter chuckles under his breath.

"Eleven-thirty," Ruthie overrides me.

"Fine, but not a minute later. Understood."

"Yes, sir."

"You kids have a good time. And, Colter. Not a hair on her head, feel me."

"I'll keep my hands to myself if that's what you mean."

"Lips too."

"Oh, my God, Dad. Stop." Rochelle grabs her date by the hand and drags him out the door.

I hear them leave and Ruthie goes back to the kitchen. I follow her. "We need to talk." I place my beer on the counter and fold my arms across my chest.

"What about?" She sprinkles candy over the cupcakes.

"Alexa."

Ruthie looks up. "What about her?"

"She can't move in with us. We don't need to involve ourselves in whatever trouble she's gotten herself in."

"Let me worry about it. You're a man so you don't understand these things. It won't be permanent. I'm sure her parents will come around. I'll talk to them, but in the

126

meantime, I think she's safer here then out there on her own. Don't you?"

I know she's right but having my greatest temptation and one weakness under my roof is asking for trouble I don't need. "Why don't I talk to her father and see what I can do?"

"Sure. Whatever. Help me get these boxed up, will you? I promised I'd drop them off to Lucy for the bake sale for the new uniforms for Ro's squad."

"Sure." I swipe one for myself and Ruthie swats at me.

"These aren't for you." She comes in for a kiss. One I don't want to give, but one I know I can't deny. Keeping her happy is important more so now than ever. Her tongue presses against my lips and as much as I don't want to, I give in. Gripping the back of her head, I hold her where I want her, but inside my head it's not my wife I'm kissing.

Closing my eyes, I see Alexa clear as day. The image slices through me like a damn knife piercing through my heart. Why the hell did she come back? I break away from Ruthie when she practically purrs and starts rubbing up on me like a kitten.

"I don't have to take these just yet. We can take advantage of having the house to ourselves, honey."

"I gotta get to the clubhouse."

"James, you said you'd try."

"I know what I said."

She shoots me a seductive smile. One that doesn't have the effect she was hoping for. Down on her knees she yanks my zipper down and undoes my belt. "Let me send you off properly then." The bitch strokes my shaft and licks her lips. I may not love her, but I'm sorry enough to let the cunt suck my dick.

Wrapping her lips around the head, she goes to town on my dick, working hard to make me come. I grip the back of her head and fuck her face as hard as I can, hitting the back of her throat with every deep stroke. "That's it, you dirty fucking slut. Suck me till I come down your throat."

She gurgles, nearly gagging on me, but I don't stop. Tears escape the creases of her closed eyes as she suctions that mouth around me tighter.

"Fuck yeah, Ale-Ruthie. Swallow for me." If she heard my slip up, she doesn't show it.

Unable to take anymore she pops free, my warm seed still spurting out onto her lips. Her tongue darts out to capture the rest and lick me clean. When she's finished, I tuck back into my jeans and get ready to leave.

"I've been thinking."

"Yeah?"

"I want another baby."

"A baby?" My heart seizes in my chest. The last thing I want is to have another kid with this bitch.

"Yes, James. Ro is getting older. Soon she will be off to college and starting her own life. We always talked about trying for a son, but then you fucked everything up and went to prison. I know that's all in the past. I just don't want to wake up one day and have any regrets. I stopped taking my birth control."

"Don't you think the timing is bad. We can hardly be in the same room together and you want to bring another kid into the mix. Why? You think it will make me stay? Keep me on a leash?"

"No. I want more for us. I want you to be my husband again. My father wants someone to pass his legacy on to."

"You father? What the fuck does he have to do with this? You been running your mouth to him again behind my back?"

"No. But if I want to talk about our marriage with my father I can. You don't control me, James."

"That's the truest thing to ever leave your mouth. Why would I want to have another baby with you when I can barely stand the sight of you? You weren't always such a miserable controlling cunt."

"Take it back."

"Or what?"

"Don't push me. You won't like it when I push back. Remember that." She flips her hair over her shoulder and storms off.

She forgets that if I go down so does she.

Fucking hell I didn't see this coming. I scrub a palm over my face and tug on my beard. Another kid. Over my dead body will I have a son. I'm not tainting my bloodline with any more of Lion's DNA. It's a wonder Rochelle is a good kid. With Ruthie as her mother and my sorry ass for a father it's a motherfucking miracle she isn't as fucked up as the rest of us.

Chapter Thirteen

MURDER

"Looks like you have the weight of the world on your shoulders." Papa pulls out the chair next to me.

"Just got a lot of shit on my mind."

"This don't have anything to do with Rochelle and Colter does it?"

"Naw. I'm not stressing that. I know he'll treat my girl right. He has you for a father."

"I'll take that as a compliment." He takes a hard pull off his longneck beer.

"You should. He's a handsome little fucker too."

"He does look like me, don't he?"

"Fuck he's a spitting image, man. Except for that white in your hair." I chuckle and he shakes his head. Papa got his name for his looks. Namely his hair. Going white at his temples and a few other spots like an old man. "You should be proud."

"I am. We may be in-laws one day."

"Slow down. Rochelle ain't getting married anytime soon."

"Keep telling yourself that. What's got you looking ready to shoot the clubhouse up?"

"Ruthie wants another kid."

"And you don't?"

"Hell no. Having Rochelle is plenty. I'm not ready to go back to sleepless nights and diapers. Long past that stage in life."

"I can understand that. Sometimes though I think it'd be nice to go back. Shit was a lot less complicated back then."

"Ain't that the fucking truth," I mutter and finish off my beer.

"Need another?" Kristen nabs my empty bottle.

"No thanks, darlin'. I'm about to ride out, but I'm sure Papa here could use some company." I push my chair back as she drops into his lap.

"Later, brother."

"I'll see you at the wedding." His head falls back, and he howls with laughter.

"Fuck off," I grumble and shove a cigarette between my lips.

"Who's getting married?' I hear Kristen ask as I walk out.

Asshole thinks he's real funny. That shit ain't nothing to joke about. I've decided I'm locking Rochelle in her room till she's thirty.

Rolling up to the house, I'm not ready to have Ruthie and Alexa under the same roof, but don't have much of a choice. I park my motorcycle in the garage. Walking into the house I hear giggles coming from the kitchen.

Fuck. I shoulda stayed at the clubhouse tonight. Anywhere else but here.

"We're in the kitchen, James," Ruthie calls out.

I stomp into the room, relief washing over me when I see it's only my wife and daughter sitting at the counter eating the left-over cupcakes.

"I see you made it home in one piece." I rub my palm over the top of Rochelle's hair, scuffing it up.

"Ugh, Dad," she whines.

"You have a good time on your date?"

"Our little girl is growing up. Had her first real kiss tonight."

"I don't need to hear that shit."

"Whatever." Rochelle rolls her eyes. "Do you want a cupcake?"

"I'm good. Alexa not staying over?"

"She's here. I think she's taking a shower or getting ready for bed."

"Right. You girls don't stay up too late."

"We won't."

Ruthie shadows me to our bedroom and closes the door. "Did you think about what I said?"

"Nothing to think about."

"I want a baby."

"Ask your boyfriend then."

"Why are you being like this?"

"Like what exactly? Reasonable. An adult. You think another kid will magically fix this?" I shrug my shirt over the back of my head and toss it into a nearby hamper.

"I don't know but don't we owe it to ourselves to try? To my father to carry on the family."

"I'm not fighting with you about this." I kick my jeans off and grab my pillow off the bed.

"What are you doing?"

"Going to the couch."

"Rochelle has a friend over."

"And?"

"I don't want her gossiping at school that Rochelle's dad sleeps on the couch."

"Who gives a fuck about what some school kids think?"

"I do. It'll get back to the other cheer moms."

"You're fucking ridiculous you know that." I shake my head and go to the living room, grabbing a spare blanket from the hall closet as I go. Flopping down on the couch, I grab the remote and turn some action movie on. I toss and turn until about two in the morning when I hear someone in the kitchen. I peer over the back of the couch and see Alexa standing in front of the sink. Her blonde locks hang down her back and the pale green shorts she's wearing hug her ass. I should roll back over and pretend to be asleep, but find my feet carrying me to the kitchen because I'm a damn glutton for punishment.

"Can't sleep?" Alexa jumps at the sound of my voice and turns to face me. Tears rolling down her cheeks. On reflex I go to her, wrapping my arms around her, pressing her head into my chest.

She gazes up at me. "I'm sorry. I thought I could do this but being back here... Brings the nightmares back."

"It's okay." I kiss her forehead, and she tilts her head up more, her lips calling to mine like a damn siren calling to a sailor at sea. "Is there anything I can do? Ruthie takes sleeping pills. I'll get you one if you think it'd help."

135

"No. No pills." She shakes her head. "I know you're mad at me for coming back, but I couldn't do it. I couldn't go out into the world while knowing you were back here. I don't have anything if I don't have you in my life."

"Lex, we can't do this."

"Yes, we can." Her sweet breath fans over my mouth, and like a magnet I'm drawn straight to her. My hands roam to her hips, and I lift her onto the counter, her legs hooking around my waist. Dipping my head, I capture her mouth with mine, greedily taking whatever I can get of her.

"Why can't I give you up?"

"Because you love me," she whispers and kisses my palm.

I step away and shake my head. I take one look at her, and I know I am so damn fucked I need a new word for how gone I am for her. I must be crazy. My wife and daughter are right down the hall. Either of them could wake up at any moment and find us together.

"Go to bed. I'm gonna talk to your folks about you coming back home tomorrow."

"I'm not going back. You can't make me."

"You can't stay here."

"You want me to go say the word."

"You know that's not what I meant."

"Is it because of your wife?"

"Don't go there."

"Why? If you can't be honest with me then who can you trust?"

"I trust you, Lex, it's me I worry about. I can't keep my hands off you, baby."

She pops off the counter, padding barefoot across the room, quiet as a mouse. Circling her arms around my waist, she whispers, "I don't want you to." Her nipples rub against me, poking me through the thin fabric of her tank. I want nothing more than to strip her bare and kiss her all over.

I breathe her in, getting a whiff of her coconut scented shampoo.

"Get some sleep."

"I don't want to sleep." Alexa's dainty fingers slip inside the waistband of my boxer briefs. I grab her hand, preventing any further contact.

"Alexa," Rochelle calls out.

"Go." I move away from her.

Alexa nods and exits the kitchen. I grip the edge of the counter and let out a breath. I need a joint.

Out in the garage I fire one up. Then like the sorry bastard that I am I jerk off to thoughts of fucking Alexa bent over the hood of my wife's car.

**

"I'm sorry, sir, but you can't go in there. Dr. Neville is with a patient."

I narrow my eyes on her. "Tell him James Thatcher is here to see him about his daughter."

She finally looks at my cut and recognition dawns on the receptionist's face. "Right away." Her throat bobs, and she nearly trips over her own feet as she scurries down the hall.

A minute later the door opens, and the weasel shows his face. "You have no business coming here. We have nothing to discuss."

"That's where you're wrong. Your daughter needs a place to live."

"I no longer have a daughter."

"No you don't. Alexa is dead to you, but I'll tell you what you're going to do. You're going to furnish an apartment to finish out the school year and supply her a car. And if you don't not only will I make a call about the abuse she endured living under your roof, but I'll also see to it you lose your license to practice."

"You don't scare me."

"No?" I lift him by his throat and laugh as he struggles to free himself. "Don't even think about it," I warn the woman at the desk when she goes to pick up the phone.

I drop him.

He rubs at his neck. "Alexa won't get a dime from me. Might as well pass her around at your clubhouse, but to be honest I doubt she'd be worth the trouble."

I lean in close. "If I were you, I'd sleep armed and with one eye open. If I see you even look in her direction, I'll buttfuck your world so hard you'll beg me to end your meaningless life."

The worthless asshole pisses himself.

"I'll see myself out."

I'm almost out the door when he calls out, "Wait." I turn back, and he cowers under my stare. "Let me write a check."

"No. You lost your chance to do the right thing."

"What do you mean?"

"Alexa doesn't need you to take care of her. I've got her covered."

"You come back, and I'll press charges for assault."

"Right. One eye open." I slap his shoulder then depart.

Chapter Fourteen

"What's up with you?"

I shrug at Rochelle. "I don't know what you mean."

She taps her finger against her chin. "Hmmm. You seem...I don't know happy."

"You say it like that's a bad thing."

"It's not, but there's something different about you. I don't know. You're kind of glowing."

"Glowing?" I shove her shoulder and she giggle snorts.

"Yes. I can't explain it."

"I mean I'm living away from my folks. I'm working on getting my grades back up after all the time I missed when I was gone."

"Does this mean you get to graduate?"

"I get to graduate if I can stay on track and don't miss anymore school."

"Dude. That's amazeballs."

"Who says amazeballs?" I make a face and grab another slice of pizza.

"I do. It's a popular phrase."

"Whatever you say."

"Colter doesn't complain." She grins.

"I bet he doesn't. Are you guys official now?"

"Yeah... I think so."

"You think?"

"I mean I know he isn't dating anyone else and he calls me his girl."

"I'm glad you guys finally got together. I was getting sick of you two making puppy dog eyes at one another."

Her eyes roll. "We do not do that."

"You so do but it's sweet. You guys are super cute together."

"We are, aren't we?" I nod. "When are you going to start dating again? Colter said Tanner thinks you're hot."

"I'm seeing someone."

"Since when? And why do I, your best friend in the entire world not know about this?"

"He's older so we have to be careful." I bite into my food.

"How old? It's not Todd is it?"

Hearing his name, my mind flashes to him pinning me down on the floor in this same room. Midchew my stomach rolls in the worst way. I drop the slice and cover my mouth, running for the bathroom.

"Alexa what's wrong?" Rochelle yells after me as I drop to my knees and pray to the porcelain throne.

All the food and soda I consumed comes rushing up so fast it shoots out my nose.

"Can I do anything?" I shake my head, but she gathers my hair and pulls it back. "Want me to get my mom?"

"No. I felt a little off earlier." I wipe my mouth with a tissue and flush it with my dinner.

Rochelle steps out in the hall and I clean up.

"I think I'm going to take a nap."

"Fine, but I want to know who this new guy is."

"New guy? Who has a new guy?" Ruthie questions, coming down the hall with a laundry basket pressed to her hip.

Her mom would kill me, Rochelle too, if they knew that James is my guy. I'm his dirty little secret. His girl on the side. The other woman. I should feel guilty, but I don't. I love him so much it physically hurts when we aren't together.

"I've just been talking to someone in an online chat. He's in college," I mumble.

"Well be careful you never know if you're talking to a real person or not."

"Of course."

"What are you two doing just standing in the hall?"

"She threw-up," Rochelle volunteers.

"Are you okay? Need me to get you anything?"

"No. I think the pizza was just too greasy or something." I can't say being in this house is hard. That one of the worst experiences I've ever endured began in the living room and sometimes I experience flashbacks of that night.

"I'm having dinner with some friends tonight, but if you need me to stay home I can."

"I'll be fine. Ro will look after me."

"All right. I'm leaving in about an hour and won't be back till late. You girls behave yourselves."

"We will, Mom."

I go into Rochelle's room and flop on the twin bed her mom had James set up for me until I find something more permanent. My staying here is temporary. Ruthie says I can stay as long as I want, but I know she'd change her tune in a heartbeat if she knew the truth.

That I've been fucking her husband behind her back.

James has been gone for a few weeks now. Gone on what Rochelle called a run for the club. I wanted to ask her more about it but didn't want to seem too interested in her dad. I only stay here to be close to him and he's not even here.

I miss him. I wish I knew when he was coming home.

Rochelle keeps staring at her phone and giggling. Part of me is jealous. Her and Colter don't have to hide their relationship. He can take her on a date and not have to worry who might see them together.

The bedroom door opens, and Ruthie lets us know she's leaving. The minute she's gone Rochelle jumps up and slides her shoes on. "Colter's picking me up. Do you wanna go or stay here?"

My stomach is all gross still, and I'm not in the mood to watch them sucking face all night. "I think I'll hang here. You go. Have fun. You don't need me tagging along every time the two of you go out."

"I don't mind. Colter doesn't either. He could invite Tanner."

"I'm afraid I'm coming down with a stomach flu or something. I wouldn't be any fun. And I don't want Tanner getting the idea I like him or something."

"Okay…but if you change your mind call me and we'll come back for you."

"I'll probably sleep."

"Fine." she huffs. "See you later."

"Bye."

With everyone gone I realize this is the first time I've been alone in the house since that night. Panic bubbles in my chest, flooding my veins with anxiety. I take a deep breath and close my eyes. I know Todd can't hurt me anymore. I'm being silly. I can't finish the pizza but that doesn't mean I can't continue the movie Rochelle and I had started.

I'm about halfway through the movie when I hear a motorcycle pull up. My pulse races. James must be home, and it will be the first real moment I will get him to myself since I started staying here. I dash to the bathroom to make sure I look halfway decent considering I threw up earlier. Fingers slipping through my hair to undo the knots, I gaze at my pale appearance, and pray he's as excited to see me as I am him.

The movie still plays from the living room, the Tv casting a soft glow on the walls of the dark room. A man sits in the recliner with his face shielded to me. A lighter flicks, and the moment I catch a whiff of the minty smoke, I gasp.

I slap a palm to my lips immediately but it's too late. He sees me, and I see the face of the devil when he glances in my direction. "I'm surprised to see you here. I guess the last time wasn't enough. Come back for more?" he stands as I shrink back at the recognition I have of the sound of his voice washing over me like my worst dream come true.

My head screams for my feet to move but they are rooted in place.

"I..I don't want any trouble."

A deep but hoarse chuckle rips from his throat. A sinister sound that is a warning that my body recognizes. Goosebumps pebble across my skin. The room seems to drop in temperature. I'm chilled to the bone. "No one's going to save you now. I should've known I couldn't count on Todd to finish the job. This time I won't make any mistakes." He takes a drag off his cigarette. His lips pucker to blow out a smoke ring and my skin crawls.

There's only one way for me to go and that's to run back down the hallway and barricade myself in one of the rooms or go out a window. Distracted by my own thoughts I'm not prepared when he grabs me, pressing the ember of his cigarette into my arm using the hand tattooed with a lion's head wearing a crown. I cry out, kicking with all I have, but I'm powerless against his strength.

The Lion as I now call him carries me kicking and screaming to the master bedroom. He drops me on the bed, and I attempt to scramble away from him, doing a backwards crab crawl across the mattress, but he's too fast.

Slap. I'm backhanded, his tattooed hand connecting with my mouth, splitting my lip in two with one of his rings. "You filthy little cunt. I know all about you. Been keeping an eye on you and my useless son-in-law. First you fucked with my money, had my top seller killed, and now you've tried to ruin my daughter's marriage. Nobody fucks with what's mine and gets away with it."

"I—"

Thwack. He punches me. "Shut up. I didn't say you speak." A sharp pain like I've never experienced before shoots through my skull and my vision blurs.

Stars dance in my eyes. I know this time there's no one to save me. I never should've come back, but I couldn't stay away from James. I don't regret loving him. I only wish we could've had more time. I disappear inside my mind, getting swept away in my memories of him.

We may be a thousand miles apart for all I know, but he'll live in my heart these last minutes or seconds that I have left.

"Look at me," the hateful man screams in my face.

I refuse him, earning me a punch to the gut. *Oof.* All the air goes whooshing out of me. A tear rolls down my cheek as I struggle to escape back inside my mind to thoughts of my biker. Our forbidden love. Everything we never said.

"I said look at me when I'm talking to you." His rough hands wrap around my throat. This time I don't deny him. My eyes bulge as I struggle to breathe. I scratch with all I have, clawing at his arms, grabbing at his shirt.

"I'm going to fuck every hole you have until your body gives out." He lets go of my throat, and I try to roll away from him. I get on my right side when he starts tugging on my yoga pants, yanking them halfway down my legs. I try to fight, but I can scarcely catch my breath. "Stop moving." The evil bastard attempts to pin me to the mattress. His fingers tear at my panties, nails digging into my skin.

"I forgot my… what the fuck are you doing?" Ruthie screeches. "Get off her." She flies toward us, and I pray that she can stop him.

"Get the fuck out and mind your own God damn business."

"I. Oh. My. God. Alexa, sweetie," she cries, and he backhands her like he did me earlier. Her head whips to the side. "Have you lost your mind?" She screams.

"Do I need to tell you to get the fuck out again," he roars, towering over her with his fist raised. I should run, but I'm unable to look away. I concentrate on getting my pants back up over my hips. "This is club business and nothing to do with you."

"But she's just…"

"I said mind your own business." He moves to hit her again and she cowers away from him, backing out of the room slowly.

"Ruthie, please. Help me," I cry out hoarsely, but she's gone. Lion charges toward me. "No. Please. No," I whimper as he grabs me up by the hair and slaps me so hard, I black out momentarily.

"Get away from her," Ruthie says from the doorway of the bedroom aiming a handgun at my tormentor.

"This doesn't concern you, girl."

"I said get away from her."

"Or what? You aren't going to shoot me." With his attention off me, I try to run past him. His arm hooks around my waist before I've taken two steps.

"Let her go and we'll never speak of this again."

"I don't take orders from you. I fucking give them." He pokes around in his pocket, producing a knife for his effort. Pressing the blade to my throat he walks me toward her. "I'm leaving and taking this little bitch with me. We have unfinished business. A score to settle. This is club business."

We're standing directly in front of her now and Ruthie presses the barrel of her gun between his eyes. Oh God. If she doesn't kill him, he'll kill us both. The blade cuts into my skin. I whimper feeling the trickle of blood rolling down my neck.

Chapter Fifteen

Stick a fork in me and call me roadkill. Lion sent me up north to deliver a whore he traded off to The Stable. It's a ranch in Canada where they shoot porno flicks. I don't know why he needed me to personally escort her there, but I suspect he didn't want me poking around in his affairs.

Rolling down my street I see Lion's motorcycle out front of my house. Ruthie's car is running in the driveway, but no lights are on inside the house other than the occasional flicker from the Tv projecting on the walls and reflecting on the window. It's not unusual for my father-in-law to visit with Ruthie, but I have a bad inkling in my gut. I park, shut my bike off, and head for the door.

I don't know what gives me pause, but I open the door quietly. Slipping inside I listen and wait.

"Do-don't make me choose," I overhear Ruthie. The tremble in her voice sends me running. My pulse drums in my ears and races up and down my throat. I stop short in the hall behind my wife. In a standoff with her father she presses the barrel of my .45 between his eyes. Alexa is tucked into his chest with a knife to her throat.

My veins burn with the taste for vengeance. Tonight this bastard is going to die executioner style but not at her hands. I won't let my wife have that on her heart no matter how I feel about her. I created this madness and sadness that exists between us. Look up pain in the dictionary and you'll see our marriage. We've done nothing but hurt each other.

Placing my hand over Ruthie's on the gun, I tell her, "Take Alexa and get out of here. This is between your old man and me." The fear shining back at me through Alexa's eyes nearly cuts me in two. He put his fucking hands on her for the last time.

Lion chuckles. "Never have liked you. You think you're man enough to take me on?"

"Let Alexa go. It's me you want. You've got me."

He shoves Alexa into Ruthie and she eases her grip on the weapon but refuses to relinquish it to me. "Take her out of here," she grits through her teeth. Alexa moves to my side clinging onto me for dear life.

I have a choice to make. Save the woman I love or defend the one I married. Ruthie is Rochelle's mother, and I made a vow to love and protect her. It's no choice. Not one anyone should have to make.

"No. This is club business. Let him answer for his sins. Drop the knife or I put you to ground without a fair trial."

"If that's how you want to play it." The knife hits the floor, and he holds his palms out. "They'll never side against me."

I kick the knife away.

"Are you sure?" Ruthie asks.

"You and Alexa will stand as witnesses. He disrespected me by coming into my house and hurting what's mine." Ruthie shoots me a funny look, and I correct myself. "Alexa's under my protection."

"You sure that's all it is?" Lion motions head toward Alexa curled into my side as though I'm her lifeline.

I ignore his accusation. Ruthie doesn't need to know about Alexa and me. Not tonight. "He threatened you. Daughter or not you're my wife. I won't stand for anyone harming you. My family is my world. You know that. Your father doesn't care about you or Rochelle. He spits on his patch and club. If he moves, shoot him."

Ruthie strengthens her stance and clicks the safety off.

I squeeze Alexa's hand, but don't take my eyes off the enemy. "Go to the garage. There's rope on the utility shelf." I want to reassure her that everything is going to be fine, but the club could vote against me. Lion's been Prez a long damn time. This shit could backfire and go sideways. It could be me who is cast out and not him.

**

Emergency church is in session. Lion sits at the head of the table, but he's in chains. Ruthie and Alexa are sitting at the bar under the watchful eye of a prospect. This isn't ideal or how I planned to take the bastard out, but here we are. Nickel, Lion's right-hand man and VP glances around the room counting heads.

"I call this meeting to order. Brothers you have been called here tonight under unusual circumstances. I'm not going to waste anyone's time. Let's cut straight to it. Lion, you stand accused of breaking our code, of disrespecting a brother and his property. Murder claims you went to his home uninvited twice and assaulted someone under his protection. You are charged with not only sexual assault and battery but conspiring to deal Cloud Nine with the

Dry Ridge Sinners after we voted against the deal. Do you deny these charges?"

"Fuck you. This is my club. None of you would be shit without me. I did what the rest of you were too pussy to. That girl was in the way. Murder had no right to offer her protection. We're only here because he's pissed I fucked his little cunt first. She begged me for it. Bitch was fucking dripping she wanted it so much."

Grinding my teeth, I ball my fists, finding it hard to resist the urge to take him out right here. He's baiting me, but I'm not playing his game.

"That true?" Nickel turns his questioning on me.

"No."

Lion smirks. "He's fuckin' her all right."

"Where I stick my dick has nothing to do with what you did. This isn't about me. It's about you and what a sick fuck you are. I went to prison for killing the worm food who hurt my sister. I have no problem doing time if it means I get to put you down and ensure you never touch another hair on Alexa's head, but I wanted to do this right so there'd be no doubt that when you take your last breath it's for good reason. You're a traitor to that patch and don't deserve to wear it."

"And you think you do?"

"No, but someone better than you does."

"Enough. Grudge, bring in the girl."

The room goes quiet. Women are never allowed in on club business, but this is a rare exception. Grudge returns with Alexa and seeing her in the light…it's worse than I thought. Holding ice to her mouth she's brought to the front of the room. One glance around the table at their faces tells me my brothers don't like what they are seeing any more than I do.

Bruised and spirit broken she stands before us with nothing to gain for it but everything to lose. If the club takes Lion's side, it could mean a death sentence for not only me but Ruthie and Alexa. Papa knows if I go down Colter is to get Rochelle out of town. I may not be much of a father, but I won't let her die in my name.

Blood related or not if Lion makes it out of this, he'll wipe my family out.

"Do you understand what's being asked of you?" Nickel begins questioning Alexa.

"Yes."

"And you understand that if you lie there will be consequences?"

"Yes."

"Whatever happens in this room is to never be spoken of outside of these walls, yeah?"

"I understand."

"Good. Let's proceed." He leans back in his seat and fires up a joint. He takes a hit then passes it around the large table with our club insignia burned into the wood. A skull with two motorcycles, one on each side. "Tell us how you know our Prez."

"I started seeing this guy, Todd." Alexa pauses, fidgeting with her fingers, twisting them together at the knuckle. "He gave me a bag of weed to keep for him, but my mom found it. She flushed it then kicked me out. He was angry and wanted his money. I had him drop me off at Ja—Murder's house because Rochelle and I are friends, and I thought I'd be safer there. Todd left for a while, but then he came back…" Bottom lip trembling, she sucks in a deep breath and wipes at her eyes.

I nod for her to go on.

"He attacked me. Started hitting me, threatening me. He knocked me to the floor and proceeded to rape me. Someone else entered the house. I couldn't see him, but I could hear him and smell him. The man hit Todd and took his turn with me. He smelled like menthol and there was

159

a tattoo." She rubs a finger over the back of her hand. "A lion's head with a crown."

"What happened after that?" Reed prompts.

"Todd took me somewhere. I was gone for weeks. He kept me drugged and one day he decided to let me go. I don't know why. I expected to die. I woke up one day at a park near my parent's house. I was scared and didn't know what to do."

"That's the day I saw you walking up and down the road," Grudge says.

"Yes. Murder took me to a safe house for the night. The next day he brought me to Lily, and I stayed there for a while. Then I came back because people were looking for me. My parents put me out again so Ruthie said I could stay until I found a more permanent situation. That's where I've been until tonight. I walked into the living room. Lion was sitting there waiting for me. Again, he attacked me. This time he took me to the bedroom, and we fought as he tore at my clothes. Ruthie came home for something. She interrupted his plans. Then Murder showed up and here we are."

"Left out the part where you and Murder been fucking," my bastard of a Prez states.

"Any truth to that, Alexa?"

160

She stares at her feet, moving her head back and forth.

"Lex, look at me," I demand. Those green eyes meet mine swirling with fear. "You don't have to protect me. I've got nothing to hide."

"Going to ask you one more time," VP tells her. "Are you having an affair with Murder?"

"I asked him to take the bad away and give me something good in its place because I couldn't sleep. I couldn't eat. I could feel their touch. Smell their breath. Hear their grunts. They filled me with poison and James took it away. He showed me not all men are bad. Made sure my body healed with antibiotics. Gave me a place to hide until I felt safe and a place to lay my head. There's nothing nefarious about that. He's the best man I've ever known. He may be a killer, but he's no liar. That man sitting there." Hand trembling, she points to Lion. "That man is pure evil. His name should be Lucifer because he's the devil. If you let him walk next time it could be your daughter or Old Lady he goes after. What will you do then?"

"That'll be all. Grudge, take her back to the bar."

"Want me to grab Ruthie?"

Nickel holds his hand up. "Won't be necessary. I think we've heard enough."

**

"Your club has denounced you as Prez. You are hereby stripped of your colors and your position within the Royal Bastard MC." Nickel takes a knife and jabs it into Lion's cut to remove the President patch. "Your wife will no longer receive any benefits from the club. You will not be buried with club honors nor will we speak of you after today. Your existence will be scrubbed. It will be as though you disappeared. I, Nickel acting in my role as Vice President sentence you to death. Not only did you go against our code, but you violated one of the most sacred rules of all."

"Fuck you. Get on with it. I'd rather you put a bullet in my brain than bore me to death." His cold eyes cut to me. "I hope I put a baby in your whore so that every time you look at her and her bastard all you see is me. Whenever you sink inside that tight little pussy you remember that my dick was there first and that she moaned for me before she ever did for you."

At those words I lose what ounce of control I had left. I look at his left hand. The one with the lion's head tattoo. "Hold him," I snarl. Two of my brother's take

162

control. I go to the wall where the weapons hang. The ones we use to interrogate a difficult person of interest. I grab an axe. "Cuff him to the table."

Lion jerks but it gets him nowhere. With his hand locked in where I want it, I line the sharpened blade up above his wrist and bring it down with one swoop to chop off his hand. Blood splatters and spurts. He cries out once before passing out.

I take off his other hand. I'm saving his head for last. Tonight I'll bathe in his blood and fuck Alexa in it while he listens. Her crying out my name will be the last thing he ever hears. Tomorrow I'll sew the President's patch onto my cut.

Chapter Sixteen

"What did they ask you?" Ruthie lights up a cigarette and takes a shot of liquor.

"I'm sorry. They made me swear that what was said in that room stays there."

"Right." She takes a drag off her cigarette. "Want one?"

"No. Thank you."

"Want a drink?"

"I'm fine. Really."

"Alexa, you don't have to be strong with me. I know my father's a bastard. I see a lot of myself in you. Why do you think I latched onto James so young and got pregnant with Rochelle? I wanted out of that house. I wanted him to pay attention to someone else if you get my drift. I knew if I got pregnant, he'd make me get married, and then I'd be free, but he…never mind. It's in the past. It's over. We'll both be free. Cheers." She holds an extra shot glass up to me, and I accept it.

"To freedom." The alcohol burns down my throat. I glance around the clubhouse. This is my first and probably last time here. There are some couches pushed up against one of the walls. A stripper pole attached to a small stage in one corner. We're seated at the large bar that takes up most of the room. On the wall there are framed photos of motorcycles and club members.

"I do have one question." I look back to Ruthie. The way she is staring at me so intensely sets me on guard. "Something my father said…are you fucking my husband?"

My face pales. "What? No. No way." I shake my head. "Why would you ask me that?"

"I'm sorry you've been through an ordeal. I don't know what I was thinking. It's been a long night. I should take you home."

"No."

Her gaze narrows on me. "Something wrong?"

"I can't go back there. Not after tonight. I can't do it."

She starts to say more, but a man by the name of Reed comes for me. "Ruthie, you're free to go on home to Rochelle. Alexa is wanted for more questioning."

"But…where's James?"

"Busy. Get on home now." He gives her a look and grabs me at my elbow. "This way." Ruthie scowls at my back as I retreat down a set of stairs that leads to the clubhouse basement.

It's dark and cold down here.

Reed jerks me to a stop outside of a steel door. "Through there. Murder wants to see you."

My heart hammers in my chest. He could be sending me to my death. I don't know this man or what the club voted to do with James and Lion. Ruthie's under the impression that they will side with her husband, but she wasn't in that meeting with them. The tension in that room was so thick I could scarcely breathe.

I take a step back. "He wants to see me down here?"

Reed laughs darkly. "Sweetheart, you've got nothing to fear with me. I heard your story. No one here wants to put you through more pain." He opens the door and lightly pushes me through. I jump when the door slams shut behind me.

I'm in a small, poorly lit room, but there is another door. I enter the next room, and that's where I see him. James. Standing shirtless with his back to me.

"Hey," I call to him. He turns slowly. At first glance he appears sweaty. Shiny even under the glare of the light bulb swinging from the ceiling over his head. "What is this place?"

"C'mere." He extends a hand to me, and I place my palm against his. James curls his fingers around mine, pulling me in close. In this moment I realize he's covered in blood when it rubs off his chest and onto my white tee. "Look at me, Lex."

"Wh-wha-what is happening here? Why are you? Is that…is that blood?" my knees begin to buckle.

"Stay with me, baby. Got something I need you to see."

"I don't think I want to." I attempt to break free from him, but he doesn't let me go.

"You're in my world now, sweetheart. There's no backing out now. My brothers know all about us and who you are to me. No one will ever hurt you again or they'll face Lion's fate."

"And what is his fate?"

He tugs me further into the room. Red. I see red liquid pooled on the floor in a puddle. It's everywhere. On a steel table rests a single hand. A hand with a crowned lion's head tattooed across the back. "I think I'm going to be sick."

"In through your nose and out your mouth, babe. Breathe."

"Is that his...his hand?"

"I took his hands." He pulls me flush against his body covering me with more of Lion's blood. James's erection presses into me, but I try to ignore the fact that he's turned on. There's a man's hand on the fucking table. My head spins as I continue to take in the scene around me. There's a wall to the right with any weapon you can think of on display. Swords, knives, guns, heavy tools. Whatever you can imagine it's there.

"What do you mean you took them?"

"See that axe?"

I gulp then nod. I see it. Covered in blood.

"Wanted you to see with your own eyes that the bastard is never going to touch you again."

"I don't know what to say." My heart races. He killed his father-in-law. He killed him for me. That's two men who have lost their lives because of me and I'm not sorry.

Should I be feeling guilt or remorse? Maybe. I only have relief.

"Don't say anything. Gimme' that mouth." Touching his mouth to mine, James consumes me with his kiss. Stroking my cheek, he smears blood along my jawline. "I'm going to fuck you right here covered in his blood. This is my oath to you that from here on out you're mine, and I'll kill any motherfucker who dares to come between us or touch what belongs to me. Make no mistake, Alexa. I protect what's mine, and I'm a territorial son of a bitch. Lion said he fucked you. That you moaned for him. Now the last thing he will ever hear are the sounds you make for me."

"What do you mean?" I ask, but I already have my answer. Strapped to a chair unable to move or look away because his eyes are being forced open with some metal device connected to his face to pry them open, Lion stares at me. Where his hands should be are bloody rags that's soaked through wrapped around the stubs of his arms. I don't know how he is still alive. There's so much blood.

Oh God. I'm going to faint. My eyes roll back, and I sway on my feet. James catches me. "I know you're freaked the fuck out."

Freaked doesn't quite match what I'm experiencing. Hell, I don't know what I'm feeling but when James comes at me again, kissing me deep and wet all the crazy and the blood seems to melt away leaving the two of us in a space in time where there is only us. He lifts me onto a table with my back to Lion thankfully.

"Need inside you, baby." He tugs on my shirt, yanking it over my head. Lips trailing along my neck he sets me on fire. "Want you crying out my name." He nips at my collarbone. I come alive for him.

Only him.

My biker.

My killer.

My man.

Rolling my nipple between his thumb and finger, he teases my sensitive skin until it hardens. I cry out when he grabs hold the waist of my pants and practically rips them off me, tugging them down my legs as though they burn him to the touch. "This is going to be hard and fast, but I'll make it up to you later."

Shoving my knees apart, he moves between them, sliding my ass to the edge of the table. I wrap my legs around his hips. Leaning back on my elbows using the table to support me I watch him guide his thick cock inside me. The sight is carnal, filthy even, but beautiful.

"Always ready for me," he mutters. Gripping my hip, he pulls out then slams back in with brutal force. The walls of my pussy contract and stretch around him, greedily. Murder fucks hard. That's who he is right now. One man but two different identities. James is soft and sweet. His biker side though is a rough and savage killer who takes what he wants. Right now, he wants me. I belong to him. Both sides of him.

"Uh. Uh," I pant out as he thrusts deeper and harder. My ass slides in the blood on the table. It should turn me off, but when I'm with my man nothing else matters.

"Fuck yeah, Lex. Take it." His hand slides up my throat and gives me a squeeze, then moves to my chin. His thumb rubs blood over my lips but right now I don't care. We're animals fucking in his kill. Stripped bare and raw, covered in blood like demons. I suck his thumb between my lips and moan, giving that bastard forced to watch a show.

Murder fucks me like tomorrow may never come. He leans forward to kiss me, surging further inside me. So deep, I swear he's rooted there. My stomach drops and my knees shake. My sinister killer sweeps his tongue inside my mouth, and I fall apart at the seams unable to hold on any longer. My body jolts, and I cling to his shoulder for assistance.

"I'm gonna come, Murder."

"That's it. Come all over my cock." He slides in and out at a slow pace, staring down at his dick as he moves in and out.

Body quaking, I cry out his name, "Yes, Murder. Fuck me, baby."

"Never felt anything better than you, Lex." He jerks inside me, finding his own release. Murder separates from me, and his essence runs down my thighs. I'm bruised and dirty, but I've never felt more alive. "There's one thing left to do."

I watch in both horror and fascination when he takes possession of the axe.

"You can go to the other room and wait, or you can watch this piece of shit leave this world. Your choice but you got about ten seconds to make your choice."

"You said I was part of your world. I see that it can be ugly. Scary even. But it can also be beautiful. You gave me that. You gave me your love too even if you never say it…I can sense it in your actions and your touch." If I ever want to be his Old Lady, I've got to prove to him that I'm strong enough. That fail or fly I'm going to be his ride or die. Even if I'm not sure I have the strength for this, I know how to fake it till I make it. I've been doing it to survive my whole life. "I'm staying. I want my face to be the last he sees."

Murder's gaze meets mine. Filled with fury but I see resolve there too.

Filthy, naked, and possibly deranged I force myself to keep my eyes on Lion up until the moment his head rolls across the floor.

Chapter Seventeen

"No fair. Why do you get an apartment?" Rochelle pouts, and Colter shoots me a knowing but sympathetic smile as he drops my last box on the kitchen counter. We've seen each other in passing at The Devil's Playground. The clubhouse of the Royal Bastards MC. He knows all about my secrets I'm sure.

Rochelle doesn't know her grandfather raped me nor that her own father killed him for what he did to me. Ruthie wants her kept as far away from the club as possible. She made me promise not to tell her, but one day she will find out. She's dating Colter, and I hate keeping this a secret from her. She's happy with him. I just hope that when the truth does come out that she'll accept my being with James. That she'll be happy we found each other.

Ruthie brings in my new bedding. It makes me feel super shit that the wife of the man I'm sleeping with is decorating my apartment. James told me to smile and go on. Said that one day things will change, and we'll be together for real. I want to believe that with all my heart. I trust him. It's just sometimes they share these looks I'm not part of. They whisper, and she'll smile at him the way I do.

I keep wondering what she would have done had I confessed the truth when she asked me if I were fucking her husband. Would she have washed her hands of him? Would she have fought me for him?

"Alexa, James and the guys will be here in about fifteen minutes with the last of your furniture. If you don't need anything else, I'm going to take Rochelle out for lunch. Some mother daughter time." Pain flashes behind her eyes, and I realize she must be taking her out to break the news that her grandfather is gone.

"I'm all good. Call me later, Ro?"

"I'll probably be back over. No way is my bestie getting her own apartment without me."

"Slow down. Your dad isn't ready to let you fly from the nest just yet." Ruthie guides her daughter toward the door.

"You coming with us, Colter?" Rochelle grins at him and my stomach drops. That joy on her face is about to be snuffed out.

"No," Ruthie answers first. "It's just you and me today, kiddo."

"Dad wants me here to help carry the heavy shit." He flexes his muscles, and I roll my eyes.

"Catch up with me after then?"

"You know it, babe."

"All right enough of that. Let's go, Ro."

They leave and I start to work on unpacking the kitchen stuff Ruthie gave me. She said it gives her an excuse to get new stuff for hers. Colter's gaze pierces through me. "What?" I look over at him and he shifts his focus out the kitchen window to the parking lot.

"They're here."

"That doesn't answer my question."

He scrubs a palm over his head, then pulls his dark hair back to show off the shaved sides. "How long are you going to lie to them?"

I stare at the floor. "I don't like doing it." I meet his gaze, hating the judgment being thrown back at me. "She's my best friend, but you need to understand that I love him."

"Doesn't make it right."

"I never said that it did. Are you going to tell her?"

He scowls. "No. It's not my place, and I don't want to be the one to hurt her like that. I'll leave that to you. I'll be there for her when it's all said and done. But you need to tell her."

"I know that. I just can't. Not yet."

He nods and the front door opens. I smile at James and hope he can't tell its forced. "Someone order a couch?"

"You didn't have to do that."

"I wanted to." He enters followed by Colter's dad, Papa. If I didn't know better, I would swear they are brothers. Both of them are tall and muscular but not in that body builder way. They're lean and tone. Tattoos of dark elements. Reapers. There is something otherworldly about them. I can't put my finger on it.

"Colter," his dad calls him over. "Let's get this furniture moved and there might be some date money in it for you. We passed Ruthie and Rochelle on our way in.

Your girl mentioned wanting to go to a movie." He wraps an arm around his neck and roughs up his hair.

They disappear out the door.

"Shouldn't you be helping them?"

"I will but first, I've been dying to do this for days." Stepping into my space, his hand cups my jaw, then he kisses me soft and slow. It's been two weeks since everything went down with Lion. James has been busy being named the new Prez of the Royal Bastards. I don't know the details because well its club business. I only know he's been taking a lot of meetings and cleaning up Lion's mess.

Then there's Ruthie. I know she's suspicious, and we have to tread carefully. I mostly worried about Rochelle. I told her that I thought he was hot once and she pinched me so hard I had a blood blister.

Breaking away, he grins at me. "Things are going to be different, Lex. You'll see, baby. This is just the beginning." I pray he's right. I don't know how much more bad I can handle. "I better go help."

"Yeah." I nod. "You do that." I kiss him again.

It didn't take them long to bring up the couch and get my bed set up. Colter and Papa are gone and now it's just James and me. I collapse on the couch, and he drops next to me, slinging an arm around me. His lips meet my forehead and I let out a happy sigh. I wish this meant he'd be living with me. I know better though a girl can dream.

I stare at the kitchen and imagine myself preparing him dinner and him coming in after a long day with the club. I'd have him a cold beer waiting next to his plate. He'd smile at me and tell me about his day over dinner.

Someday we'll have that.

One day we won't have to hide our love.

One day I'll be his Old Lady, and he'll be my man for real.

His cell phone goes off. I shift so he can dig it out of his pocket. Mouth turned down he swipes a finger across the screen. "Yeah? Just finishing up putting this shelf in the closet. I'm almost done. Gimme' about ten minutes. I'll get it. That bad, huh? Right." He pauses. "Love you too."

I stiffen at his words. Hearing him say what I long to hear so freely to her hurts more than I want it to. The call ends and he goes to his feet.

"You're leaving, already?"

"Yeah, Ro isn't taking the news of her grandpa that great and Ruthie needs me to grab her favorite ice cream on my way home."

180

"Of course." I attempt to smile, but I know he sees through me.

"What's wrong, babe? You not like the apartment or something?"

"It's fine. Great really. I just I've missed you is all. I feel like I never see you."

"I'll come back later tonight or in the morning."

"Okay."

"Don't be a brat. You know I've got a family."

"Then you should go. Don't let me keep you." I lick my lips and he looms over me, dropping his knees to the cushion on either side of me.

"You know I'd stay if I could."

"You gotta go. I understand." I turn my head to stare at the wall, folding my arms across my chest.

"Don't be mad."

"I'm not mad."

"Babe, you're totally pouting."

"Am not."

"Fucking are too." He grabs my chin and jerks my face toward him. "Give me a kiss. I gotta ride out."

"I'm sure Ruthie'd be glad to."

"Fuck," he groans and goes to get up.

I grab his arm. "I'm sorry."

181

"No, you aren't but you can make it up to me before I go." He places my hand over his crotch. "Want in that mouth." He undoes his zipper. "And don't fucking tell me to go home to Ruthie for it."

I lean back on the couch and yank his jeans from his hips. His erection juts in my face and he rubs the head over my lips. Tongue darting out, I taste the saltines of him.

I part my lips as he grips the back of my head. "Open wider. Good girl," he praises me, and all those bad feelings slip away.

If loving him were a religion, down on my knees worshiping his cock is how I'd pray.

My mouth burns, stretching to accommodate his girth.

"God damn, pretty girl. That feels good." He tugs my head back to glide in and out slowly. I flatten my tongue against him and suck. James makes love to my mouth. I'm lost to him. There isn't anything I would do for this man. My heart is so full I could burst.

He works his cock in out slow then fast building the tempo with each time he passes between my lips, hitting the back of my throat. I gag on him. Tears burn in the crease of my eyes ready to fall any moment now. He pulls out, smearing precum over my lips.

"You gonna swallow like a good girl for me?"

I nod and murmur, "yes," wrapping my lips around him again.

"Fuck." His phone goes off again. "So damn close." He freezes and goes for his phone. "What?" he barks at whoever is on the other end. "I said I would. When I get there." He ends the call and slings the phone. "Let's test out that new mattress." James kicks off his boots and drops his jeans. He loses his shirt somewhere between the living room and bedroom. Laying back on the bed he holds his cock up. "Get up here and ride me till I come."

I undress quickly. Sinking down on him. I roll my hips, moving side to side in slow motion. "Was that your wife again?"

My man slaps me on the ass. "Shut up and keep doing that right there. Last thing I want to think about when I'm inside you is another woman."

I smile big at that. Using his shoulder for leverage, I bend forward to kiss him. His breath fans over my lips. "You taste like my cock."

"Then I guess I better not kiss anyone else tonight."

He shoves me to my back and moves into missionary position, settling between my legs to guide himself in once more. "You go around kissing anyone else and I'll kill them."

"That a warning?" I gasp when he smacks my clit.

"No. It's a fuckin' promise. Don't toy with me and say stupid shit like that, Lex. Not now. Not ever. This pussy." Thrust. "Belongs." Thrust. "To me," he says breathily, his warmth spreading through me as he gets off. Lips to mine, James kisses me briefly and rolls away. "Gotta go."

I flop down on the bed wearing a pout.

He smirks. "Yeah. I owe you one. I'll take care of you next time."

"You're not coming back?"

"Probably not with the way Ruthie is breathing down my neck."

"She asked me you know…about us. I told her there was nothing going on of course."

"She believe you?"

I shrug. "I guess so. She did buy all this new stuff."

"Right. I'll call you." He starts out of the bedroom.

"James?"

"Yeah, babe?"

"I love you."

He fucking winks at me in response, but he told Ruthie on the phone. My heart cracks, and it takes everything in me not to cry. My bottom lip wobbles. I hear him cursing under his breath in the living room. Part of me wants to scream at him and tell him not to come back while the other half wants to beg him to stay. All I want is three words, and he refuses to give them to me.

Chapter Eighteen

"What's up with you?"

"Nothing."

"That's the third nothing I've gotten from you since I got here." Alexa is being all funny. She's not even dressed like she normally would be. Wearing an oversized sweatshirt and workout pants, her hair is piled on her head in a messy bun.

"It's not important right now."

"Babe, look at me. I've not seen you in weeks. So whatever it is, I want to know."

Alexa chews on her thumbnail, refusing to look me in the eye.

I let out a sigh and pull her to my side of the couch. "I can't fix it if I don't l know what's wrong." Ruthie has been clingy as ever since the shit with her old man, so I've kept my distance from Alexa though it's killed me to do so. "Is this because I've not been around much lately?"

"No," she answers quickly. "I know you had your reasons. There's something I want to tell you, but I'm afraid of how you'll react."

"Whatever it is we'll figure it out." I kiss her temple, and she hugs my waist.

"You say that now…" she trails off.

"Lex, cut the bullshit and spit it out."

"You know how Rochelle told you I wasn't feeling so hot."

"I remember you had that stomach bug or whatever it was that's been going around. You still feeling sick?"

"Um…the thing is…it's not a stomach bug. I was late."

I go rigid. "You were late."

"I didn't get my period, and I kept getting nauseated every morning. I took a test."

"You telling me that you're pregnant?"

"Yes," she whispers.

I sit forward, resting my elbows on my knees.

"Are you mad at me?"

"Why would I be mad at you?"

"Because you're married, and Ruthie's already asking questions about us, and now…"

"It's mine?"

"I've not been with anyone else if that's what you're asking."

"I'm asking."

"Wow. Okay. If that's what you think. That I went and got pregnant to try and trap you then..."

"Then what?"

"Then you can leave."

"You want me to go?"

"Do you want to go?"

"Fuck." I flop back on the couch. "I don't know. It's a lot to take in." I scratch the back of my neck. "You want to keep it?"

"You want me to have an abortion?" Unshed tears glitter in those gorgeous green eyes, and I know I'm acting like a complete dick.

"There's a lot going on with the club. Timing is bad."

"I get it. You don't want us. I don't need you, Murder. Go ahead and be like everyone else in my life I ever gave a damn about. Use me and throw me aside. It's all I'm good for, right? A hot piece of ass on the side because your wife got fat. You don't care about me. Do you?"

"Shut your fucking mouth," I warn. Her using my road name is pissing me the fuck off right now. I know she's doing it to be a smart ass.

"Just go. I'll be fine. I've survived worse." she sniffles.

"You don't know shit. Putting words in my mouth. Telling me how I feel."

"That's the problem. I don't know how you feel. Do you care about me at all? Do you love me?"

"Do I love you?" I snort. "What do you think this is? That I just put up anyone I fuck in an apartment and pay their bills. That I'd risk everything for a piece of ass."

"You never tell me."

"Tell you what?" I grit, getting in her face.

"That you love me!" her voice goes high, and she chokes out a sob.

"I show you, pretty girl. I bust my ass every day trying to get closer to divorcing Ruthie so we can be together."

"Then why won't you leave her?"

"I can't lose Rochelle." She blanches at my words.

"Rochelle would want you to be happy."

"There's things you don't understand."

"I'm trying, but you aren't giving me anything in return."

"Ruthie knows something I did, and she can use it against me to send me away for the rest of my life."

"What did you do?"

"I can't tell you."

"Can't or won't?"

"Both. But it's because you're better off not knowing. I'm trying to protect you."

"Protect me. Protect me from what exactly? I watched you kill Lion. I know you killed Todd. Who better to keep your secrets than me? I'm the one who loves you. I'd never use any of it against you. I'm not your wife. I'm not her. I'm nothing fucking like her."

"Be patient with me." I tuck her back into my side. "I don't want to fight with you."

"I don't want to fight with you either, but this baby is real, and I need to know that I can count on you. You're either with me or you're not. I'm all alone here."

"You deserve better than me, Alexa."

"I don't want better. I want you. The question is do you want me? You swore to me that I'm yours. Are you a man who goes back on his word?"

"I'll always take care of you. I don't want you to worry about that."

"Take care of me. Do you hear yourself right now? I don't want you to take care of me. I want you with me. I need you."

"Shit. Lex, do you know how scared I am to be happy?"

"You're scared?"

"I'm terrified, babe. Anytime I get a little good I fuck it up. You're more than good. You're the best God damn thing that's ever happened to me. So yeah, you scare the fuck outta me."

"Do you want to be with me or are you going to be a coward?"

"C'mere."

"No. No more. You tell me how you feel about me or leave me alone. I can't keep going like this. I need to know where I stand in all this."

"Fuckin', love you, Lex. I can't get any realer than that. That what you want to hear?"

"I want you to be honest with me. Honest with yourself. Don't tell me what you think I want to hear to spare my feelings. If you don't love me then say it. I want to hear it come out your mouth."

"Do you have any idea how adorable you are when you're mad?"

"I'm not mad. I'm hurt and tired. There's a difference."

I stroke her loose hairs that fell from her bun away from her face. "Listen to me, I'm not a man that shares his emotions easily. I have a lot on my mind, but I shouldn't be making you feel like shit. You being pregnant, it's not ideal. I won't lie to you. It doesn't mean I don't care about you. That I don't fucking love you. I never planned on having any more kids. But this baby didn't ask for my fucked up shit and neither did you. We'll take it one day at a time." I press my hand to her belly. My heart hammers in my chest. Alexa smiles at me, and I wish my worry would ease, but it's there in the back of my mind, lurking like an enemy waiting to strike.

"One day at a time," she agrees softly.

"How about this day, you get naked."

"Ugh." she rolls her eyes. "Is that all I am? Your first stop on your way home when you want to get your dick wet?"

"Fuck. I can't win with you today."

"I don't want to fight, James."

"Then stop nagging me to damn death. If I wanted my ass chewed, I'd go home to Ruthie, but I came here to you." I move in, crowding her space. "Kiss your man, Lex."

Her lips part, and I smell the chocolate she was eating when I first got here. "Are you my man?"

"Yeah, babe. I'm your man."

Arms going around my neck, she launches herself into my arms and cries into my chest. Fuck me. I hold her close, breathing her in. We stay like this for what seems like hours. Me just holding her, giving her light touches, and gentle kisses until she calms down. Her tears stop and my heart cracks because I know I will never be able to give her what she wants. What she deserves. A man who can devote his all to her. I'll try like hell to be that man for her, but I have my club. I have my wife and daughter.

She'll never be first. Not until I get my shit straight.

"Go for a ride with me."

Alexa swipes her thumbs under her eyes. "Is that a good idea?"

"It's dark. Come on."

She smiles big and my heart skips two beats. There's never been anything prettier than when she smiles at me. "There's my pretty girl."

"I'll change."

"Wear your boots."

"Okay."

Alexa and I ride through downtown Charleston. Her arms wrapped around me. Her tits smashed into my back. I squeeze her knee when we roar toward the clubhouse. "I need to make a stop."

I've not brought her back here since the shit that happened with Lion. Not since I became Prez. I pull through the gate and give Grudge a chin lift. He shakes his head but keeps his mouth shut when Alexa takes off her helmet.

"This won't take long." I lead her inside, I motion for Nickel to follow, and we go straight to my office ignoring the whispers and stares. Let them fucking talk as long as they don't say shit outside of these walls or to my wife. Alexa needs to know that I trust her. My club needs to realize she's part of my life.

"Sit." I look to Alexa, and she drops her ass into my chair. I stand behind her and Nickel sits across from us. "What's the word on the Dry Ridge Sinners?"

"They're stirring up trouble with Grim and his boys in Kentucky. Heard Rebel is involved with Lil' Bit."

"Not our concern. With Lion gone, it looks like they've got other interests to keep them occupied."

"I agree. Anything else?" he grins at Alexa, and I want to knock that smug smirk off his face.

"Eyes off her tits. Alexa is pregnant."

Nickel whistles. "You don't waste no time, do you?"

"When I'm out of town I want eyes on her. Got me?"

"I hear ya, man. I'll look in on her."

"Good and I don't need to tell you that this stays between us. Don't need Ruthie catching shot of it and pulling one of her stunts."

"Cool. Cool. Always a pleasure, Alexa." He winks at her, and I want to gouge his eyes out. Nickel sees himself out before I knock his head off his shoulders.

I spin Alexa around in my chair bracing my palms on the arms of the black leather armrests. "You're leaving again?"

"Can't say for sure, but I'm trying to work out a deal for some extra income. Got a baby on the way. Shit ain't cheap."

"This your way of saying we're in this together?"

I shouldn't fill her head with false hope, but where Alexa is concerned, I can't seem to think straight. All I want is to be with her and soak up the light that shines so

196

bright within her. She's good and sweet. And the demon inside me is drawn to her like a moth to a flame wanting to possess and control her in every way.

"I'm saying I gave you my word, and I intend to keep it. I'm working out the rest. You want my honesty. There it is."

"I hear you."

"I know it's not enough for you, but I'm getting there, Lex. I'm trying."

"That's all I want."

"Good." I dip my head to kiss her. The instant her tongue touches mine I go rock hard like a damn schoolboy seeing naked tits for the first time.

"Now what?"

"Now I'm going to bend you over this desk and fuck you."

"You think so. What if I say no?"

"Then I'll try to convince you."

"And if I still say no?"

"You planning on denying me of what's mine?"

The left corner of her mouth twitches. "I'm still deciding."

"How about why you think about it I do this." I drop to my knees and jerk her pants down. Alexa spreads her thighs for me opening the gates to my personal heaven. I devour her pussy like a man enjoying his last meal.

Chapter Nineteen

"Come on. You haven't done anything fun in forever." Rochelle pouts at me. "I can't believe you actually came over. You always want me to come to your apartment." She rolls her eyes. "Mom probably thinks you don't like her cooking or something."

"It's not that. Your mom's cooking is fine. I've just had a lot going on. I missed too much school where I had that stomach bug that wouldn't go away, so I had to talk to my mom to have her withdraw me and sign me up for this online course so I can get a diploma."

"You talked to your mom, how did that go?"

"Not great, but she came through for me for once."

"That's good."

"So who is throwing this party and why should I go?"

"One of Colter's friends. And no, it's not Tanner though he will be there. He still thinks you're hot."

"Fine." I don't tell her that I only came over to see if her dad was home. He's been gone more often than not. I know he's negotiating a deal to bring in more money. I guess Lion made some bad investments that left the club on the brink of being broke.

"Yay." Her hands clap together. "You're not wearing that though, are you?"

I glance down at my yoga pants and pinch my oversized flannel that hides my growing baby bump. "What's wrong with what I'm wearing?" I frown.

"It's a party not whatever this is." She waves a hand down the front of me "You can wear something of mine. It's not a big deal."

"I can change on the way it won't take a but a few minutes to grab something from my apartment."

"Okaayyy." Her brows draw inward. "You wear my clothes all the time."

"I've gained a few pounds, it's no big deal."

"Colter should be here soon. I think tonight could be the night if you know what I mean."

"Oh. You sure you guys are ready for that?"

"I don't know. Maybe. We've been dating exclusively and he's no virgin. Guys have expectations."

"He's not like pressuring you, is he?"

"No. He's not like that."

"You're right. I'm sorry." Colter is one of the good ones. "How about I help you get ready for your big night."

"You sure you're okay? You know if you want to talk, I'm here."

"I'm good." What I can't say is oh by the way I'm pregnant. It's your dad's kid. We're in love, and I hope one day you'll be okay with us being together. I've imagined the conversation in my head a gazillion times. None of the imaginary scenarios I've created have ended well. Rochelle can't know the truth. Not yet anyway.

"You've not mentioned the guy you were so hush hush about lately. You still talking or whatever?"

"Kind of…complicated."

"This is the older dude, right?"

"Mhmm. He works out of town a lot so you know."

"I thought you said he's in college?"

"Did I?"

"When am I going to meet him? You haven't even given me a name. I'm your best friend. If you can't tell

201

me about him, then maybe it's not a relationship you should be in."

"I don't want to fight about this. You know how nuts my parents are. They'll like have him arrested or something."

"Can they do that?"

"I don't think so, but the threat would do plenty of damage."

"Well enough about this mystery guy. Tonight we're having fun."

"Woo. Fun." I hold up a red V-neck shirt. "What about this with your ripped jeans?"

"You think it'll look okay?"

"Colter's a motorcycle man. He'll love you in anything honestly."

"Like you know a lot about motorcycle men." She giggles. "Wait. It's not someone in my dad's club, right?"

"What makes you ask me that?"

"Nothing. It's just I thought I heard Colter and his dad talking about you being at the clubhouse, but I must've heard wrong. Or maybe they were talking about a different Alexa."

"Probably."

"Girls, Colter's here," Ruthie yells down the hall.

"Let's go."

"Ro, wait. Promise me you guys will use protection."

"Yeah sure. I mean you and Todd must've done it like a million times without anything though, right? And you didn't get pregnant."

"Something like that," I lie. I hate lying to Rochelle, but I don't have much of a choice.

Colter barely speaks to me, and I wonder if he knows that I'm pregnant. We're about to go out the door when James enters through the garage. I didn't even hear his motorcycle pull up. Was he already here and hiding out there the whole time? His gaze meets mine briefly and I smile. He scowls at his shoes. Is he upset that I'm here?

"Where are you kids headed off to?"

"A party. We just gotta swing by Alexa's first so she can change."

He arches his brows at me, and I kinda do this weird shoulder lift thing while trying not to draw attention to myself.

"We don't want to keep you guys. Your father and I are going to dinner. It's the anniversary of our first date." Ruthie grabs his hand and kisses his cheek.

My heart carves itself out of my chest. He's taking her to dinner. That doesn't sound like a man who is trying to leave his wife. I want to scream for Ruthie to stop touching him. To tell her that I'm having his baby, and that it's me he loves and not her, but I can't do that.

I can feel his gaze on me as I stare at the floor biting back my tears. Does he know that this is torment for me? Does he even care? His wife just ripped my heart out. This…us…our lies…its' tearing me apart.

"We should go," Colter says, and I'm grateful. I need to get out of here. I need away from Ruthie. James too, before I break.

"Happy anniversary," I mumble and start out the door. I'm halfway to Colter's Camaro when I hear my name.

"Alexa."

"What's my dad want with you?"

"The um car…the car I might get. I asked if he'd look at it for me."

"Oh. Okay."

I wait for Rochelle to get in and close the door before I turn back to him.

"What is it?"

"Where are you guys going?"

"Why do you care?"

"Lex, you know things are tense right now."

I want so badly for him to take me in his arms and tell me everything will be okay, but I know he can't. It's agony to have him right here and yet so far away. I'm tired of pretending. "I don't think I can do this. Watching you with her. Not be able to touch you when I want. I love you, but this is too much."

"You know the score, babe." He shoves his hands in his pockets.

"Yeah so why do I feel as though I'm on the losing team?"

He steps forward and I step back. My heart is hammering all the way up in my throat. If he touches me it will all be over. The truth will be exposed, and I'll lose him and Rochelle forever.

Speaking of the wicked cunt. Ruthie steps into the garage. "Everything okay out here?"

I sniffle as he turns to face his wife wishing he'd make a stand and tell her he's done with her, that he's going to be with me, but he doesn't. I don't know if I'm angry or sad. "Have fun on your date. I hope you have an amazing night."

"You girls be careful," she calls out, and I look back just in time to watch her plant a big kiss on his lips. The same mouth that feeds me such beautiful lies. I want to ask her how my pussy tastes considering her husband loves it so much, but I refrain.

My only consolation is seeing him tense and pulling away from her, but it changes nothing. She's still his wife, and I'm on the outside looking in. No matter what he says I'm all alone.

On the way to my apartment I keep trying to figure out an excuse to get out of going to this party and come up with none. Not any that Rochelle would buy or accept without pitching a shit fit, and I can't blame her. I've been a bad friend lately. No friend at all. I hate all the lying. I hate not being able to share how much I love her father. That she's going to have a sibling. That we're connected for life.

I go through the motions. Nod when I think I should as Rochelle chatters about Tanner and how I should give him a chance while I get dressed, careful to keep my back to her.

"Maybe," I lie. "I guess he's okay."

"Okay? The guy runs track. He's hot."

"You're right. I'll talk to him, okay?"

Rochelle frowns at me. "I don't know what's with you, but you gotta relax." She takes a swig from her bottle of Strawberry Hill. She's been drinking it since we pulled out of her driveway.

"I think I'm still not over that stomach bug."

"Oh no. You aren't canceling."

"I didn't say I was." I slip my black ballerina style flats on, turning to face her hoping the swell of my stomach isn't all that noticeable.

"Have a drink of this."

"No thanks."

Her eyes narrow on me. "Why?"

"Because I don't want to." I leave her in my bedroom and hope she'll drop it. "What time does this party start anyway?" I look to Colter and he shrugs.

"You're pregnant?" Rochelle gapes at me, eyes on my protruding stomach.

"What?"

Her gaze widens. "You won't drink. You're gaining weight in your belly. You were sick but only in the mornings. Oh. My God. Alexa." She grabs my bottle of vitamins I forgot were on the counter and rattles the contents.

"Ro, drop it. Please."

"Admit it."

"What?"

"Say it. You're pregnant."

"It's good for my hair and nails is all."

"Don't lie to me. You've been doing a lot of that lately." She throws the bottle and the cap falls off. My pills scatter across the tile of the kitchen floor.

"Don't be like that. You're a hateful drunk." I bend to start picking up the vitamins.

"At least I'm not a liar." She towers over me, venom dripping from her.

I peer up at her with tears streaming down my cheeks. "Yes. Fine. Okay. You caught me. I'm pregnant. My life is a mess. I'm barely holding it together. Are you happy now?"

"Who's the father?"

"Please don't ask me that. I don't want to talk about this right now." I wipe at my cheeks and stand to face her, abandoning the mess for later.

"Why is this guy you're seeing such a secret? How old is he, Alexa?"

I look to Colter hoping he'll I don't know help me in some way. "I can't tell you."

"Oh my God. Is it...is it Colter?"

"No. No way. I'd never do that to you, and he wouldn't either."

208

"Is this why you two whisper behind my back? We're supposed to be best friends. Best friends don't keep secrets like this unless they have something to hide."

"Babe. You know how I feel about you." Colter goes to hug her, and she takes a step back. "Don't shut me out, Ro. Alexa, you better tell her the truth right now or I will," he threatens.

"So you know. You know who Alexa has been seeing for months, but me her best friend. I don't get to know. Screw you both." She grabs Colter's keys off the counter and stomps toward the door while we chase after her. She enters the driver's side, and Colter hops in the passenger seat. The car starts, and I can't bear the thought of her mad at me. I can't let her think that Colter and I ever would go behind her back. I slide into the backseat as she peels out of the driveway then slams on the brakes. "Both of you get out."

"You don't even have your license. Just a permit. Trade me places. My dad will kill me if he finds out you were driving my car," Colter begs her. Rochelle hits the gas and swerves to miss a car parked on the side street.

"Rochelle," I scream. "Okay. I'll tell you. Just please stop the car."

For some reason she speeds up.

"Rochelle. Stop the car." I go for my seat belt, and Colter tries to reason with her. "You're not thinking clearly, and you've been drinking. Don't drive mad."

"You're both liars," she screams.

"Colter hasn't lied to you. He's not to blame in this. Be mad at me. I'm the one keeping secrets and lying to everyone. I lie to you. Your mom." I can't hold back my fat tears as they roll down my cheeks. "I'm sorry."

"My mom?"

"Ro, please stop the car."

"Tell me his name. Right now."

"James." Her gaze meets mine through the rearview mirror. Time freezes in place.

"James who?" she whispers.

I suck in a deep breath. "I think you know."

"Ro, look out," Colter screams, going for the steering wheel. It all happens so fast and yet so slow. Metal clinks. Glass shatters. The seat belt I'm wearing jerks me back in the seat. The car skids across the road. I knock my head against the back-passenger window as the vehicle rolls three or four times down an embankment, I've lost count.

I'm shaken, but I think I'll be okay. My head throbs, and I can't think clearly. "Ro, Colter. You guys good?" No one answers me, and my blood runs cold. Chills fan up and down my arms. I focus on the front seat of the car. Colter is slumped forward with blood gushing from his forehead. A chunk of glass protrudes from his eye. Bile lurches in my stomach and claws its way up my throat, burning for release at the gruesome sight. "Rochelle?" I cry. The whole driver's side of the car is smashed in. Her body is twisted at an odd angle partially under the steering wheel and partially hanging out of what's left of her door. Neither of them was wearing their seat belt. A woozy sensation washes over me, and I touch my forehead. I glance at my fingers seeing my own blood. My hand goes to my stomach. My baby. Please let my baby be okay.

I black out and when I come to, I have no idea how much time has passed.

Oh God. It's growing dark, and all I can hear is the water churning in the nearby river. "Rochelle, please answer me. I'm sorry. I take it all back. I take it all back." I blink trying to get my tears to stop but it's not working. "Colter. Tell me you guys are okay. Don't shut me out." I pull on my seat belt, but it won't budge. "Someone help. Help," I scream till my throat goes raw.

"Can anyone hear me?" A man calls out, trying to open Colter's door.

I go to speak but my voice dies in my throat.

He gives up on the other door and yanks mine open. "I'm ok," I manage to croak out.

"Don't move. I've called 911."

"I need to help my friends."

He glances to the front of the car and drops his head, scrubbing a palm over his mouth. Reaching around the seat he checks Colter's pulse first.

"Is he breathing?"

"I'm no doctor. Can't be sure."

"Rochelle?"

"I can't reach her from here."

"I need out of this car."

The man pulls a knife out of his pocket and cuts the strap of my seat belt.

I lean forward to touch Rochelle, but the man stops me.

"I wouldn't," he warns.

"She's going to be okay. Right?"

He ducks back out of the car. "Over here." He waves his arms.

I climb out of the car on shaky legs.

Sirens wail in the distance, growing closer with each passing second though they seem like hours. Please let them be okay. *Please, God, save my friends.* I drop to my knees and pray. I beg for forgiveness. I'll give anything.

I'll take it all back.

I'll give him up.

God if you're listening please hear me.

Chapter Twenty

I can't breathe. I can't speak. She's gone. Both of them are. It's all my fault. I did this. I killed Rochelle and Colter. I heard them as I was being loaded into the back of the ambulance. One survivor. Minor injuries. The seat belt saved my life. I'm alive and they're dead.

"Alexa, honey." My head snaps up at the sound of my mom's voice. The curtain to my bed in the ER is drawn back. "Sweetheart." She rushes toward me, and I wrap my arms around her.

"She's gone, Mommy. I killed her. I killed my best friend."

"Shhh," she shushes me and kisses my forehead next to my bandage. I think it's the only real affection my mother has shown me in years. "You did no such thing. You weren't even driving. None of this can be pinned on you."

"Colter...Rochelle. They were mad at me." I cry harder. Snot bubbles out my nostrils. "It's all my fault. I killed them. Why didn't I die too? I should be dead. Not them."

"Can't you give her something to calm her down?" I hear her murmur to someone.

I curl up in a ball on the hospital bed and pray for God to take me too. This has to be a bad dream. It can't be real. My best friend can't be gone. She just can't be. Every time I hear footsteps I look to the crack where my curtain is pulled watching for her shoes. It's always a nurse or someone here for another patient. My mom had to go fill out paperwork for the insurance or whatever. I keep praying she's going to come back any second now and tell me there was a mistake. That Rochelle and Colter will be fine. That they are here too, and I can see them any minute now.

Heavy footsteps sound in the corridor. I can sense him before I see his riding boots through the crack. James is here. How do I face him right now? How do I look this man I love more than my own life in the eyes and tell him that it's my fault his daughter is gone? I hold my breath waiting for him to open the curtain and tell me he hates me. That he wishes it were me who died in Rochelle's place. It's my greatest fear—losing him for good, and it's about to come to fruition.

The curtain is yanked back but it isn't James. "I was sent to check on you. You need anything?"

I shake my head. "How..." I struggle to find the words.

"Not good, but he did ask me to make sure you were okay."

"Okay." I laugh bitterly. "My best friend is dead, Nickel. Nothing is okay. It should've been me."

The handsome man blows out a breath. Colorful tattoos snake up his arms.

"What are you doing here?" I hear my mother question as she enters behind him.

"Ruthie asked me to see how Alexa is."

"Can you take me to them?"

"You're not going anywhere, young lady. Not until I speak with the doctor."

Nickel shoots me a wink and steps out. I'm sure he was sent as my bodyguard or to make sure I don't take off. Maybe both. Perhaps he's here to kill me for what I've done.

"Does dad know?"

"Your father didn't want me to come, but you're my daughter. I tried to raise you right, but you keep going down these dark roads, and I'm not sure what more I can do."

"Love me. That's all I've ever wanted from either of you, but you refuse to give it. Why? Why am I so bad? Why doesn't anyone love me?"

"You don't know what you're talking about."

"You can't even say it, can you?"

"Say what?"

"That you love me." A tear slides down my cheek and drips onto my hospital gown.

"You're being silly." She fusses with my blanket, ignoring my question. Blowing off my feelings as though they don't matter. That I don't matter. I've never mattered in her eyes, and I never will.

"Mom?"

"What?"

"I'd like you to leave."

"Excuse me?" her brow crinkles revealing the lines etched on her forehead.

218

The doctor enters the exam room before I can argue with her. "Hello, Miss Neville." He flips a paper on my chart and smiles at me. "I see you've had stitches. Your bloodwork all came back good. You have a mild concussion, but nothing to be concerned about. Everything seems normal with your pregnancy."

Flames lick up the back of my neck. My mother's hand goes to her clavicle. I have no doubt if she were wearing pearls, she'd be clutching them now. "Did you say pregnancy?"

He looks to my mother who appears on the verge of passing out. "And who are you?"

"Her mother." Her head snaps in my direction. "You're pregnant," she hisses the word as though it's toxic.

"Seems so."

"Is it by that wretched Todd? I knew it. I knew this would happen." She shakes her head, muttering under her breath about how wicked I am.

"Do you have someone here to drive you home and to look after you?"

"Yes."

"Okay. I don't see any reason to keep you any longer. You're a very lucky girl." He hands me my release papers and exits.

"Your father will have a coronary. I don't know why you continue to pull these stunts."

I ease off the bed. I'm sore and bruised. I've been here for hours. All I want is to crawl into my bed, pull the covers over my head, and hope that when I wake up this was all some horrible nightmare.

After I change back into my clothes, Nickel is waiting for me, and I'm grateful. I thought my mom showing up might be a good thing for our relationship, but I was mistaken. She's never going to change. The woman will never see me as anything other than an inconvenience and a failure.

"What are you doing getting yourself twisted up with biker trash? He's not the father, is he?"

"No, Mother. He's a friend of Ruthie and James. You know the people who've done nothing but take care of me since you and Dad put me out. You don't even know them."

"I know enough. They'll only drag you down with them. There's no hope for you. You're a lost little girl who can't see she's destroying her life. You'll ruin everything in your path, including your bastard baby."

"Hey, lady," Nickel snarls. "Watch your tongue or I'll cut it out your mouth after your husband watches you suck my dick." He grabs his crotch, and I don't know who appears more mortified her or the nurse who just overheard the exchange.

"Well, I've never. Don't call me again, Alexa."

"I won't," I whisper to her back.

"You okay?"

"You want the honest answer or the universal fine?"

"Right. I brought a cage so no worries about riding on my bike." Out in the parking lot Nickel helps me into the cab of his truck. "You want to get food or anything?"

I shake my head. "I can't think about food right now. How are you so calm?"

"I figure it like this. Death is a natural part of life, but my being upset right now won't help or change anything. What I can do is what my Prez asked of me and that was to make sure you were good and have what you need. I compartmentalize shit."

"Can I see him?"

"Got orders to take you to your apartment and stay as long as you need me to. I'm sure you can understand that Ruthie is losing her shit and your man ain't in the headspace for anything or anyone right now. That includes you."

I nod. It's probably for the best I don't see him or Ruthie for that matter right now. Because once I do, he will hate me forever.

Chapter Twenty-one

MURDER

"This is nice, isn't it? Just the two of us like old times." Ruthie smiles over the brim of her wine glass before taking a hearty sip.

"I don't know what fucked up fantasy you've been living in, but this has never been us. If this were like old times, we'd be having takeout pizza and sitting on crates while Rochelle played with her blocks."

"Don't be a sourpuss. We've come so far. Our little girl is growing up. You're the Prez now. Everyone looking up to you. I'm the envy of all the other Old Ladies. They're all jealous of us you know. We finally have it all. Don't act like you don't enjoy it."

"Maybe if I wasn't spending all my time cleaning up all the shit deals your father made. And the chaos he left in his wake. The shit he did to not only Alexa but other members of the club. Was fucking their wives in front of everyone to humiliate them. Had a brother bring his Old

Lady to me and promised if she disappointed me, I could have his sister and daughter too."

"He what?"

"You heard me. So no its not all fun."

"Did you fuck her?"

"What are you gonna do if I did?"

She stabs her fork into her steak, cutting the meat quickly.

"Cat got your tongue?"

"I don't want to fight. Have you given anymore thought to a son now?"

"You think I want another kid? Think I want to bring a son into this fucked up club and hope he fills my boots one day?"

"It's what you're supposed to do. You have a status to uphold."

"Don't tell me what I'm supposed to do. Coming here with you tonight was a fucking joke. Just like our marriage."

"Now you're only trying to hurt my feelings."

"Didn't think you had any left." I top off my beer and wish I could smoke a damn joint right about now. My thoughts are miles away with Alexa. She's pregnant and has no business going to a damn party. What am I gonna do…ground her? Tell her she can't have friends? The look on her face at the house earlier about damn near killed me. Would serve me right if she found someone else. Sometimes I wish she'd quit me. But I know if she did, I'd just drag her back into my world.

My cell phone goes off. It's the clubhouse. "Gotta take this," I inform Ruthie when her cell starts buzzing too. I'm happy for the interruption. "Talk to me."

"Cops are here looking for you. They won't say why," Grudge tells me.

"I'll be there in ten."

Ruthie gives me a funny look.

"What?" I snap.

"That was Mrs. Medoza from next door. She says there's a cop looking for both of us. What did you do?"

"What the fuck makes you think it's something I did?"

"Let's just go see what this is about. Do I need to get our lawyer on the phone?"

"Not yet." I pay our bill, and we ride out to the clubhouse. When we arrive there's a police cruiser sitting outside the gate. I roll up next to them and cut off my bike.

"You James Thatcher?"

"What's this about?"

"Is there somewhere private we can talk?"

"Here's fine." I throw my leg over my bike and Ruthie gets off after me.

"I wish you'd reconsider taking this matter elsewhere. I'm sorry to have to tell you that your daughter was involved in a single vehicle motor vehicle accident."

Ruthie clutches my hand. "Is she okay?"

"Ma'am." His gaze darts to his shoes and the world seems to tilt off its axis. "I wish I could tell you differently, but Rochelle Thatcher was pronounced dead at the scene along with her passenger Colter Riggs. An Alexa Neville was transported to the hospital with minor injuries."

My legs nearly give out. I drop to the pavement. His lips keep moving, but all I hear is static. Rochelle, my brown eyed girl ready to set the world on fire since the day she was born. The first person to show me what it truly meant to love someone else and put them first. The baby I cradled in my arms, slept with her on my chest the first three months of her life because she'd cry whenever I put her down. I watched her take her first steps. I swore I'd always protect her. That she'd never want for nothing. My child is gone from this life and onto the next.

226

Ruthie's blood curdling scream forces me to snap my head up. The officer has his arms around her, offering the comfort I'm unable to give. "Not my daughter. Not Rochelle," she sobs. "Please. No. You've made a mistake. James, tell him he's made a mistake. It's not her. Tell him." She falls to her knees. The gate behind me opens up. Grudge picks Ruthie up. Nickel holds a hand out to me.

I'm supposed to be strong, but nothing prepares you for the loss of a child.

**

One of the officers I spoke with called it a tragic accident. Said Rochelle was driving, and they believe toxicology reports will show she had alcohol in her system. None of it makes sense. Rochelle had her permit but knew not to drive unless her mom or me were with her. She nor Colter were wearing their seat belts, but Alexa was. I need answers and there is only one person who can give them to me.

Ruthie is at her mother's. Had to give her a damn sedative to knock her ass out. I wish someone would put a bullet in my head and make the pain stop. It's more than I can bear. I can't drink or smoke it away. I don't do pills and will never stick a needle in my arm but fuck me if I'm not tempted by the thought of making this ache go away if even for an hour. Never knew anything could hurt like this. Hurts so damn bad I want to drive straight into oncoming traffic.

I have Slick drop me off at the apartment. When I walk in Nickel is asleep on the couch. I tap his shoulder and send him on his way. He doesn't hesitate. I think he knows by taking one look at me now isn't the time to offer his condolences. There will be time for that later. Right now is the time for Alexa to tell me what the fuck happened to my daughter and why she's still breathing and Rochelle isn't. My brain knows that the seat belt could have saved her life, but my heart can't accept the truth. Not until I hear the details from the only person alive to tell the tale.

I enter the bedroom. Alexa isn't in our bed. She's standing at the window staring out at the moon. The moonlight spilling through the window casts a glow on her. Her blonde hair hangs over her shoulder, wet and dripping onto the carpet. Standing in a tank top and bikini style panties I can see the perfect shape of her growing baby bump. The sight is beautiful yet haunting. I wonder if losing Rochelle is my punishment for knocking Alexa up.

Her gaze meets mine. "You came."

"You okay?" Angry and heartbroken I'm still drawn to her.

"No. You?"

I shake my head, and she crosses the room to where I stand frozen in place. I kiss her forehead next to her stitches. "I'm glad you're okay." I am fucking grateful I didn't lose her too.

"I'm not. Rochelle...Colter..." her voice cracks.

"Shh." I pull her into my arms. "The baby's okay?"

"The doctor said I have a mild concussion, but the baby looks good. I got to hear her heartbeat."

"Her?"

"They did an ultrasound. They couldn't tell the sex. But I think maybe it will be a girl."

I swallow down the knot forming in my throat.

Her trembling fingers stroke my cheek, and I rest my palm on her belly. "I'm so sorry, James."

"Yeah. Me too. I know you've been through a lot tonight, but I need you to tell me what happened."

"I will. I'll tell you everything, but first will you hold me? Please. All I've wanted is you."

I kick off my boots and lead her to bed. "You're freezing."

229

"The cold reminds me that I'm still breathing. That my heart is still beating when it shouldn't be."

"Don't talk like that." I tuck her into my side, stroking the rough pads of my fingers up and down her arm.

"You say that now."

"What's that supposed to mean?"

"When I tell you...you're gonna be done with me, and wish I were dead, but don't worry I wish it enough for the both of us."

"Tell me now," I growl.

"I love you." she cries. "I love our baby. I loved Rochelle."

Chapter Twenty-two

Tears blur my vision. My chest constricts. I find it hard to breathe, but I know I have to tell him. I have to tell James everything even if it means I will lose him forever. It's what I deserve after what I did. "I need you to know I never wanted to hurt you. Rochelle. Hell, not even Ruthie. She's been good to me, and I don't deserve her kindness. I don't deserve you, but I love you, James. I love you so much that it makes me physically sick and thought of losing you…I wish I had died tonight. I don't know why God didn't take me instead. Maybe there is no God."

"Lex," he starts, but I press my finger to his lips, and he kisses the tip.

"Please listen. I need to say this."

He stares at me long and hard, and I can't find the words I need to say to him. My heart is going to beat out of my chest.

"Easy. Breathe. You being this upset isn't good for the baby." He blows out a whoosh of air. "Let it wait till morning. I think we've both had enough bad for one day. Whatever you want to tell me I sense it's nothing good. Nothing I'm gonna want to hear. It won't change the fact that my daughter is laying on a metal slab at the funeral home. Won't change the fact that Papa has to bury his son. I don't know if there's a God, but never wish yourself dead, Lex. Not for me or anyone. Tomorrow I have to make arrangements for Rochelle. Tonight I need you to be you. Be strong for me. Need you to make everything else disappear in the way only you are capable of. I need you, pretty girl. I need you to remind me that I have something worth fighting for."

His hand slides to my hip then curves to the shape of my stomach. Our lips meet, tongues connecting in a slow dance that only we know the steps to. Nothing or no one can bring me to life like he can. His warmth washes over me giving me false hope that we can survive this.

"Even on the worst fucking day of my life all I wanted is you, babe. Couldn't get to you fast enough."

232

"You shouldn't want me. You should hate me, and you will. You're going to leave me. You won't want me or this baby. You'll stop loving me."

"Stop pushing me away, Lex. You asked me to take your pain away now I'm asking you to do the same." He swipes his fingers along my cheeks then kisses the last of my tears away.

"You give me too much credit."

Hooking his thumbs along the waistline of my panties, jerking the white lace over my thighs in one swift motion he says, "Need you skin to skin." My tank top is pulled up over my head and tossed to the floor.

"However you want me, I'm yours." I help my shattered man out of his clothes. I've never seen him like this, and it's all my fault. The sight of his broken spirit nearly kills me. It's my fault. All of it. Him. Us. Ruthie. Rochelle. Colter. All the hurt leads straight back to me. I destroy everyone I love.

"Want to bury myself so deep inside you I disappear," he whispers into my ear, teeth sliding against the shell. I want it more than he knows. To disappear. For us to get lost and never find our way back.

"Follow me into the dark and leave all your troubles behind." I brush my lips over his.

"Let me lose myself in you for a few hours." Dragging his lips down my throat, he nips the thin skin there with his teeth, and I scratch my nails down his back. We do our best to crawl inside one another to escape our heartache.

Hot, thick, and rock hard, James guides his cock inside me. I gasp at the welcomed intrusion. He doesn't move. His gaze meets mine, tortured and uncertain of what the future holds.

"Don't talk. Just listen." He caps a palm to my lips. "I know I've had a fucked up way of showing it, but I do love you, Alexa. I love you more than I can ever show you. I'm in a bad way. My head is in a dark place. I'm gonna say and do shit I don't mean. I'm gonna hurt you, baby. I don't want to, but I will. I'm angry at the world. I want to watch it burn." He removes his hand.

"I'll give you the match," I promise, and he has no idea how true my words are. When I tell him what happened, I'll be first on his list. The thought of losing him terrifies me, but we'll always have tonight. Our love will live on forever in our baby and in my heart. A tear escapes, rolling down my cheek.

"Don't cry, pretty girl."

"I wish you hadn't done that."

"What's that?" He slides out and back in slowly, rolling his hips in the most delicious way.

"Told me you love me."

"Why?"

"Because I'm never going to be able to keep you." I slide my palm down his neck to rest over his heart. "It hurts. The thought of you not belonging to me and not wanting me. It's killing me. I won't survive if you leave me."

Threading his fingers through mine, he brings my palm to his lips, kissing the soft contours. "I ache for the day I get to truly make you mine, Lex, but right now I'm no good to no one. Not you. Not my club. I've failed everyone. But I needed you to know the way I feel about you. No more words. I'm gonna show you."

His tortured soul mates with mine. Fevered kisses. Broken promises painted and fractured on my skin with the imprints of his teeth. Body moving with mine like the whisperings of poetry in a darkened alley between forbidden lovers. We are one. The rest of the world forgotten. Nothing else matters but this. Tonight. Us. Our love.

My biker making love to me like only he can.

Skin ablaze he takes me in every position I've ever imagined while discovering new ones I want to experience over and over again with him. Only ever him. Every I love you that leaves his mouth is a blade stabbing into my heart. My sins bleed out through my sweat begging to be unleashed onto the world. Soul aching, I cry out his name. The bitter truth daring to drip off the tip of my tongue slow like honey.

"Fuck yeah," he grunts, hammering me into the mattress. The headboard knocks against the wall. James grabs my pillow and places it between the two to stop the noise. With slow, deep, punishing strokes he regains his torturous rhythm, dragging me to the edge of my orgasm and snatching it away again. Over and over again.

He will be the death of me because this man will haunt me forever.

His heavy breaths. The airy scent of his cologne and leather. Liquor and smoke flavored kisses. The erratic tempo of his heartbeat when he makes love to me. But most of all the way he looks at me with those dark, feral, hungry eyes.

Flipping me to my stomach, he positions me, face down, ass up. *Slap*. A hand connects with my left ass cheek, curving to the stinging globe with raw possession.

"Come for your man, Lex." Gripping my hips, he thrusts deep and hard hitting me in the right spot continuously until I shatter beneath him. "That's it, baby. Give it to me. Let go." I give it all to him, my love, pleasure, and pain.

Flexing his hips, surging forward, driving into me relentlessly he soon follows, painting the ink of his passion across my backside.

"Know one thing."

"What's that?"

"I didn't think it was possible for you to get any prettier but look at you." He massages my breasts hugging me from behind. "Fuckin' thicker. Hips getting wider. Gotta say, I'm loving you pregnant, baby." Giving me one last kiss between my shoulder blades, he gets off the bed and goes into the bathroom for a towel. "Made a mess of you." He grins as I stare up at him sideways, supported on one elbow. "Looking picture perfect." He quickly wipes me then drops back on the bed, tucking me into his side, palm splayed along my ribs.

I wish he could hold me like this forever.

Sliding his hand over my baby bump, he lets out a heavy breath. "You think of a name for the baby yet?"

"I don't know. Maybe JJ for a boy. For a girl maybe Elodie. I haven't really given it a lot of thought."

"Rochelle always wanted a little sister," he shares, and I freeze. Her name is a slap back into our harsh reality. We escaped it a short while, but we can't pretend that Rochelle's not dead and that life is simple. "I wish she'd get the chance to know her brother or sister. To know how happy you make me."

"She knew," the words tumble out before I know what I'm saying.

"Knew what?"

I lick my lips, tears already staining my cheeks. "About us. That's what I wanted to tell you. She kept harping on me to go out with this guy. Tanner. I blew it off as long as possible, and she begged me to go to the party with them. We stopped here since I needed to change, and she offered me a drink of her wine. I declined and said I wasn't in the mood to drink. Ro started in on me. Making accusations that I wasn't her friend because I was keeping secrets. She found my prenatal vitamins and I tried to lie. Told her I was taking them for my hair and nails. But you know her. She's smart and stubborn. A lot like you. We argued about my being pregnant and the identity of the father. Rochelle thought I was sleeping with Colter behind her back. We both denied it, but I couldn't tell her it was you. I didn't want to hurt her. She got angry and grabbed Colter's car keys."

I stop momentarily to catch my breath. James has gone so quiet and still. His silence scares me, but I know I have to persevere. He needs the truth. All of it. No matter how much it hurts I owe it to him. I owe it to my best friend. "Colter ran after her, and so did I. She got in the driver's seat. Colter in the passenger. I slid into the back as she was peeling out the driveway. We begged her to pull the car over, but she was so upset and not thinking straight. I don't know where she got the wine. When Rochelle drinks she gets a mean streak. I swore to her I'd tell her the truth if she'd stop the car, but she kept speeding up until I blurted out your name. She looked at me like she hated me through the rearview mirror." I'll never forget that look. "The next thing I knew Colter was jerking the wheel, and in a flash the car went rolling and when it stopped, I think they were already dead. I passed out then help came. You know the rest." I finish and wait for his response.

A chilling sensation creeps up my spine at the loss of his touch. The bed shifts, and I dare to look over. His back is to me. Head in his hands, elbows resting on his knees.

He's so silent I can't stand it. I need him to say something. Anything.

"James." I crawl toward him and go to wrap my arms around his shoulders, craving his touch.

He flings me back so quickly I nearly go sailing off the other side of the bed. "Don't fucking touch me," he growls.

"I'm sorry."

"You should be."

I hug my knees to my chest and watch him get dressed. "I know you're angry."

"Angry?" he snaps and glares at me with such malice my heart stops beating. The hate shining back at me breaks me into a million tiny pieces. "I could kill you. Snap your neck like a fucking twig, but that'd be too easy. Want you to suffer with the knowledge of what you did. Of what you took away from me. You stupid girl."

"I know it's my fault. If I could take it all back I would. I begged God. I promised I'd give you up. That I'd give anything to bring her back. I prayed for him to take me instead. I love you. The last thing I ever wanted to do was hurt you."

"Hurt me? You've fucking carved out my heart. Stay the fuck away from me. Don't come to the clubhouse. I don't want to hear your voice or see your face. You're dead to me."

I rush to him. "I love you. You said you loved me. We're having a baby, James. You can't just shut me out."

"Only reason you're still breathing is because Rochelle loved you. Maybe your father had it right when he said you destroy everything you touch."

At his words I fall to my knees. He could have said anything to me, and I could've taken it but not that. I've lost him just as I knew I would but the pain. Nothing could have prepared me for what I'm feeling tonight watching him walk away without so much as a glance back.

Dear God, if you're listening hear me now. Take me. Kill me because I can't be in a world where he doesn't want me. Where he doesn't love me. I can't do this without him.

Chapter Twenty-three

Months later

I pop the tab on another beer and chug. I glance up when I see Ruthie standing in the way of the Tv. "The fuck do you want?"

"Heard from one of the other cheer moms that Alexa is in labor."

"And?"

"I thought I'd go check on her. Victoria is such a cold woman. Alexa must need someone there for support."

"You aren't to go near there. Stay away from her. You hear me. You go to that hospital and I'll kill you with my bare hands."

"Jesus. You're a nasty drunk. It's not her fault, James. Rochelle loved her like a sister and what my father did to her...I."

I sling my can at the wall and Ruthie flinches. "Fuck that bastard. I hope he's rotting in hell. You're not Alexa's mother. If it weren't for her our daughter would still be here."

"You can't know that. You gotta stop this obsession with Rochelle's death. I know you blame yourself and punishing Alexa is easier, but it won't bring our daughter back. I miss her too. I lost her too and so did Alexa. You act like you're the only person allowed to grieve for her, but you're not alone. Stop pushing everyone away. We all lost her."

"Fuck you, cunt."

"Wow. Okay. Fine. You don't want me to go, I won't, but you need to stop this. You have a club to run. People depend on you. I depend on you. I need you to act like a man. Sober up and take a damn shower. You stink." She picks the beer can up and slings it back at me. "I love you, but you're a real miserable bastard. I don't know why I keep trying to save this marriage. You're determined to be wretched and alone. If you aren't careful, you'll get your wish. I'm dropping this gift basket off at Alexa's apartment. I hope when I get back that you've got off your ass."

"You're not doing a fucking thing for Alexa." I stumble toward the garage.

"What are you doing?" Ruthie huffs behind me as I glance around for something to put a stop to this bullshit.

Bingo. I grab a sledgehammer and start fucking slinging. Beating the fuck out of Ruthie's Corvette.

"James! What the serious fucking fuck are you doing?" She screeches behind me, but I block her out.

Filled with rage, images of Rochelle and Alexa dance before my eyes. The windshield cracks splintering into a web pattern like the fragments of what's left of my heart.

Losing control, I slip off the deep end consumed by violence and regret. I exert all my energy as Ruthie watches from afar unable to stop me.

Visions of Alexa cloud my thoughts. Her gorgeous green eyes. The way she looks at me as though I'm her damn hero. How sweet she tastes. Heaven being inside her and hell living without the temptation of her.

"James. Stop this. Stop it right now," Ruthie continues to yell.

Bitch is right about one thing. Rochelle is gone and nothing will ever bring her back. I drop to my knees surrounded by the wreckage I've created. A wife I hate.

245

Another child coming into this fucked up world. I should be there. No matter how bad shit is between Alexa and me, she shouldn't be alone. Not for this.

"Call Nickel. Tell him you need a new car." I drop the sledgehammer with a loud clang.

"You're in-fucking-sane, you know that?"

"I'll have a prospect clean this up later." I get up and walk down the driveway to my bike.

"Where are you going?"

"Got somewhere I need to be."

Palms sweating, I shut off my bike in the visitor parking lot. I've not seen Alexa since the night Rochelle died. If she attended the funeral, I didn't see her. I know I fucked up, but I'm not sure I've got it in me to make it right. I got no business being a father. If I had been a better one to Rochelle, she'd be alive. Papa wouldn't have lost his only son. Losing Colter completely turned him white headed.

I enter the gift shop and spot a grey teddy bear. I'm a sorry bastard. I don't know if we're having a boy or a girl. I pay for the bear and grab a small vase of flowers. It's not gonna fix us but it's a start of an apology for not handling shit better when she told me what happened.

Stepping off the elevator to the labor and delivery floor of the hospital I run straight into Victoria. Her mother. Wrinkled old bitch who has probably never had an orgasm in her life.

"You have no business here."

"I got as much right to be here as anyone if not more than you."

"Oh, I know all about you. How you took advantage of my daughter when she was weak and in trouble. You preyed on her vulnerability and put these stupid ideas in her head, but you and I both know she deserves better. That you'll never be the kind of man who will do what's best for her or this child."

"You don't know what Alexa needs. You turned your back on her when she needed you the most."

"And you think you're any better than me." She shakes her head, and I don't argue because she's right. I walked out. Treated her just like the rest of them. I hang my head in shame. "You even think of stepping one foot in that room and I'll make one phone call and see to it that you're rotting in a cell. Alexa doesn't want you here. You're not fit to be a father. If you really care about my daughter, you'll do the right thing and stay away. I won't allow you to ruin her life any further. I've spoken to a good family. They are prepared to adopt the baby."

"That what she wants?"

"It is. My lawyer has drawn up the papers. It will all be handled discreetly. No one will ever know you're the father. I can drop them off to your clubhouse later today. Alexa can move on with her life, and you can go back to being the trash that you are. My husband is willing to look the other way this one time. We can make sure Alexa gets a good education and marries a decent man. One who will provide her everything you can't give her. Go home to your wife, Mr. Thatcher. Worry about rebuilding your family, and I'll take care of mine. Look at you."

"Yeah." I snarl, staring at my wrecked knuckles, bloody and scabbing over from the damage I did on Ruthie's car. "Tell me one thing. Boy or girl."

"If you must know it's a girl."

Fuck me. All the air goes whooshing from my lungs. The vase slips from my grip, shattering against the dingy white tile. Without another word I give her what she wants. I leave. She's right. I can't be the man Alexa or this kid needs. I don't have it in me.

Alexa deserves a do over. A fresh start like I tried to give her in the beginning but was too damn selfish to follow through on. This time I'll be a better man. I'll do the right thing. I gotta let her go for good.

I drive to the clubhouse and get lost in liquor and easy pussy. I drink myself into oblivion but still no matter who I fuck all I see is her. My pretty girl with her tempting red lips. Those gorgeous green eyes haunt me. All I want is her, but I'm no good. A rotten bastard who will only ever hurt her.

After I fail to fuck away thoughts of Alexa, I stagger down the road to Rochelle's grave. I drop to my knees in the dirt. A storm brews. Thunder roars in the distance and lightning crashes. Rain pelts against my skin but nothing can wash away my sins. I grip the grass, digging my nails into the soil of the earth.

"I don't know what to do," I mutter to the headstone. "I fucked everything up. I let you down, Ro. I wanted to be a good father. I didn't want to love her, but I wanted her more than anything, and I've paid the price for giving in to temptation. I'd give anything to see you just once. To tell you I'm sorry I disappointed you. Give me a sign, princess." I look up at the dark clouds rolling overhead.

When I don't get a response, I let out a roaring scream and punch the ground. I'm beaten down and defeated. I don't know what the hell to do. Maybe

Rochelle would have been better off had I not killed Dusty. The man Ruthie moved in when I was in prison. The murder Ruthie helped me cover up. The one she holds over my head.

"James." Ruthie's hand touches my shoulder gently.

Fuck. Is this my sign? *Is this what you want, Rochelle?*

I grab her hand, clutching onto the only person I have left.

"Do you know why I wanted to be with you all them years ago?"

I shake my head. Her words intrigue me. I don't know why she's here, but I'm listening.

"Because I knew I could count on you. You'd never let me down. I never told you because I was ashamed, but my father…Alexa wasn't his only victim. I see a lot of myself in her. Wanting to escape a bad home life. Looking for a hero. I've watched the two of you, and I want to believe there's nothing going on. I'm not blind though. The way she looks at you. She's in love with you. Maybe it's all a crush or in my head."

"There was someone but not her," I lie.

"If you can say it's over with whoever she was and that there was nothing between you and Alexa, then I believe you. I don't think it's a coincidence we were both drawn here, honey. We're meant to be together. I knew it all them years ago just like I know it now. You're best I've ever had and all there will ever be for me. Come home with me. Let me take care of you for once."

Maybe it's regret or guilt. Maybe it's all the alcohol fueling me, but I know I need to make a change.

Chapter Twenty-four

"I got your bag. Everything is ready to go. Your father scheduled your induction. You just get into the bed and relax," my mother orders, practically pushing me onto the hospital bed. "It will all be over soon, sweetheart. You'll see things are better this way. Time to move on with life and look to the future."

When James turned his back on me, I was alone and on my own with no one to count on but my parents. Our relationship isn't great, but they are all I have. I don't blame him. I knew he'd hate me. I hate me. No one wishes it were me who had died in that wreck more than I do. Rochelle should be having the time of her life with Colter. Experiencing all her firsts with him. Now neither of them will ever have any of it. I did that. I took that away because I was selfish. James lost his daughter and Papa had to bury his son.

I can't bear to be in my apartment because all I think about is Rochelle, Colter, and James. Mostly James. I knew I'd miss him. Only I wasn't prepared for how greatly. I can't eat. I can't sleep. He's all I think about, but this baby is coming, and it's up to me to do what's best.

My mom knows a couple who have offered to adopt. I'm conflicted. Ideally it makes sense. I'm in no position to take care of a baby. I don't have my diploma. I'm eighteen and on my own. The lease will be up on my apartment soon. My parents say I can come home if I give up my baby and finish school. I don't want to depend on them. I'm scared though. I don't know what to do. I'm lost and heartbroken.

Nowhere to go. No job. No one wants to hire me because I'm a dropout and pregnant. My life is a mess, and it's my fault. I made the choices that put me in this situation. I gave my heart and body to a man who hates me. He doesn't love me, nor does he want to be a father to my child. However, despite it all I owe it to him to call him and tell him that our daughter will enter the world

254

today. That he lost Rochelle, but he's gained another child.

"Where's my phone?"

"Let me see." She pilfers through my overnight bag. "I could have sworn I stuck it in this pocket. We must have forgotten it."

"I need my phone now."

"You don't need it. You want it. Big difference. Besides you need to focus on delivering a healthy baby for the Mahoney's. Your father and I went through a lot of trouble finding someone who could be discreet and pay for your hospital bills. Having a baby isn't cheap, Alexa."

"I don't need a reminder. I just want to take some pictures when she's born."

"I thought we agreed that it's best if you don't hold her or do any of that stuff. Don't need you getting attached and changing your mind."

"She's still mine. If I want to hold her and take a million pictures I will. Now get me my phone, Mother. You promised I could call James."

"I can call him."

"Will you really call?"

"Now why would I lie? Really, I do wonder about you sometimes."

I turn away from her to hide my tears. If she sees them, she'll just tell me I'm acting emotional and to toughen up. Part of me thought if I called him, he'd come. That all he needs to realize we can still be a real family is to hold our child.

"I'll be back with your phone. It's probably in the car, but if you need anything your father is doing his rounds, and one of the nurses can page him."

"Just get my phone," I mutter, biting back a sob.

She exits the room, and I let out the tears I've been battling all morning. A nurse comes in to check my vitals before administering the oxytocin to induce me. The process is slow moving until my water breaks. That's when the contractions really kick in. By the time my mother brings me my phone, I'm dilated to seven and wondering about my epidural.

"Did you call James?" I ask through gritted teeth as another wave of pain hits me, my belly tightens, and I want to die. I need my epidural. I'm not strong enough to do this without pain meds.

"No. You said you wanted to do it."

"Just give it to me please." I go up on my knees and rock back and forth wishing more than anything he'd walk through that door. That he'd rub my back and hold my

hand while promising me everything will be okay. "Ahh,"
I cry out. "It hurts. I need my epidural."

"You don't get drugs. Your father thought it best you
experience the true pain of the consequences of your
actions."

"Why? Why would you do that?"

"You need to learn that you just can't go around
doing whatever you want. There's a price to pay for every
wrong step you take. Maybe you'll think twice about
spreading your legs to biker trash in the future."

Another pain rips through me. "Just fucking call
him," I scream.

"Your father will be in soon to check you. It's almost
time. The Mahoney's will be here shortly to pick up the
baby as long as she's healthy."

"No. I want to spend her first night with her. You
can't do that. I didn't sign anything yet."

"Really, Alexa. You can't expect to keep her. You'll
never make it on your own."

"Call James."

"Wake up, you fool. He's not coming. He doesn't
want you or his bastard. He never did. He used you.
Preyed on your weak nature."

He promised me. He swore I could count on him.

"No. He'll come if you call."

"I didn't want to do this, but you leave me no choice. I spoke with your precious James and you know what he said. He said that you were a delusional little girl with a crush. He denied everything. Now I don't know who the father is, but you've got to stop this behavior. But since we need his signature for the adoption, he signed the paperwork if we promised to keep it all discreet. You should be ashamed, lying like that on a married man. A man who took you in. He wants nothing to do with you. They all blame you for what happened to Rochelle and her boyfriend. You think he wants to see you. Hear more of your lies. That man said to tell you to keep away or he'd be forced to take actions to shut you up for good."

"I hate you."

"Well, darling girl, the feeling's mutual. You think I want to be here cleaning up the mess you made of your life? I'm here for the sake of your father's reputation. He has a status to uphold in the community."

"Get out."

"What?"

"You heard me, Victoria. I want you to leave. I don't want you or your help. I'll take care of my baby on my own."

"The Mahoney's are good Christian folk. And if you play your cards right you father has arranged a husband for you. One of his doctor friends. He's a bit short and going bald but with your prospects I think you should count your blessings that anyone is willing to marry you or take your child."

"I don't care if they have all the money in the world or if God himself comes down to put my child in their arms. It'll happen over my dead body. Now get the fuck outta here so I can birth my daughter in peace."

"If this is what you want. Then fine. Have it your way, but when you and that baby are hungry and homeless don't call upon me."

"Don't worry." I breathe in through my nose and out through my mouth, attempting to control the pain. "We don't need you. We don't need anyone." Not James either. I can do this. Somehow. Someway.

The second she leaves I collapse into a heap of pain and tears.

Another contraction rips through me so violently I feel as though my spine will tear itself free from my body. I go blind momentarily from the agony. I blink and attempt to stand. I can see my cell phone on the other side of the room laying on top of my bag. If I can get to it, I can call James myself. Another contraction hits me, followed by another, and I go to my knees, screaming for the nurse.

My monster prick of a father rushes in and goes into doctor patient mode.

"No. I don't want you here." I attempt to shove him away.

Thwack. His hand whips across my face. "Calm down damn it. Right now, what matters is delivering your child safe and healthy. Now get back to bed so I can examine you. Don't know why you are up to begin with. Where is that stupid nurse?" he curses under his breath ushering me into the bed.

I don't want him to touch me but am left without a choice as my baby doesn't want to wait any longer.

"I can see the head," he announces as the nurse finally shows up.

Fifteen minutes later my gorgeous Wylla Mae is cradled in my arms screaming her head off as I kiss all her fingers and toes feeling more love than I could ever imagine for this one tiny person who has been the source of so much trouble and heartache.

"Hello, my tough baby girl. It's just you and me, but I will always love you and protect you. I named you Wylla because it means faithful. And Mae after my friend. Rochelle Mae Thatcher. She would have loved you. She's your big sister, and I bet right now wherever she is that she's your guardian angel."

Wylla Mae and I are both released from the hospital the following evening. Me with more stitches than ought to be humanly possible and her healthy as can be. I have no one to call. I keep telling the nurse my ride is running late.

I've gotten as desperate as calling Nickel but he's not picking up. I even thought about calling Tanner, Colter's friend. That's how sad and pathetic I am. I have no friends. Rochelle was all I had, and I killed her. No one is coming. No one cares about us.

"Knock. Knock." I glance to the door of my room and see Ruthie.

My heart jumps to my throat. "Wha-what are you doing here?"

"I meant to come sooner, but I've had some car trouble." She rolls her eyes. "Anyway, the nurse said you were released and asked if I was your ride. Do you need a ride?"

"I couldn't ask you to do that."

"It's no trouble. I figured your mom would be here."

261

"We aren't speaking."

"Okay. Well I'm here. Do you have a car seat?"

"I do at the apartment."

"No problem. I will run and get it. You and this little sweetie." She rubs a finger over my sleeping daughter's dark hair. "You sit tight, and I'll be back in a flash." She starts back out the door of my hospital room.

"Ruthie?"

"Yeah?" her voice wobbles slightly.

"The key. It's in the front pocket of my bag."

"Right." She fishes it out and flashes me a tense smile.

I swallow hard once she's gone. Does James know she's here? Did he send her to check on us? Does she know the truth? Did she come to see for herself that I gave birth to her husband's love child.

I have too many questions and no one to ask them to.

Chapter Twenty-five

"You really didn't need to go to so much trouble." My stomach churns as Ruthie busies herself in the kitchen boiling bottles.

"Rochelle would have been glued to your side if she were still here. I don't know, Alexa. Seeing you. It makes me feel closer to her if that makes sense." She dabs at her eyes. "Sorry. I get so emotional at times."

"Don't apologize. You miss her. I do too."

"You were like the big sister she always wanted. I want another baby, but James feels it's too soon after Rochelle." My heart clenches in my chest hearing his name. She has no clue that my daughter belongs to her husband. I'm a terrible person. She's grieving the loss of her daughter, and here I am flaunting my baby in her face in the apartment her husband pays for. "Between us, he's having a rough time. Losing Rochelle changed him, but it brought us closer together. I know you and Ro were friends, but I think being a mom now you can relate."

"Sure. I'm glad I guess that things have gotten better for you guys. I didn't know you were having trouble," I lie.

"Things were rocky but last night." She winks. "We well reconnected you could say. Before long our babies might be playmates. I think James will come around, and well if we are lucky, we conceived last night. He was just…" she lifts her shoulders and smirks all dreamily.

I'm going to be sick. Bile burns in the back of my throat. He was with her. While I was in the hospital crying for him, he was fucking his wife. I deserve it. I know I do. But her words and the bitter truth of it all still fucking cuts into my chest and rips my heart out. He was never going to leave her. Not for me. He never loved me, did he? It was all sex.

My head spins as the realization takes root. He used me. I was nothing but the other woman. My heart hammers in my chest so fast. I can't breathe. Is this what a panic attack feels like? Or am I truly dying?

"To be honest with you, Alexa. Rochelle isn't the only reason I'm here."

Sweat beads across my top lip. My stomach plummets to my feet. Oh shit. She knows. She's going to tell me that James and her want my baby or to stay away. My mind races as she smiles at me.

"My father."

"I…I'm sorry what about him?"

"I know this might be a difficult conversation to have, but I know what he did to you, and I was wondering…well I got the impression that your daughter might be my half-sister. So if you need anything at all I want you to know that you can count on me. He may have been a bad man, but what he did isn't your fault. Your mom may not be in the picture, but you've got me. James too. I know he's been cold and distant since the accident, but he knows you need us."

I'm going to faint. She thinks Wylla Mae belongs to her rapist father. I swallow hard not knowing what to do with this information. Do I agree with her lie or make up a new one?

"Don't feel obligated. Your father. Wylla isn't. Um. Tanner. You remember him. Colter's friend. It was a onetime thing, and he doesn't know. I don't have any plans on telling him."

"You need to tell him."

"I will just not right now. It's complicated. You see he has a girlfriend, and I don't want to cause any problems for him. I don't want or need anything from him. It's just ya know. Whatever," the lies just keep coming.

"You poor dear."

"I'll be fine. Truly. I'm putting in applications, and I'm sure once I find a car and a babysitter, things will work out for me. I'm thinking of moving to another city even. Fresh start and all that." I still have the bank card James gave me. I never touched that money. I could use it for Wylla and me. He is her father and he gave it to me.

I hope there is still money in the account anyway.

"Not to pry, but you aren't prepared for this baby at all. It's okay to ask for help. I know you're strong. You don't have to prove that to me. No one has to know. Not even James. It can be our secret. You didn't get a baby shower. I want to do this for you. So let me see what you have."

Heat shoots up my spine. She's right. I didn't think any of this through. I don't have anything besides a few basic things. Not even a crib. A fat tear rolls down my cheek. "I…"

"You know what. It's okay. You just kick back there on the couch. The baby is asleep in the carrier, and you should sleep when she does. I'll prep a bottle or two before I leave. You've got enough diapers to cover you for now. Leave it all to me."

It's too much. I can't allow her to do this and yet I have no one else. My mom was right. I'm lost. I don't know what I'm doing or how to take care of a baby at all. A small sliver of my heart was holding onto hope I'd be doing all of this with James. Now look at me. I'm his wife's fucking charity case.

Ruthie hums to herself moving through my apartment, changing things around, and making notes on a pad of paper she got from the junk drawer in the kitchen. I close my eyes and sleep sucks me under.

**

"Shh. They're still asleep. Try to be a little quieter will you."

I blink.

"Where should I put this?" a guy's voice sounds close by.

"Take it to the bedroom," Ruthie tells him.

"Got it."

I open my eyes in time to see Tanner packing a big box toward my bedroom.

Holy shit. Why is he here? This is bad. Real bad. He can blow my secret out the water. I'm torn between trying to get rid of both of them or pretending I'm asleep a bit longer. Wylla Mae wakes up with a startled cry, and I instantly jump up. So much for faking my sleep.

"You want me to get her?" Ruthie offers, and I shake my head.

I glance around the room while I get Wylla from the carrier. "Ruthie…it's too much." There's so much stuff.

"Nonsense. I only bought the essentials. I have a little surprise for you." She motions toward the hall. "Figured you need a nudge in the right direction."

I look over to see Tanner smiling sheepishly at me. *Shit.* "Hey, Alexa." His cheeks redden when he says my name.

"Hi. Can you hold on a second? I just gotta." I point to my baby's stinky butt and move past him.

"I gotta get going, Alexa. I think you and Tanner have some talking to do. I'll check back in on you, but if you need anything give me a call."

"Okay. Thanks." This is all too much and too damn strange.

"I'll see myself out." She waves and slips out the door.

I lay Wylla down on my bed realizing I forgot to bring her diapers and wipes with me. I can sense Tanner hovering over my shoulder. I can't believe Ruthie did this. She had no business dragging him here. This has nothing to do with him.

"I don't want to sound rude but what are you doing here? No hold that thought. First can you um grab me a pack of wipes and a diaper out of the living room?"

He scratches at the back of his neck. "Yeah. Sure."

"Great. Thank you."

I get her onesie unbuttoned by the time he returns. "Here you are." He places the items next to her on the bed. "What the heck is that?" his face screws up, deep blue eyes widening.

"What?"

"Her bellybutton."

"Oh. That's from her umbilical cord. Um one more favor. I need an alcohol swab from my bag. It's in the chair in the living room."

"How about I just bring you the bag?"

"Good idea." I still have no idea what he's doing here. I change my baby's diaper while he's fetching the bag for me. "So what are you doing here?"

"Um. I don't know for sure, but Rochelle's mom called my mom and said she needed my help with something. She made me go shopping for baby stuff and had this weird conversation with me about responsibility and being a man. It made me super uncomfortable. I got the impression she thinks I'm the father of your baby, but I know that's not possible so you wanna tell me what the hell is going on?"

"I'm so sorry for dragging you into my mess. It's my fault. I hope she didn't say anything to your mom." I clean the umbilical cord and snap the onesie back.

"Not sure. But why does she think we slept together?"

I grit my teeth. He ought to have full transparency. "Because I may have told her that we had a one-night stand that resulted in my baby."

"I like you, but my parents will kill me if they think I got you knocked up."

"I'm sorry, Tanner." I cradle Wylla Mae to my chest. "I don't expect you to lie for me. It's just…I can't. People can't know who the father is, and I had to tell her something. She was asking questions, and I didn't have answers. If you mom asks questions, tell her it was a misunderstanding."

"You're beautiful," he blurts out. He blushes and stares at his shoes. His head snaps back up. "What I mean is whoever or whatever they're the one missing out. I've thought you were the prettiest girl in all of West Virginia since the fifth grade when my family first moved here. If people think that you...that we. Then I'm okay with that. I've been wanting a shot with you long as I can remember. You might not think of me that way, but maybe one day you will."

"That's sweet. Probably one of the nicest things anyone has ever said to me. I'm not looking for a boyfriend, but what I could really use tonight more than anything is a friend."

He smiles at me. Tanner has one of them golden smiles. Perfectly sculpted lips and a chiseled jaw that'd cut glass. Any girl would be lucky to have him. Because sure he's cute, but he's sweet and kind. The kind of guy most parents would love for their daughter to bring home. The guy I shoulda been dating, but he's not the one I love. My heart belongs to a royal bastard in every sense of the word. As hurt as I am, I still ache for James.

"How about we get this crib set up?"

"I'd like that. Thank you, Tanner." I shift my baby girl to my other shoulder and kiss his cheek. I don't know if I will ever open my heart to another man, but maybe one day.

Chapter Twenty-six

"What's all these charges?" I flip through my bank statement. "Why you buying fuckin' pampers? Something you wanna tell me?"

Ruthie tucks her dark hair behind her ear. "I bought them for Wylla Mae."

"Who the fuck is Wylla?"

"Alexa's daughter. I felt so awful for the poor girl. She has no help. Her parents are dreadful people, and she meant so much to Rochelle. It felt like the right thing to do."

I steel my facial expression, not wanting Ruthie to gauge my reaction to the news Alexa kept our daughter. My chest squeezes so damn tight I'd swear I'm having a heart attack if I didn't know better. She didn't give her up. Our little girl. Fuck me. Fuck me hard. "Since when do you give a shit about what happens to Alexa?"

My wife laughs. "I told you. Her baby might be my half-sister."

"Cut the fucking bullshit. What kind of game are you playing at?"

"No game. It's the truth." She moves in, slinging my papers out my lap. "You know visiting with her…brings back all those good memories. When we first had Rochelle. I want a baby, James, and you're going to give me one."

"Why in the hell would I do that?"

"Because you love me and want to make me happy." She kisses my jaw and I pull away. "Don't be like that. We deserve a second chance don't, we?"

"How many times we gonna try and get it wrong?"

"As many as it takes. Make a baby with me." Her hand slides down my neck. "I want a baby, honey. Do this one thing for me."

I jerk away. "Having another kid won't replace Rochelle. Won't change a damn thing."

"I bet I can change your mind."

"You think so?"

Her lips move to my ear and the words she whispers, sends an artic chill down my spine that's so damn cold my blood could freeze.

"The fuck did you just say to me?"

A coy smile plays at her lips. "You heard me, lover. Give me a baby, and I'll grant you the freedom you crave. Now take off your pants."

**

"What ya need?" Grudge rubs his jaw.

"Want you to do something for me."

"Name it."

"Ruthie. Gotta funny feeling. Need you to keep an eye on her. You see her talking to anyone or doing anything weird. Let me know. Keep it between us. Don't let her know you're following her."

"I can do that. You can count on me, brother."

"Good." I grunt, and he takes off.

I light up another blunt and Nickel flops down in the chair across from me. "Let me get a hit of that."

I reach it across the table. "How'd that last run go?"

"A-Okay. No problems. Even picked up an extra twenty-five percent for a job well done."

"And the other side detail. She still using the account?"

"Yeah. Man, look. How long you gonna keep this shit up?"

"Keep putting money in it. She see you?"

275

"Nope. Though I did see something I'm not sure you're gonna like." He passes the blunt back.

I take another hit. "And what's that?"

"Not sure if I should tell you or let you figure that shit out on your own." He grins and reaches for the Mary Jane again.

I take another hard puff before handing it over. I cough and slap at my chest. "Can't do that."

"Brother, I respect the fuck outta you, but that's your God damn kid. Ruthie sniffing your ass every time you make a move or not."

"I'm not ready to see her."

"Alexa or the kid?" he hands the blunt back.

"Both, but mostly Alexa. Bitch burns through my veins like heroin."

"Hardest addiction to kick."

I blow out a ring of smoke. "Exactly. I see her and all I wanna do is rip her clothes off and fuck her till neither of us can see straight." I take another hit. "Did that little fuck stick she was seeing leave town?"

"Yeah. He got smart. Likes his pretty boy face too much. I don't get you." He shakes his head, and Kristen slides a beer in front of him and replaces my empty.

"Yeah well that makes two of us. Besides it's better this way."

"Better for who? You're fucking miserable. Married to a cunt."

"Watch it. That cunt is still my wife and pregnant with my son."

"Fuck. For real?"

"Yeah. Wanted to wait to say anything until we knew for sure."

"Then congrats, Prez. Guess you won't care that I saw Alexa working the pole at the Lion's Den." He smirks and knocks back his beer.

"The fuck did you just say?"

"Me and a few of the boys swung by last night on our way back into town. Gotta say…fine piece of ass like that had my kid no man would be tossing singles at her ass and seeing her titties. And what a fine ass and rack she has. Having that baby did her body good. She musta been drinking a helluva lot of milk."

I shove my chair back and jump up. "What time is it?"

"I'd say it's about time you got your head out your ass and claimed your bitch before someone else moves in."

I ignore him as he laughs. All I see is red and I'm about to be a bull in a china shop. I climb onto my Road King and ride out. I'm gonna spank her ass. Alexa has no business working in a dump like this. I've been funneling money into an account for her. Plenty enough to cover her rent. any bills, and to make sure the baby won't want for a damn thing.

I park and light up a cigarette. Fucking place is booming. Then I see it. A fucking poster by the front door. Alexa in a black leather bikini straddling a Harley looking like every man's wet dream come true.

I snatch the poster off the brick and wad it up.

"Hey, man. The fuck?" One of the bouncer's snarls at me.

I step into his space. He takes one look at the President's patch on my cut and realizes his mistake. My club owns this shithole. Hence the fucking name Lion's Den.

"My bad. Go on in."

"Want all these taken down." I grunt and shove the poster into his chest.

"She's our main feature," he mutters.

I don't give a fuck what they think she is. Alexa isn't gonna be their anything for much longer. Gonna jerk a damn knot in her head. Since I'm here I might as well scope shit out and see how Marco is running the place since we gave Lion's man Dingo the boot. I grab a table toward the back. I don't know if I want Alexa to know I'm here. Been months since we've been face to face. Since we've touched. Since I walked out the door on her and didn't look back.

I pull out my phone and dial Slick. "Got a job for you. Need the apartment wired and a room setup for surveillance in the basement. No one else on this. I don't have time to get in touch with the Reapers to do it nice. I want it done now. Get in and out." I end the call. Should have done that shit months ago. Least I can see my kid without Ruthie knowing or being tempted by Alexa.

I signal one of the bitches working the floor to bring me a shot. Marco better get some hot ass in here because once I take Alexa out the rotation, he'll lose business. Knocking back one shot after the next, I sit through a few sets wondering when Alexa will grace the stage.

My cell buzzes with a call from Ruthie. I send her to voice mail. I'm not in the mood for more of her shit right now. I need a fucking break. The crowd moves closer to the main stage, growing louder. The lights dim. "Ladies

279

and gentlemen the reason you're all here, welcome to the stage Lexi."

I sit up at the sound of a motorcycle roaring onto the stage. The bouncer shuts it off leaving Alexa on the back with the spotlight shining on her. Seeing her riding bitch on another man's biker is a punch to the gut even if it's all for show. *Play With Fire* by *Sam Tinnesz* filters through the sound system. Dressed in a black leather bikini top, Daisy Dukes, and knee-high boots like on the fucking poster, all the blood in my body shoots straight to my dick at the sight of her. Smoke covers the floor of the stage. The lighting switches to red strobe lights and an image of fire pops up on a loop on the screen behind her.

Is this a fucking strip show or a theatrical production? I snort to myself and do another shot.

Alexa leans forward, practically humping the seat of the bike. I already want to charge the damn stage, sling her over my shoulder, spank her ass raw, and fuck her brains out. Been months and the attraction I have for her seems to only grow stronger. After her little display on the motorcycle, she trades it for the pole.

Rubbing up and down it seductively she unbuttons her shorts, teasing at what's beneath them—my own personal paradise. All them years of cheerleading paid

280

off. Her routine appears effortless. She loses the boots and denim shorts. Strutting across the stage in fishnets and a thong, teasing at removing her bikini top, the crowd loves her. I watch powerless to stop the performance. It hurts like hell knowing she's meant to be mine, and I can't have her.

It's for her own good. She wouldn't understand why I've made the choices I have. I'll carry the burden of it till the day I die, aching for her. Unable to stay away, I inch closer to the stage, bulldozing my way through any motherfucker who stands between us. My pretty girl commands attention and fuck me she's got mine. My cock swells, craving her sweet pussy.

Chapter Twenty-seven

"The fuck you think you're doing?" James grips me by the elbow and drags me into one of the private lounges of Lion's Den, the strip club I've been dancing at to support Wylla Mae and me.

My heart leaps to my throat at the sight of him. I've done as he said. I've stayed away. I've not asked him for anything. I used the account he set up for me a few times out of basic necessity until I started working here. I never thought I'd be in this situation. Taking my clothes off and flashing my tits and ass for a little cash. I have a daughter to support though, and for her I'll do whatever it takes to give her the world.

"What's it look like? I'm trying to earn money to take care of my daughter."

"She's my kid too."

"Ha." I laugh in his face as he backs me up until the backs of my knees hit the couch. "My daughter doesn't need a damn thing you got to offer her. Why don't you run on home to Ruthie and play house?"

He grabs my chin, his gaze burning with fury. "You don't know what you're talking about."

"Right. Okay. I heard you're having another kid. Congratulations." Some members of his club stop in often and Mitzi, one of the dancers who has taken me under her wing fucks Nickel. She doesn't know James is the father of my child, but she loves to gossip.

"What happened to you, Lex? This..." his hand rubs down my side, and I shiver. "Taking off your clothes for money... I don't like it."

"You don't have to like it. You don't get to tell me what to do anymore. You gave up the right when you signed your rights to my kid away. I got your papers." They were stuck under the door of my apartment. When I saw that he signed his rights away that was it. The last shred of hope I had that we'd be together gone. He's proven he'll never change his ways and that he doesn't give a shit about us.

"What papers?"

"Oh, you know what. Fuck you."

"Fuck me?"

"Yeah." I get back in his face. "Fuck. You. Murder."

"Fuck me?" he growls, and I shrink back, falling onto the black leather couch.

He looms over me all broody and still the sexiest man I've ever seen. Those dangerous dark eyes bore into me. Warmth tingles through my veins and to regions I wish wouldn't get excited by his presence, but I'd be a liar if I said I wasn't attracted to him. I look for him in every man I meet. It hurts to admit that, but it's true. He's all I will ever want, and I hate that I do. Want him. I try so hard not to think about him, but it's hard when I look into my daughter's brown eyes and see his reflecting back at me.

"I hate you. I hate you so much I need a new word for how much."

"You don't hate me, Lex." He jerks my legs apart and grabs me between the thighs. "You're just mad because I'm not yours to fuck anymore, but I'm feeling generous tonight." His hand moves to his belt.

"What are you doing?" I try to move but he holds me in place with one hand while undoing his jeans with the other.

"Gonna fuck you, baby. Give you some dick so maybe you'll lose the attitude and remember who you belong to."

"Stay away from me."

"You know you want it. Fucking soaked and panting for it."

"You're drunk."

"Miss you, pretty girl. Miss the feel of you. The way you'd cry out and beg me for this cock."

"I'm not having sex with you." I shove against his chest, and he doesn't even budge an inch. No, he rips my fishnet stockings and yanks my thong clean off.

"Been months since I've been inside you. Months since I've felt peace. And one look at you, and all my anger and pain fades right away. Why is that? Only thing that can bring me any peace is you?"

"I don't give a damn what you think you feel or know. I'm not yours, and I never will be again."

"You'll always be mine, Lex."

"You're delusional."

"Shit is complicated." He slides a finger inside me, and I melt at the connection. My eyes roll back in my head when he adds a second digit to the mix. "There's my girl," he grits, coming in for a kiss.

I roll my lips inward to deny him, but my body hums for him. Craves his touch.

"Playing hard to get?"

"No. Stop it. I'm not yours. I don't want this. I don't want you." I push at his shoulders.

"Liar. So full of shit they can smell you in Kentucky. Kiss me," he demands. His liquor tainted breath washes over me.

"Eat shit."

"How about I eat your sweet cunt instead?" he drops to his knees to worship me. Rubbing his face between my legs he kisses my clit, sucking the sensitive skin. "Fuck, Lex. Best pussy." Squeezing my tit as I try to wiggle away from him, he ignores my cries of protest. "God damn, I don't know what I've missed more. Eating you till you come or you riding me till I blow."

His filthy talk shouldn't set my soul on fire, but it does.

He strokes himself with one hand and plays with my pussy with the other. Can't fight it or deny it. As fucked up as it is, I want him. I want him so bad I could cry. Against my better judgment I lay back and stop resisting. Getting a grip on his hair I ride his fingers while he tongues my clit until I come. I've not been with anyone since him. Tanner tried. He was patient and sweet, but eventually his patience gave out and he took off.

"That's it, Lex. You don't want me. Don't like it when I do this either, right?" He grins then laps at my pussy, licking me like he can't get enough.

I'm still in the throes of my orgasm when he snakes up my body and shoves his thick cock inside me. A shudder and jolt ripples through him as my pussy contracts around his dick.

"Fuck, baby. Fuck. Nothing better. So damn good. Your pretty little pussy curves to my dick." And then he's moving fast and furious, fucking me as if his life depends on it.

We're feral animals rutting. Heavy grunts pass between us. Teeth nipping and tasting. Sweat dripping, blood pumping, bodies slapping together in a rhythm that's erotic and primal. He kisses me hard and deep. I hate myself for loving him. For loving how well our bodies fit. How he knows what buttons to push. How to play my body.

I wish I could be stronger, but when it comes to this man, I'd do almost anything he asks of me just to be with him. I'm pathetic. I lift my hips, seeking him out, wanting him to go deeper and harder.

"No more dancing, Lex."

I go still. I found one thing I won't give him. "You don't get to tell me what to do."

He draws out and slams back in. "Promise me."

"Get off." I press against his chest.

"I don't like it. Don't want my brothers staring at you and imagining fucking what's mine."

My hand flies up and whips across his cheek.

Nostrils flaring, he wraps a hand around my throat and gives me a squeeze in warning. "Don't ever fucking do that again."

I gasp. Tears sprint down my cheeks, hot and fast as though they are racing. "Let me up."

"You're mine, Lex. Told you I'm a possessive bastard. We're through when I say, and I didn't fucking say." Murder fucks me harder than before as though he needs to remind me or possibly punish me.

Our gazes meet. He gives me his imperfectly perfect smile then pulls out to finish on my belly. Dropping his forehead to mine he holds still a beat before pushing away.

"I'm not gonna stop ya know. I don't need you or your false promises. I can take care of myself. Like always."

"Lex…I." he drops his head then snaps it back up in a flash. Intense and snarling, his eyes narrow on me. Angers pours from his stare, rolling off him in waves. "I warned you. You're in my fucking world. You don't get to decide when you leave. If I want to fuck you, you'll spread them legs for me. If I give you money, I expect you to spend it on my God damned kid."

I jump up and grab a tissue from the side table to wipe my stomach off. "I'm going to say this one more time. I'm not your property. Wylla Mae is my daughter. She doesn't belong to you. You don't know her. You've never held her. Fed her. Changed her. You know nothing about what it's like for us. You wanna fuck someone…go get one of your whores at your clubhouse. Or better yet why don't you go home to your wife you're so devoted to and ask her how my pussy tastes, huh?"

In one swift movement he's back in my face, hand on my throat again. "I should just knock you up again."

"I'm not Ruthie," I grit in his face, holding back my tears. "Go home to your pregnant wife and stay the hell out of my life. I don't want you. I don't need you and I sure as fuck don't love you. Leave me alone, Murder."

"Not till you get it through your head that this is the way shit's gonna be until I say otherwise. Anyone touches

289

what's mine…" he grabs me between the legs again. "I'll fucking kill them. Behave accordingly. Don't fuck around on me. Do as your told."

"I'll fuck anyone I want when I want."

"Babe, you're really pissing me the fuck off."

"Get used to it." I jerk away from him and stomp down the hall to the dressing groom. Screw him. I don't need this shit. Not from him. Not after everything we've been through in the past year.

Chapter Twenty-eight

MURDER

The second I stumble through the garage door Ruthie flicks the kitchen light on. I throw up an arm to shield my eyes as I squint. 'The fuck you doin'?"

"Do you have any idea how worried I've been? Do you know what time it is?"

"You're not my mother." I shrug past her and kick off my boots, making my way toward the bedroom.

"I needed you and I couldn't reach you."

"I've held up my end."

"I'm spotting blood. I called the doctor and he said I should come in first thing but if gets worse to go to the emergency room."

Fuck. Fucking fuck. This is the second miscarriage in the past year. Her first happened a few months after we buried Rochelle. I don't love Ruthie. Nor do I want to raise another child with her, but I don't want to lose my son. My future depends on this pregnancy being viable. I lay my cut over the back of a chair and step out of my jeans. "I need a shower."

Ruthie comes in close and starts sniffing me. "You're wasted? You smell…" She sniffs my face. "Like another woman. Like pussy. You're fucking around on me? After everything?"

"I agreed to another baby. Never said shit all about keeping my dick in my pants."

"I assumed that was obvious, James. Don't toy with me. You know what I'm capable of," she says with a sneer.

"I'm getting in the shower then I gotta head back out to handle some shit for the club. I'll give you a ring to see what the doctor says."

Her hand moves to her hip, but I slam the bathroom door in her face before she can start flapping them damn jaws with more of her nagging bullshit. I'm in no damn mood. Alexa is under my skin. I'm disgusted with myself. I know I'm a sorry bastard. I knew not to go to that club and be that close to her, but I did it anyway. In the shower I punch the white tiles until my blood runs down them. I fucked up. I'm supposed to protect her not be the man hurting her. Yet I can't seem to stop. If I stay away, I can't breathe. If I get too close, I drown myself in her and hate her for it. I'm fucked in the head.

You've never fed her.

Held her.

Changed her.

Alexa's words echo in my thoughts as the hot water sprays down on me. It hurts because it's the truth. I don't deserve that little girl. By the time I get out of the shower Ruthie has gone to bed. I've tried to force myself to feel something for her, but when I look at my wife the only emotions inside me are regret and loathing. I hate her but can't bring myself to kill her because we got one thing right. Rochelle.

I ride out. When I reach my destination it's quiet. All the lights are off. I let myself in with the spare key. The kitchen is tidy, save a few empty bottles in the sink and a can of powdered formula on the counter. I flick on the light over the stove. In the living room there's a stack of baby clothes folded on the coffee table with a full basket next to it on the floor. On the end table sits a framed photograph of Alexa in the hospital, holding our daughter. I trace the rough pad of my finger along the smooth glass making out their faces.

You've never fed her.

Held her.

Changed her.

Creeping down the hall, I'm careful to keep my movements light and silent. I pause at the bedroom door. Alexa is sprawled out in the center of her bed in nothing but a thin tank top and a thong. I want nothing more than to strip down and crawl into bed simply to hold her, but I can't. At the foot of the bed is a white crib.

The baby fusses and Alexa stirs. I don't want her to know I'm here and yet I'm not ready to leave. In three steps I'm leaning over the crib and glancing down at Wylla Mae for the first time. Bald headed and big eyed she kicks her legs out, slobbering on her tiny fists.

She resembles Rochelle at this age. I stroke the top of her head, surprised to find that she does have hair it's just fine and blonde. A spit bubble blows out her mouth. I go to leave but she cries out. The sound splits my heart in two. Alexa doesn't budge at the noise this time. It's been a long time since I've held a baby, but I pick my daughter up gently, being careful to support her head and bottom.

"Hey, baby girl." I whisper, strolling to the living room, patting her back as I go. Her sweet baby smell washes over me as I drop my ass to the couch. Laying her across my knees I stare at her. It's been a lifetime since I've done this, but I'm sure not much has changed. "You got my eyes," I note, studying their brown color.

Her legs kick my belly.

"You're a strong little squirt." I pick Wylla up and cradle her to my chest. "I'm sorry I'm not around for you. Life's not fair, and I got my reasons. Things you're too young to understand. But I stay away for your protection. There are people who'd use you to hurt me. An evil woman who will hurt your mom if I'm not careful, and I can't and won't allow that. You're too important to me. You need your mom more than you will ever need me. But I want you to know that I love you. Love your mom too. You were born out of the love we share. No matter where this life takes us, I'll watch over you." She grabs a handful of my beard, tugging on the whiskers and cooing.

"One of the hardest things I've ever had to do is walk away from you and your mother." This sweet, pure child of mine pats my cheek as though she understands. "You got your whole life ahead of you. I'll be damned if I let you pay for my sins. Only want the best for you. To give you that no one can know you're my flesh and blood. I lost one daughter then you came along. I was told someone else would raise you. I tried to make my peace with that, but your mom changed her mind. Gotta tell you, Wylla Mae, I'm damn glad she did." I kiss the top of her head and close my eyes soaking her in. Committing this moment to memory because it can't happen again. I can't afford to be weak. Not when her future depends on it. I gotta do this for her. For Alexa.

"She likes you," Alexa whispers, startling me.

"I don't know about that," my voice comes out hoarse. "Listen…"

"No. I'm done listening to your broken promises and lies. You can't just show up in my life whenever you want. I still love you though I know I shouldn't. I thought you loved me too, but this…whatever we are is far from love, James."

"I wish I could tell you what you want to hear. Give you the life I promised. But this is all I can give. You said you'd take me any way you could have me. Did you mean that?"

A tear slides down her cheek. "It's not enough."

"Doing the best I can. There's shit you're better off not knowing. Can you trust that I wish things were different, and I'm fighting like hell to stay away for your own protection."

"Did someone threaten me?"

"Nothing for you to be worried about."

"Don't shut me out."

I get up and hand Wylla Mae to her mother. "This is how it's gonna be."

"Just tell me why. Make me understand. Give me one reason. A real one."

"Not tonight."

"Then when?"

"When the time is right." I stroke her jaw, and she turns into my caress. "I love you, Alexa. You can question everything else but never doubt the way I feel about you or our daughter. I'm doing what's best. I need to know you'll wait for me. As long as it takes to pull us through the other side of the mess I've made of things."

"I'll wait for you, James, but don't make me wait too long. I need you. We need you."

"You gonna keep dancing?"

She shrugs, and I contain my anger even though my blood is boiling at the thought. I don't want to fight with her in front of the kid. "I need to change her."

"I can do it."

Her brows shoot up. "You want to change her diaper?"

"Yeah."

"Okay. Her stuff is on the changing table in the bedroom. I'm going to make her a bottle." She shoves Wylla Mae back into my chest.

A putrid smell wafts up from the back of her sleeper and something wet touches my hand. "Fucking hell," I mutter.

"Did I forget to mention that she's wet?" Alexa rolls her lips inward fighting her giggle, but I hear it under her breath. Serves me right though.

"She's more than wet." I stomp down the hall and lay the baby on the changing table. First damn thing I do is clean my hand off with a baby wipe. "All right." I rub my palms together. I can do this. It's just a shitty diaper. No big deal. I unsnap her sleeper and go to undo the latches on the diaper when she rolls to her side, and that's when I see it. Greenish yellow nasty fucking oatmeal looking shit streaked up her back. I throw a hand over my mouth and gag. "What has your mother been feeding you? Alexa," I holler. "I'm gonna need a damn hose."

Wylla Mae blows a spit bubble at me then kicks her legs, making it worse.

"You're lucky you're cute." I scowl at her and she babbles at me.

"Just like her dad," Alexa says from behind me. "I started her bath."

My heart squeezes in my chest. This is how it should be, and I feel like a rotten bastard that I gotta leave soon with no idea when I'll return. But she said she'd wait for me. As long as it takes.

Part Two

Chapter Twenty-nine

Present day

I climb on my bike. The past eighteen years play on a loop like the scenes of a movie as I roar down the highway. The first time I saw Alexa. Pure trouble. Pure temptation. Losing Rochelle. A pain I thought I'd never come out the other side from. Watching Wylla Mae grow up without me. Seeing her evolve into a beautiful young woman and completely flourish despite all the shit life threw at her for being tainted with my blood. Watching Alexa go from man to man ruining every good relationship she had. Bringing men into her life she had no intention of settling down with. Anything or anyone to dull the pain. A free bird who never wanted to be caged by any man but me. Punishing herself for what happened with Rochelle and Colter. Hating herself for loving me.

She hit a breaking point when Wylla Mae was eight. The kid had a cold. I remember it like it was yesterday. Alexa called me. She never called, but she sounded so damn desperate, I couldn't stay away. It killed me to see Alexa and Wylla Mae. That little girl was the spitting image of her dead sister. Like the daylight to Rochelle's dark. Every time I looked at Wylla all I saw was the child I lost and another I couldn't be there for. Hurt like hell. Like a curse I couldn't break. During this time Ruthie kept suffering miscarriages. A never ending cycle of loss and grief.

Life was hell and the devil was fucking me at every turn.

Took Easton Reed with me to check in on Alexa and my daughter. When we got there the house was a mess. The house I bought them because even though I couldn't enjoy it with them I wanted them to have the best. I knew she was having one of her breakdowns. They always came on around Rochelle's birthday or the anniversary of the accident.

This time was worse than any of the others. She'd taken a bunch of sleeping pills trying to chase her demons away. I had no choice but to send Wylla Mae away with East. If Alexa was gonna die it wouldn't be in front of our daughter. I forced my fingers down her throat, made her expel what she could. Thank fuck she didn't take enough to do any real damage. I wanted to kill her myself for being so damn stupid.

"I forgive you, Alexa, but now it's time to forgive yourself, because so help me if you check out on me, I'll soon follow you to hell to torment you for all of eternity. She needs you, Lex. I can't be the man she needs, but you're wasting your life away. Pull yourself together or I'm gonna take Wylla to live with Lily."

I spent the weekend putting her back together. Got her in to see a shrink to deal with her survivor's guilt. Our relationship shifted after that. I stopped fucking her. She'd gotten with Easton. A damn good man, but they weren't right for each other. Alexa's always belonged to me and life had other plans for East. Fucking bastard fell in love with my Wylla Mae when she became an adult.

I wanted to be angry. Wanted to cut him down. But I know one thing in this life. You don't choose who to love. It just fucking happens.

Fucking Ruthie. Bitch played me all these years. Cheated me from a life with Alexa and raising my daughter. All she wanted was one more child to replace the one we had lost, and she'd destroy the evidence she had on me and the club. Sounded easy. Simple even. But she could never carry past five months. Each new loss was another stab to my heart. Another broken promise. Another year lost to a woman I despise. A woman who plotted behind my back with East's cunt ex to kill Wylla Mae and Alexa.

Alexa took a bullet to the abdomen protecting our daughter. Ruthie better count her fucking blessings that Alexa lived.

Now she's on the run. Knows that if she shows her face in West Virginia I'll end her pathetic life. I want her to suffer and always look over her shoulder for what she did to me. For the hell she put Alexa through.

I roll up to Alexa's unannounced. She's been avoiding me since her doctor gave her the all clear after her shooting. I'm running out of patience. It's time we set shit straight face to face. No more dodging my phone calls and refusing to see me.

I know I've got a lot to make up for, but hell she hasn't been no saint. I cover the peephole with the pad of my finger and ring the doorbell. I wait and nothing.

I ring the bell four more times. I'm *this close* to breaking in.

She promised me she'd wait for me. It may have taken us a long motherfuckin' time to get here, but I'm here to collect on that promise she made me all those years ago.

"I know it's you. I don't have anything to say to you," her voice filters through the door.

"Well I got plenty to say to you. So you can listen through the door if that's your choice, but we're having this conversation."

"Fine."

I take a step back and wait for the door to open but two minutes pass. She's called my bluff. Fuck it. I'll use my key. I fish it out my pocket and go to stick it in the lock to find she's had them changed. Not that I blame her after the shit she's been through, but I keep eyes on her house all hours, night and day. Sometimes my own.

"Let me in, Alexa, or so help me I'll kick the damn thing in. Need to see your face. Gonna give you to the count of three." I suck in a breath and get ready to force my way in if need be, but I hear the lock click.

The door swings open and there she is, big pouty red lips. The prettiest thing I ever laid eyes on in all my days. Olive green eyes glittering with the tiniest flecks of gold. Body made from sin and for loving me. A body I've taken advantage of more times than I can count. A body I can't live without.

"You have five minutes then I want you gone." Stepping to the side she allows me inside. The door closes the second I pass through it nearly catching me on the ass.

Folding her arms over her chest, she stares at me hard enough to turn my bones into stone then crush me to dust, but I've never been one to back down from a fight, and I won't start today.

"Tick tock."

It's now or never. Time to lay it on the line and remind her that no matter what's happened between us. No matter what Alexa will always be mine. "All these years...wasted them. Coulda been happy. You and me, babe. Coulda been kissing you. Having that sweet cunt in my bed. Got nothing to show for it. Got nothing but regret. But I'm here now."

"Go fuck yourself, Murder."

"I'm James to you."

"Asshole sounds fine to me. Or dickhead. Prick. Asslick."

My lips twitch. "Only ass I ever licked was yours."

Her cheeks bloom pink.

"Shut up."

"You loved every damn second of it too."

"For one night of passion I bought myself a lifetime of pain. You've taken everything from me. I wasted twenty years on you. I'm done throwing my life away."

Alexa flinches when I step toward her.

"Don't ever be fuckin' afraid of me. Never ever lay a hand on you in anger, baby. Always treated you with respect."

Alexa snorts. Tears streaming down her cheeks. "You kept me all these years, giving me money, buying me a house. A car. I was your paid whore. Your filthy secret." Wiping her tears away she shakes her head. "You don't know how to love anyone but yourself and the ghost of a daughter who hated you."

"Take that shit back," I grit through my teeth. The light in her gorgeous green eyes appears snuffed out, and it breaks me into about a million pieces knowing I'm the one who did this. I'm the one who broke her and made her feel unworthy of love. Of my love. I turned her into the bitter woman who has a hard time trusting men. Who won't let anyone in out of fear of being hurt again. Who craves love desperately but pushes anyone away who gets too close including our own daughter because she thinks she isn't loveable, but I love her. I always have.

"No. Rochelle hated you in the end."

"You want to hurt me. I get it. I hurt you, but don't do that. Lex."

"Why? Truth hurts."

I wrap an arm around her, pulling her closer as she pushes against me but failing to loosen my hold. "That why you get so damn mean when I say I love you. Because you know it's true?"

"She knew what you did. You did what you always do. Murder someone to solve your problems. Rochelle told me how you killed that guy your wife had moved in while you were doing time. Said he was the only father she ever knew, and you took him from her. She tried to forget but he haunted her dreams."

"Fuck." I let her go. Alexa always knows where to hit me the hardest. Each time worse than the last. I stare at my boots unable to gaze into her eyes and see the ugly truth. I know my sins. I don't need reminding.

"Then you treated Wylla Mae, the little girl who'd done anything to make you proud like trash. All she ever wanted was a father and you denied her. Denied me of all I ever wanted."

My gaze flickers up, registering the change in her tone. The anger has left her, and the single emotion left is pure sadness. "And what's that?"

"All I ever thought about was being your Old Lady. How good it'd feel to tell everyone you were my man. That you loved me. That we shared a beautiful daughter together. All it ever was…all we were was a beautiful lie. A lie I told myself over and over again hoping one day it'd be the truth. You don't love me. You never did. So stop pretending."

"How long you gonna keep trying to shut me out, pretty girl?"

"As long as it takes for you to get it through that thick head of yours that I'm done."

"I say when we're done, and we're far from over." I grip her chin seeing the fire blazing dancing in my eyes reflected in hers.

"I'm not one of your club whores. I'm damn sure not your wife so back the fuck up and get out of my face."

"Don't want no whore. Don't got no wife either."

"Bullshit."

"You think I'd stay with Ruthie knowing she was behind those bastards putting their hands on you. Bitch is the reason you were shot. Bled that fuck dry. Slit his throat ear to ear. Would done the same to Ruthie but out of respect for Rochelle's memory I let the cunt walk away. Told her I better not catch sight of her in West Virginia ever fuckin' again if she wants to keep breathing. I ever hear anyone breathe her name I won't think twice about putting her to ground for all the bullshit she's caused. Divorce was fast tracked. It's over. I'm a free man."

"Well lah-de-fucking-dah. What do you want a cookie? A blue ribbon? Gold medal?"

"What I want is you to stop being such a God damn smart ass and admit that you still feel something for me. Stop being a bitch for five minutes and hear what I'm sayin'. 'Cause, Lex. Baby, I'm trying to tell you this is our second chance at a fresh start. Leave the past where it belongs."

"Oh, I'm trying, but it's you who isn't hearing a damn thing I'm saying to you. I'm done, James. You need to let go."

"Want you to think long and hard about how good we were together."

"You must have smoked too much pot or drank too much moonshine because I remember the past just fine. I lived it and barely survived you. Maybe you're the one who needs to jog their memory. I loved you, and all you ever did was bring me down."

"I know I hurt you, but I'm here now."

"You can't change the past no matter how hard you try. We can't go back and that's exactly what I'd be doing if I give in and let you into my heart."

"So you admit it. You love me."

"I've never not loved you. It's never been in question has it?"

"Guess not. But I shouldn't have to remind you that I loved you too. Since the first time I laid eyes on you, I knew you'd be my ruin. And I wanted you anyway. Took whatever I could get knowing it'd never be enough for either of us. You've always had a hold on me, pretty girl. Think back long and hard. You'll see and when you do, you'll come to me."

"Don't hold your breath."

"You'll see, Lex. I'll be waiting." I brush my knuckles along her cheek, and her face softens. "Come back to me, baby. Promised you'd wait for me as long as it took."

Unshed tears glitter swirling in those flecks of gold as she stares at me. "James," my name leaves those sweet lips.

I bring my mouth down on hers, hard and true pouring every ounce of love I have for her into the power of my kiss. I won't lose her. I'm not so proud now that I won't swallow my pride and go to my knees to beg for one more shot to make it right. To give her the life she deserves. Show her the love she's always craved.

Alexa sweeps her tongue against mine tasting of home. Her body melts into mine, and I walk her backwards toward the stairs. She stops abruptly. Palms pressed to my chest she breaks our kiss. "Look at me, James."

"Got my full attention, babe."

"You and me…we'll always be unfinished business. I've made my peace with it, and now it's time that you do too. I'm putting the house up for sale. I'm doing something I should have done a long time ago. I'm leaving. This time I'm not coming back. I'll always love you. You have two choices. One we say goodbye now or two you can follow me upstairs and give me something to remember you by, but after…I'm done. I walk away, and we go our separate ways. I can't do this anymore. We're

314

not getting any younger. Don't you want something more for yourself?"

"Everything I want is right here and so help me, Lex, if you think you're packing up and walking out on me I'll chain you to my bed and spank your ass until you give me what I want."

"Okay."

"Glad you see things my way."

I go to kiss her, and she clamps her mouth shut going still.

"Gimme' that mouth, baby."

Her head moves side to side.

"You and I both know you don't want to deny me." I shove my hand down the front of her jeans, and she's fucking soaked like I knew she would be. "Don't want me, babe. We both know you're a fuckin' liar."

"I hate you."

"Because you know I'm right. We belong together. Fate brought us together. Waited my whole damn life for someone like you. But I fucked it up. I know that."

"I'm done with this conversation. I'm drained. I've got nothing left to give you. So save your energy, and put it toward building a relationship with your daughter."

"Already had a chat with Wylla Mae. She knows where my head and my heart are. Said I needed to fix us then she'd talk to me."

"There's nothing to fix. I'm not repeating past mistakes."

"Wanna talk about the past, Lex? I'll tell you how I remember it all going down between us." I curl a finger inside her, and she moans. "Yeah, baby. Let's talk." I kiss along her jaw, take away my finger, and toss my woman over my shoulder.

Chapter Thirty

"Put me down." I wiggle and shake, but all I manage to do is force James to tighten the hold he has on me.

Strutting into my bedroom he dumps me on the mattress. Lifting his leg, he kicks the door shut and locks it. "Not leaving this room till you catch on to what's going down. Got something I can tell you now after all these years."

"What's that?"

"Shit that Ruthie was holding over my head all these years. It's over."

"Ruthie?" I sit up. He has my attention.

"Yeah." He sits on the edge of the bed and hangs his head. "I should've fucking killed her. Put a stop to her bullshit years ago. Fuck."

"What did she do?"

317

"She always knew about us. Was blackmailing me. The night I took care of Lion…after Rochelle died, Ruthie threatened you. Both of us. Bitch claimed she had evidence. Our fingerprints, a video…the axe I used in a secure location. If she turned that shit over to the FEDS like she was claiming to do unless I gave her another child…Wylla Mae woulda grown up without a mother. We'd both gone to prison."

My breath hitches in my throat. I can't even process this information. "Why would she do that?"

"Fuck if I know. Jealousy. She blamed us both for Rochelle's death. Said she took one look at Wylla Mae and knew she was mine. Thought I had it under control. But she kept having miscarriages. Loss after fucking loss. I didn't want them babies, but I still felt that shit."

"I'm sorry you went through that, but what changed?"

"Knew she hired those dumbfucks who hurt you. Told her I'd let her live if she gave me what she had on you."

"Jesus." My stomach does a somersault.

"I did what I thought I had to for you and our girl."

"What did she have?"

"The axe." He lets out a sinister laugh from deep within his gut. "Bitch played me. Once she was gone, I had the damn thing checked for my fingerprints. But better than that it wasn't even the same one. She knew the weapon and too many details though. Someone inside the club fed her information on me."

"Who would have done that?"

"Maybe Nickel. Can't ask him now being he's dead." He scrubs a hand over his head.

"Thank you for telling me."

"But?" he stares at me with those dark eyes that have tortured me for years.

"It doesn't change anything between us. Too much has happened, James."

He grabs my hand. "Baby, I've been in hell all these years. Unable to touch you whenever I wanted. Unable to raise my daughter. You think I'm just gonna give up after all we been through. I prayed you'd find a better man. I thought that man was gonna be East, so I stepped aside and tried to make peace with the fact that I was gonna be stuck with Ruthie till the day I took my last breath."

"Let's not talk about East." I make a sour expression at him.

"Heard you was pretty rough on him and Wylla Mae."

"I was. I could see our daughter going down the same path as me, but East is nothing like you. I didn't want the Old Lady life for her, but she's happy."

"Thank God for that." His lips twitch into a wide smile.

"Yeah. So now I know about Ruthie."

"You trying to kick me out?"

"What'd you think would happen? That you'd show up and tell me about her betrayal and I'd be relieved? Throw myself at you?"

James shrugs. "A man can hope."

"I don't hate you. Sometimes I wish I could. I want you to find happiness. It's just not going to be with me."

"You need to go get in the shower and get ready so I can take you to the BBQ at The Devil's Playground to show you off."

"Have you lost your fucking mind?"

"Never claimed to have it to start with." He moves in close, breath fanning over my lips smelling of cigarettes and coffee.

"Don't."

"Don't what?"

320

"Assume I'm going to kiss you."

Hands sliding up either side my throat he holds my stare. "Who says I want to kiss you?"

My mouth drops. "You don't?"

"Do you want me to kiss you?"

"I…"

"Yes or no question, babe."

"Stop it."

"Stop what? I'm asking you. Do. You. Want. Me. To. Kiss. You?"

My pulse spikes and my stomach dips. "You're making me nervous."

"Since you wanna be all shy I'm gonna make this real simple for you. I'm gonna go start the shower. You're gonna take these clothes off and clean up. I'm gonna start making some calls about selling this house and mine then see what's what with a piece of property I've had my eye on. Then we're going to the clubhouse so I can have a beer with my woman. Sound good?"

"Sounds crazy."

"Never said I was sane." He moves to stand.

"Hey," I tug on his hand.

James peers down at me. "What?"

"You forgot something."

"Nope. Think that covers it."

"You forgot to kiss me."

My man smiles big and wide flashing me his teeth through the unruly jungle that makes up his beard. He comes in slow and sweet, cupping my jaw as he descends back to my bed. Mouth fusing with mine he makes love to my mouth softly.

James pulls away much too soon for my liking. "Know what?"

"Hmm?"

"I think we're gonna be late."

"Very." I pull him in for another kiss knowing I must be insane. He's giving me everything I ever wanted. I'd be a liar if I said I'm not terrified that I'm going to wake up and find this to all be a dream. Ruthie kept us apart for the past eighteen years. Put us both through hell. I never thought this day would come. He's saying and doing all the right things, but every bone in my body screams for me to run fast and hard. I don't know if I'm strong enough to give him my heart a second time. "Can it really be this easy?"

"What's on your mind?"

"Ruthie...after everything. She's just gone from our lives? She's walking away and leaving you alone for good. I don't trust it."

"I've got Grudge tailing her. If she makes a move, I'll know."

"Okay."

Brushing a knuckle along my cheek, he murmurs, "As natural and easy as breathing."

"What is?"

"Being with you. I want to do it right this time, Alexa."

"I think it's a little late for that."

"Just get in the shower. Wylla Mae will be there."

**

James rides through the gates of the clubhouse and rolls to a stop in his parking spot. I reluctantly follow him off the bike and allow him to hold my hand as we go around back to where everyone is hanging out by the picnic tables. I'm only here because our daughter is supposed to be. I scan the crowd for Wylla Mae's face not finding any sign of her.

"Heard the good news, Prez." James let's go of my hand to do some sort of weird back slapping hug with a brute of a guy. The name on his cut says Viking. I've seen

323

him in passing but don't really know the guy. He's a tall blond with tribal tattoos running the length of both his arms in full sleeves. "Ding dong that bitch is gone. Fuck me." His gaze roams over me. "Looking fit as fuck, Alexa." He releases James and comes straight at me. Hands going to my hips, lifting me into a spinning hug. Viking plants a sloppy wet kiss right on my mouth.

"Hands off my Old Lady," James snaps through his gritted teeth at the guy.

I slide down his tree trunk of a body and return to James's side.

"Shit. Didn't waste no time. No disrespect meant, man. I'm gonna go see about a beer."

"Yeah you do that before I stick a boot in your ass."

"He seems friendly."

"Too damn friendly." He tucks me into his side.

"I feel like everyone is staring at me."

"That's because they are." He chuckles and I punch him in the rib.

"Ugh. This was a terrible idea."

"Want everyone to know that after all these years I finally got the girl."

"We'll see." I can tell he wants to argue by the way the corner of his mouth twitches under his facial hair. "You need a shave. Starting to look like a mountain man."

"Didn't hear no complaints when I had my face buried between them legs. C'mon. Let's get some grub."

We move through the crowd. James pausing every two steps to bullshit with another club member. Some of them I know. Many of them I don't recognize. Holy must be new. I'm happy to see Slick is still around after all these years. He's always been good to me. When I heard the news about Nickel it bothered me more than I expected it to. He was the club VP and always looked out for Wylla and me from afar under James's orders, but I found comfort knowing I could always call on the man for anything. I hadn't needed to for some time. Not with Easton Reed always ready to swoop in and save the day for Wylla Mae like some sort of damn hero riding on his Harley instead of a horse.

I should've seen it coming. East and Wylla Mae falling in love. The two of them were always drawn together like magnets. Even when she was nothing more than a child they had a bond no one else could compete with. I finally spot the two of them by the buffet style table. East is loading her plate down with macaroni salad.

Her hands rests on each side of her baby bump. Their baby girl is due in a few weeks. I can't believe I'm going to be a grandma. Seems like only yesterday I was pregnant with her. I squeeze James's hand and motion to our daughter. He gives me a squeeze then a nod.

"You came." Wylla smiles big and after all these years I'm still never prepared for the pang of guilt that hits me when I look into her eyes and see the resemblance she holds to Rochelle. Like my deceased friend she has her father's big brown eyes.

"Your dad said you'd be here."

"I told him to invite you. Grab a plate. Pam will be offended if you don't eat. She's been prepping for this all week."

"Okay." I don't think Pam will be too torn up if I don't pay my compliments to the chef, but I keep that to myself. Link's woman never has liked me. Always turned her nose down at me because I was the other woman. Old Ladies don't hold any love for a clubwhore. And though technically I never played the part that's how she viewed me. I get it, but I never crossed that line. I only ever dated single club members. It was all to get under James's skin. Not that it matters now. It's all in the past. "I'll meet you at the tables."

East gives me a nod. I'm accepting of him as my son-in-law, but there's still an awkward tension I'm hoping will fade soon. We never were compatible, and I'm glad my daughter has him. I've never seen a man more devoted than he is to her.

I grab a hot dog and squirt some mustard on it. Pam keeps giving me this funny side eye glance. I'm surprised she's biting her tongue. She's always been a woman who doesn't hold back. I know James wants me to fit in and get along, so I make sure I get a heaping pile of her potato salad even though I don't really care for it. When I get to the end of the table where the coolers are, she approaches.

"Hey."

"Hey yourself."

"So you and Murder finally stepping out together. Ink isn't even dry on the divorce papers and you can't help yourself."

"I get that you don't like me. I don't particularly care for you either, but what happens between Murder and me is none of your business." I balance my plate on one hand and dip my hand into the cooler for a beer.

"Maybe not but we look after our own."

"Then you should already know that he's a man who gets what he wants. For the past eighteen years that's been me. It'll still be me till he says otherwise."

"Be nice, big sister." Roane's Old Lady, Jules joins us, holding her boy Jasper on her hip.

"I'm nice," Pam says with a grin that tells a different story.

"Right and I'm Santa Claus. Alexa, it's nice to see you."

"You too. Your boy sure is growing fast."

"That he is. Big and strong like his daddy."

I shoot her a friendly smile. "See you around I suppose."

"We hope so. Don't we?" I don't miss the elbow she shoves into Pam's rib as I move past them to join Wylla Mae.

Chapter Thirty-one

"So you and Dad seem cozy today."

"I don't know what you mean."

"Don't play dumb with me. I know when you're lying." She smirks and shovels another bite of pasta in her mouth.

"We've been talking."

"Judging by that hickey on your neck you've been doing more than talking."

"What?" I gasp, hand flying to my neck.

"Gotcha." She throws her head back laughing.

"Ugh. You're grounded."

"I think I'm too old for that now."

"We'll see about that," I mumble.

"Oh, Mom. Don't be such a sourpuss. It makes me happy to see you guys together."

"It does?"

"Yeah. I mean I still have some things I need to work through where the past is concerned, but I watched the two of you as you came around the side of the clubhouse, and well I've never seen either of you look so freaking ecstatic. That dark cloud that seemed to hang over Murder's head is gone."

"That's because he finally divorced Ruthie."

"And he can finally be with the love of his life. That's what he told me. That you're the love of his life."

I let out a breath. "You guys talk about me?"

"He's tried really hard to make amends for the past. We aren't all the way there yet, but I understand him a lot more now. Why he stayed away. Letting us go was hard for him."

"He told you?"

"Parts of it. Not everything, but enough for me to fill in the blanks that Ruthie threatened you and he did what he had to so I wouldn't lose you both."

"You forgave him?"

"I forgive you too, Mom. I just want you two to find the happiness I have with East. He wants that for you too ya know."

"Means a lot, sweetpea. I'm scared just…I'm scared. I've waited eighteen years to be with this man. What if he decides he wants to be single? He was married to Ruthie a long time."

"I guess that's a chance you've gotta be willing to take."

"I want to. I do, but part of me wonders if the timing is right." I glance in the direction I last saw him and my heart freezes midbeat. He's chatting with one of his brothers, but his arm is around a much younger woman. The way she's looking at him has me anxious. What if I'm not enough?

"If you two wait any longer for the time to be right you'll be waiting till your dead. Life moves on. You're allowed to be happy. So what he was married to that hag for years. He wasn't happy. He didn't love her."

"You're right. It should be easy, but we have a complicated past. I want it to work. I want it more than I've wanted anything in a long time." I look back to where James was standing, but he's gone and so is the woman.

"Good. Because I want you both at the hospital when this little girl enters the world."

"I wouldn't miss it for anything. Have you told him what you plan to name her yet?" I try to distract myself from wondering if he's off somewhere with whoever that bitch is.

"No. Not yet. Was afraid of setting him off, but he's been opening up a lot more about her."

"I wish you could've known her. You two would have gotten along great or butted heads because you're so much alike and yet different in your own right."

"It wasn't your fault. What happened to Rochelle and her boyfriend."

"I know that now, but sometimes that old guilt creeps back in. I hope you know I'm sorry for how I was when you were growing up. I was hurting. I punished myself and everyone around me. It wasn't fair."

"Neither was what you went through. You're one of the strongest women I know. I love you."

I blink my eyes. The stupid wet stuff is trying to leak onto my cheeks. "I love you too."

"I'd love you a lot more if you went and got me a slice of strawberry pie." My daughter rubs her baby bump, looking ready to pop any minute now.

"One piece of pie coming right up." I go to get up off the bench seat when Wylla makes a funny face.

"Oh." Her hand moves to her lower back.

"Are you okay?"

"Yeah." She hisses. "I think this wooden bench is just hurting my back."

"You sure? Want me to get East?"

"No. I want my pie. Let him be. He's having fun."

I follow her gaze to the horseshoe pit. East is enjoying a beer and the game. "If you say so."

"Just get my pie and put whip cream on it please."

"Anything else? Want another water?"

"I'm fine." She sucks in a breath but waves me off when I hesitate. "Go. Pie."

I'm slathering whip cream onto Wylla Mae's pie when an arm hooks around my waist. Furry lips brush along my ear. "There you are, pretty girl. You having a good time?"

"Mhmm." I push his arm away.

"Babe."

"What?" I snap a little harsher than intended.

"Did something happen? Someone say something?"

"Nope," I pop the P.

I start back toward our daughter when he crooks a finger through the one of my belt loops, jerking me backwards against his chest. I nearly smash the pie against my tits but manage to save it. "Stop acting like that and tell me what's eating at you."

333

"I said I'm fine."

"You're not fine damn it. Don't make me jerks them tight jeans down your thighs and bend you over my knee in front of the club. I'll spank the truth outta you if I gotta."

I lick my lips. "You want the truth? I think you're rushing into this with me. You've never been single. Maybe you should be before we try to start up again." His grip on me loosens.

"That how you really feel?"

No. "Yes."

"I'll give you time, but it won't change the outcome. You're mine, Lex. Always have been. Always will be."

I hesitate a beat then stalk toward Wylla Mae. A part of me praying he comes running and the other hoping he stays away. I'm a step away from the picnic table when she cries out. I drop the paper plate and shout for East. James is first to reach us.

"I think my water just broke," she whispers.

"Get your cage," James barks at East when he gets close. He takes off running. Everyone clears out of the way so he can drive his truck through the grass. James helps Wylla Mae into the passenger seat, and I hop in the back of the cab. "I'll be right behind you." He nods to East then shuts the door without a word to me. Not that I expected any. I'm certain he's pissed after my act of defiance.

I'm worried that he'll change his mind. Realize that he's never been on his own and want to sew all them wild oats he never got a chance at.

East drives to the hospital like a bat out of hell. I called ahead to let them know we were coming. The truck halts in front of the emergency room. A nurse is already waiting with a wheelchair. I go in with Wylla while East finds a parking space. She's preregistered so the check-in process moves quickly and efficiently.

By the time East and James park we're in her private room waiting for the doctor. The baby is a few weeks early, but I'm not worried. Her contractions are growing closer together. She's trying to put on a brave face, but I can see the pain etched in her smile.

"I hear we're ready to have a baby." The doctor grins and goes for a pair of gloves. "If you guys will give us a minute, I'll see how far Mrs. Reed is dilated."

"Come on, let's go grab a coffee. East, you want anything?"

"I'm good but thanks." His attention never leaves Wylla Mae and my heart swells a little bit more for that man. The unconditional love he has for my daughter…I know I never need to worry whether or not he'll treat her right.

James and I go down the corridor to the waiting area. I fix us both a cup of crappy, complimentary coffee. I hand off his and take up the seat next to him.

He takes a sip then stares intently at me.

"What? Why are you looking at me like that?"

"Figured out why you were all in a snit back there."

"I've not been in a snit."

"You saw me talking to Holy's sister. You were jealous and partly worried I'd want someone else. Since I first saw you in that damn red bikini, I've not wanted another woman. Have I fucked anyone else? I'm no damn saint and you've not been an angel. I know what you deserve, Lex. Baby, I'm gonna be the man who gives it to you. You can tell me all the reasons we'll never work, but I'm asking you to think about all the reasons we will."

"James…"

"No. Don't start that. Don't tell me it's too soon or too fast or whatever other damn excuse you're conjuring in that pretty head of yours. Waited my whole damn life for a woman like you. We met too damn soon, but I don't regret one moment I've spent with you. One minute of loving you or wanting you unable to have you. It's our time now. Ain't no one or nothing gonna change that or come between us unless you let it. Marry me, Lex."

"What?"

"You heard me, woman. I said marry me."

I stare at him a beat. My heart is in my throat. Words I thought I'd never hear leave his mouth. My pulse races. I think I might faint. I place my coffee cup on the nearby table to stop from spilling it. "I think you've lost your ever-loving mind."

"We both know I'm a crazy bastard. But I'm crazy about you. We can do it the easy way or the hard way. Either way this ends with you as my wife. If I gotta tie you up to make it happen I will."

"Stop talking."

"Lex…"

"I said stop talking, James." I gaze into his eyes looking for a shred of doubt. I find none. He loves me. He always has. Deep in my heart of hearts I know it. My soul knows it. "I love you."

"About fuckin' time," he mutters.

"I'm not finished." I take his free hand in mine. "You had your say now it's my turn. I've loved you as long as I can remember. You're the only man I've ever loved. I

337

resigned myself to the fact that we were never going to happen, and now here you are doing and saying all the right things. It scares the shit out of me. I'm not used to good, James. Bad is all I know. I want this, but I'm scared the moment I say yes to you that something bad will come to remind me of my place in your life and this world. I don't get the happily ever after."

Chapter Thirty-two
MURDER

"Isn't she beautiful," Alexa coos over our granddaughter. She's got a headful of dark hair. Pure perfection.

"Sure is. Gets it from her momma and her granny."

Her eyes narrow into tiny slits. "I'm no granny."

"Sexiest granny I've ever seen." I kiss her forehead.

"Shut up. You're lucky I'm holding her or I'd…"

"You'd what freeze me to death with that glacial stare."

"What do you want the baby to call you," Wylla Mae interrupts. "Nana, Grammy, Meemaw."

Alexa scrunches her nose in disgust. "Those make me sound ancient."

"What about Glammy?" East puts in.

"Not helping," Alexa mumbles.

"Neenie. G-ma. Ya Ya."

Alexa sighs. "None of them know what they are talking about. Do they?" She strokes the baby's head.

"You two gonna name this kid?"

"I actually wanted to talk to you about that. Well East and I both were wondering how you'd feel if we named her Mila Rochelle, for my sister?"

Fuck. Fuck me. Her words cut straight through my heart. Tears spring to my eyes, and I close them, battling the wetness back.

"Here take her," I hear Alexa pass the baby off. "Honey." Her hand moves along my jaw. "Look at me."

I jerk my head back and let out a breath that rattles through my chest. Turning my gaze on my daughter, I tell her, "I think it's perfect."

Relief visibly washes over her features and East gives me a chin lift.

"Why don't we give these two some privacy, and I'll take you to dinner. You gotta be hungry."

"I could eat. You guys need anything?"

East stares at his family. "Got everything I need right here."

"All right, brother. You change your mind give me a ring. Same goes for you, little momma." I kiss the top of both her and the baby's heads. "See you soon."

"Bye, Daddy." I freeze hearing her call me dad. It's the first time I've heard the word leave her lips. Been a long time since I've heard the word in reference to myself. Not since Rochelle.

"I'll be back in the morning," Alexa tells her.

"Love you, Mom."

I pull Alexa into me and we leave the hospital. When she wraps those arms around me from the back of my bike, I know this is how it's supposed to be. Took me a long motherfuckin' time to reach this point. My woman riding bitch not giving a God damn who sees. Shit feels damn good. I tap her thigh before pulling out the lot. "Where you wanna eat at? Don't give me that I don't know bullshit."

"I could go for some pizza, but let's make it delivery."

"We can call it in from the clubhouse." I roar off before she can argue. Never had a woman in my bed at The Devil's Playground other than her. Not even Ruthie. Alexa can be pissy, but that's where we're spending the night. Not taking her to the house I shared with Ruthie and sure as shit don't want to sleep in her bed either. Damn thing is hard and uncomfortable.

The party is still going out back of the clubhouse. I take Alexa in through the front and tell the prospect behind the bar to order her a pizza. Grudge is sitting at the end of the bar nursing a beer. "Gimme' a minute," I tell my woman, leaving her at the opposite end where I can keep an eye on her. "When'd you get back?"

"An hour ago. Lost track of her in the Smoky Mountains and turned back. Think her destination is Florida."

"Why you think that?"

"Her mom had family in Daytona. That's where I'd go if I were her."

"Follow up on it. I want to know where she is at all times."

"If she makes a move I'll know. Got alerts set up on her credit cards."

"Good looking out, brother."

"Anything for you, Prez." I give him a slap on the back. "Heard Wylla Mae went into labor."

"Yeah. Mila Rochelle Reed. My granddaughter." I pull my phone out and show him a few pictures. "Look how perfect."

"That's real sweet her naming the kid after Rochelle."

"Yeah. Let me know the minute you know what direction that cunt is headed."

"Will do."

I move back down the way to Alexa. I'm mad as hell that fucker dropped off his mark without calling it in with me first. I told him under no circumstances was he to pull off his detail. Not gonna make a big deal out of it tonight, but something's funny with him. Can't place my finger on it but he's giving me a weird motherfuckin' vibe.

"You get the food called in?"

"Yup. Should be here in about twenty minutes."

"Prospect, bring my food up when it gets here and a few more cold ones. Let's head on up, babe." I lead Alexa upstairs to my presidential suite. Busted out the wall of the neighboring room to make mine larger. Spent plenty nights here avoiding Ruthie. Drinking away thoughts of Alexa.

I open the door and show her inside. "It's a lot bigger than I remember." She walks the length of the room and stops at the window overlooking the back of the compound. She kicks her shoes off, and I wrap my arms around her. Looking over her shoulder I stare down to the party below. Tiki torches light up the space. Viking is in the fighting pit going up against Sandman. Viking is undefeated. Sandman is crazy to get in the pit with him.

"I like this."

"Hmm," she murmurs.

343

"Having you here."

"I like being here." Alexa twists to face me. "Grandpa," she mocks.

"Kinda like the sound of that." I grin.

"I don't know. I can't be seen with an old man. May have to get me a younger model. That Viking guy looks pretty tough."

I groan. "Don't make me kill one of my best men."

Alexa smirks and faces the window again. "That would be a shame. He's quite handsome. Big. Strong."

"You're pushing it." I get a handful of her ass, giving it a squeeze. "Yeah. Sexiest grandma on the planet."

"Stop making me feel old."

"You could be gray headed, wrinkled, and sagging and I'd still want you."

"Ha. I don't know if I believe that."

"You'll see. Years from now when I'm an old bastard and you're aging with grace I'll still bend you over and fuck you till you cry."

Alexa bursts out laughing.

"You think it's funny?"

"It's not that. I had a mental image of you with old saggy wrinkled balls and my tits down to my knees trying to get it on and one of us breaking a hip or something."

344

I smile and hug her close to my chest. Alexa just told me she sees a future with me in it. I breathe her in, thankful we've got a second chance.

We stay like this watching the scene below. Viking throws a right hook that sends Sandman flying back. He goes down on his ass out cold from the looks of it. A bang sounds at the door. The prospect, Rio, has our food and drinks.

"Leave it on the table. Grudge still at the bar?"

"No. He made a phone call and took off."

"You know who he called?"

"Heard him say it's all good. See you soon."

"Anything else?"

"No."

"All right you can get lost. Go join the party out back. You've earned a night off."

"Thanks, Prez." Rio hurries to leave. Anxious to go find some easy pussy no doubt.

Alexa flips the pizza box open. "Everything okay? You seem troubled." She grabs a slice and bites, struggling to chew through the string of cheese that's bringing all the pepperonis with it.

"I'm sure it's nothing. Just a funny feeling I got. Let's eat." I knock the caps off our beers using the edge of the table. "A toast. We can't go back and change the past, but we can start anew today."

"I don't want to change the past. It got us here. Gave us a beautiful daughter. Perfect grandbaby. We're where we're supposed to be. Together."

"I'll drink to that." I clink my bottle with hers. Then I chug before claiming her mouth. "How is it that every damn time I kiss you it gets better and fucking better."

"Practice makes perfect."

"Oh yeah."

"Yeah." She pulls me in close and plants a big one on me tasting of pizza sauce.

"I can think of something else we can practice then."

"In that case you'd better eat a lot of pizza. Like a lot."

"And why is that?"

"You're gonna need the fuel for stamina."

"I think I've got it covered."

"I don't know..." she pauses long enough to unbutton her shirt. "It could take all night."

I grab my crotch and give my cock a tug over my jeans. "I'm up for the challenge." I bring her back in, holding her gaze. Stroking my fingers along her jaw, I brush away the sins of our past. Tonight is the first day of the rest of our lives. I've waited long enough. Waited my whole damn life for her. Alexa has been more than patient. "Love you, Lex."

"I know," she whispers and unbuttons her jeans.

I want to fuck her in every damn room of this clubhouse.

A big fuck you to Ruthie and Lion.

Chapter Thirty-three

James slides the straps of my red lace bra down my arms. "Always have loved you in red."

I lick my lips. "That's why I chose this one," I confess. His dark eyes bore into me with such intensity I could catch fire. I'll never get over the way he looks at me like there's no one else he'll ever want more than me. Nothing he'll ever crave more than this. More than us. Our one spark created a wildfire that's been burning for years. Decimating everything in our path. Nothing can douse the flames. I'll burn and yearn for this man till the day I die and maybe even after in Heaven or Hell. I'd follow him anywhere. What we have is a ride or die love, and for James I've risked it all over and over again.

My motorcycle man walks me back toward the window that overlooks his outlaw kingdom. Loud music echoes through the clubhouse. The roar of engines sound.

All his men below, ready to ride for him at will. Ready to die all in the name of loyalty and brotherhood. I too am at his command. The Prez shows no mercy. I'll do as he pleases. I stare down at the party, waiting in anticipation for his next move. The heat of my man presses against me from behind as he sweeps my hair to one side.

I've tried to fight it but there's no denying that he is mine, and I am his in every way imaginable. He kisses me between my shoulder blades, carving a path down my spine with his lips, stopping only when he reaches the dimples above my ass. My body has changed over the years, and I don't have the perfect one I once did. I've gained weight. I have scars, wrinkles, and stretchmarks, but when he touches me all my imperfections fade. When James touches me, I know he cherishes every inch. Hooking his fingers under the waistline of my thong he drags the red lace material down my legs, tapping the backs of each heel for me to step out.

There's nothing better than the rough pads of his fingers on my skin except him inside me. My body

350

quivers as the cool glass of the window hits my taut nipples. James doesn't waste any time. Lining our bodies up, he enters me with one deep thrust that has me crying out in pure ecstasy.

"Always fucking wet for me, baby. That pretty little pussy is so eager and greedy. Fucking soaked." He pulls out and slides right back in. My body molded to the shape of him. Two halves of one whole. There's never been a more perfect fit than the way my pussy curves to his dick.

I brace my palms on the windowsill. When he starts to move my body…mostly my hip bones take a beating against the lower half of the brick wall that sits under the window.

He fucks me so hard my bones may crack. I can't breathe as he pounds relentlessly giving me every brutal but achingly- beautiful inch. Colors burst dancing behind my eyes. I see stars in every shade as my orgasm quakes through my body. I jolt and jerk against him.

"That's it, Lex. Come all over your cock." Yanking my hair, he tugs my head back to claim my mouth, cutting off my air, as I pant into his mouth. Sweat drips between us. He breaks away from our kiss letting out a deafening groan, spilling his release inside me.

James severs our connection. "You still on the pill?" he questions breathily in my ear.

I shake my head, unable to catch my breath long enough to answer.

"Good," he growls, pushing his fingers up in me. "What would you say if I told you I want another baby with you."

My eyes grow big and round as the full moon coming out from behind the clouds. "I'd say you've totally lost what little of your mind you have left."

"You wouldn't want another?"

I tense as he pumps his fingers in and out, about to bring me to another orgasm. "If it happened then I'd have to come to terms, but no. We're in a different stage in our lives. But it's not going to happen. The shooting. I can't carry another baby."

"Fucking Ruthie?" at the mention of her we both lose our interest in my getting off a second time.

"Yeah."

James steps away, going to the bathroom. "God damn cunt. Shoulda put a bullet between her eyes," he mutters before slamming the door.

Well that went over well. I leave him to work through his anger alone. Opening one of the drawers of his dresser, I dig out a t-shirt and slip it over my head. The black worn cotton swallows me like a tent. Sitting on the edge of the bed, I run my fingers through my hair, working out the tats. Another baby isn't something I'd want. We have a granddaughter, and I selfishly want him all to myself. I don't want to share him. I've waited too long for this. For him.

The bathroom door opens, and he stands there quietly observing me. "C'mere," he says finally, and I go to him. His arms wrap around me, and I lay my head to his chest. "Got caught up in the moment. I'm sorry that was taken away from you."

"It's okay. I don't want a baby, James, and not because I don't love you, but I'm past that part of life. I want us to enjoy it being just us. Maybe that makes me selfish, but we have Mila now. Trust me. East and Wylla are going to be calling on us to babysit."

"I do like having you all to myself."

"It has its perks. We don't have to plan around a baby. We can go and do what we want when we want."

"I can keep you naked." His hand slides down to cup my bare ass.

"That too."

"Get cleaned up and come on to bed." James releases me, and I move around him to make use of the bathroom. "There's some new toothbrushes in the top drawer. We'll shower in the morning," he says as though I don't have a choice in the matter, but I decide its best not to argue with him for now.

Making do with what I call a whore's bath I wash up in the sink then brush my teeth. When I return to my man, he's kicked back naked on the bed eating the pizza from earlier.

"Need to recharge." He grins and pizza sauce drips down his chin and onto his chest.

"You need a bib." I grab a napkin from the stack on the table. "Here." I hand it to him then crawl into bed.

"We got an appointment tomorrow to look at that property I got my eye on."

"You're serious?"

"Yeah. Why wouldn't I be? Want to get both houses on the market. That's why you saw me talking to Holy's sister. She's in real estate. I'm ready to have this every night." He reaches over and pinches my tit.

"Ow. Well who said I want this every night?" I wave my hand in his direction motioning to the naked Neanderthal getting pizza everywhere.

"You did." He drops his pizza onto the nightstand and rolls over top me, planting a sloppy pizza kiss on my lips.

"Oh sick. You still got pizza in your mouth." I shove against his chest but he only chuckles. "Ugh. If this is what I have to look forward to I'm so not moving in with you, mister."

He moves away momentarily to wash down his pizza with the last of his beer. "Hate to break it to you. Not only are you moving in, but you're gonna marry me, babe." He threads his fingers with mine as he looms over me once more, pushing my legs apart with his knees.

"You asking or telling me?"

"Definitely telling." His mouth closes in on mine. "You ready?"

"For what?" My breath hitches in my throat.

"It's happening. I'm thinking tomorrow while everyone is here."

"What?"

"Yeah. Tomorrow works."

"Hello? Works for what? Am I included in this conversation?"

"Sorry. Was thinking of where I'm getting Roane to ink my brand on you."

355

"I'm not getting a tattoo."

"Yeah you are."

"No. I'm not."

"Not up for debate. I'll hog tie you if I gotta, but my name's going on your body."

"I don't need a tattoo."

"You're getting one....right..." his lips dip to my neck. One hand moves down my side and up under the t-shirt I'm swimming in trying to get away from his crazy ass. His palm splays across my ribs. "Want my name right here."

"It'll hurt."

"I'll hold your hand."

"Oh gee thanks. How mighty of you." I roll my eyes. James pushes off the bed and goes for his jeans. "Where are you going?

"Need to make sure Holy will be around tomorrow."

"Holy? Why?"

"Need him to officiate."

"Excuse me? We are not getting married tomorrow. There's a process. Documents and a license or whatever. You can't just..." he cuts me off with a kiss.

"Pretty girl, I can, and I will. So be thinking about what you want to wear."

"We can't do it tomorrow. Wylla Mae is still in the hospital."

He frowns. "You got me there. All right this weekend then."

"Slow down. We have time."

"Nope. I'm not waiting. Want my ring on your finger. My bastard patch inked on your skin."

"We've got time, James."

"There will never be enough time for me with you in this life." With that I melt under his touch and decide I'll give this man what he wants. How can I deny him after something so damn sweet?

His cell phone buzzes from the nightstand. "Lily," he mutters as he stares at the screen. "It's late." He pauses. "Right. I can do that." He makes a face and slaps a palm to the back of his neck. I watch curiously as he makes another call. "Gamble. Yeah, it's Murder. Listen, two of my guys are coming up North. Perfect, baby doll. Yeah. Talk soon."

"Is Lily okay?"

"She will be. I think she found someone she's been looking for."

"Who's that?"

"My niece."

"I didn't know Lily had any kids."

"Lily was married. Malcom couldn't handle the rape. It changed him. Changed their marriage. He became a miserable drunk. Every time he looked at her all he saw was the face of her rapist even though I killed that piece of shit. Lily wouldn't give up on him or their marriage. She loved him. Thought a baby would fix him. Make him remember the man he once was. Only when she told him he blew his brains out. She gave the kid up for adoption. Girl named Hazel, about twenty-six years old."

"And you always knew about her?"

"Lily didn't talk about it for years. Only started looking a few years ago. It was a closed adoption."

"Poor Lily."

"Yeah. It's been rough for her. Said she felt like a piece of her was missing. So when Ruthie pressed me for a kid that shit hit close. Made me think of Lily and all the hurt she carried. If I could give Ruthie what Malcom couldn't do for Lily…I thought maybe it'd fix her, but it didn't work out that way. Every time around the third or fifth month she'd lose them."

"I can understand that. I know that was hard for you and poor Lily. I almost gave Wylla Mae up, and I can't imagine my life without her." James squeezes my hand. I can't fathom what him or Ruthie even as much as I hate her went through with loss after loss. So many miscarriages. I need to change the subject. This conversation has taken such a depressing turn I want to cry. "So who's Gamble?"

"Female Prez of the Baltimore chapter of the club."

"That's interesting."

"Don't worry, babe. It ain't like that. See her like a daughter."

"I'm not worried. I know I got you wrapped around my finger." I smirk and give him a kiss that leads to a blow job to remind him anyway.

Chapter Thirty-four

MURDER

Alexa is visiting with Wylla Mae and the baby. I needed East here for church. Grudge has gone off the radar. I don't trust it. Don't trust him. Shit doesn't add up. Him losing Ruthie. He's tailed her for years under my order. Got the prospect, Rio collecting phones at the door. I sit at the head of the table watching each brother file in and take their seat. East to my right. Viking to my left. The chairs fill up. Sandman, Banks, Crawl, Slick, Holy, Roane, Hound, and Link. No Grudge.

Rio gives me a nod and closes the door. He knows the drill. That door doesn't open till church is over. No interruptions. No women. I slam my gavel on the table with our club insignia carved in the center. "Meeting is called into order. First off I want to congratulate our VP on the birth of his beautiful baby girl."

A few whistles and cheers sound. Sandman pounds his fists on the table.

"Up first is old business but Grudge isn't here to report. If you didn't notice he's been absent a lot lately. As most of you are aware, I sent Ruthie packing after the fiasco with Lynn and those cunts plotting to kill Alexa and Wylla Mae. Grudge was supposed to escort her to the ends of the Earth. Said he lost her, but I don't trust it. Truth be told there's always been some bad blood between us due to my sister, Lily, slighted him when she turned him down after her husband died. But still I trusted he'd be loyal to this club. I'm not sure that's no longer the case."

Some murmurs resonate around the table but Holy is the first to speak up. "He came to me once for counsel. Had something weighing on his heart. Affection for another man's wife. At the time I thought he had the hots for Pam. Looking back I think I had it wrong or he led me to believe what he wanted me to assume."

"Wouldn't have been Lily, that's been too many damn years ago."

"Could been he meant Ruthie. She was still your Old Lady at the time."

"What do you want to do?" East questions.

"Let's see if he turns up but Sandman and Hound want you two on the brother. Wanna know every move that bastard makes." Both men share a look then give me a nod. "New business. Viking, want you and Holy to head up north soon as we're done here. Got a call from my sister. Swing by her center. You know the place. She'll give you the details. Ride will take you to Baltimore. Gamble has extended an invitation to you two since you'll be in her territory. Banks, how's our accounts looking?"

"Everything's up to date. Bills, dues, the girls at the club are bringing in some serious cake. It all looks good, Prez."

"Anyone have anything to add? Any grievances?" I wait a beat.

Roane holds up a hand. "Just need to know what kind of tattoos you and the Old Lady are gonna be wanting, so I can get a head start on the designs."

"I'll let you know."

"Am I officiating?" Holy asks.

"Yeah, man, so don't you two be dicking around when you get to Baltimore."

"Real happy for ya, Prez," Crawl says with a chin lift. He's lucky I don't put his ass in the dirt. He dated Alexa a few years back. I'm not too damn fond of the shit

363

I heard about how he treated her or any other woman for that matter.

"Anyone else?" I'm itching to get out of here before I lay into Crawl. No one has anything to add. "Meeting's done." All the brothers file out except for East. I wait for the room to clear. "What's on your mind, VP?"

"This Grudge situation. Man never has been a fan of Alexa, but you think he's working with Ruthie?"

"Can't say for certain. I just have a bad suspicion. That prospect, Rio. Dude said he overheard him on the phone talking about shit being all good, and he'd see them soon. What's that sound like to you?"

"He coulda been talking to that granddaughter of his. What's her name, Katie?"

"Fuck. Maybe I'm seeing what I want to, but still doesn't sit right with me. Ruthie wasn't any more faithful in our marriage than I was, but Grudge is the man I had on her."

"Think he was feeding you bullshit and reporting back to her on you and the club?"

"Someone was giving her something, man. I don't know why I never saw it before now. There's something I've not shared with anyone except Alexa and Wylla Mae knows bits and pieces. Ruthie was blackmailing me." I tell him about the shit Ruthie put me through and when I'm finished East stares at his shoes.

"Damn. I think Hound and Sandman had better find Grudge and bring the bastard in for questioning."

"You got that right." I follow him out to collect our phones.

The second East slides a finger across the screen he starts cursing and puts the phone to his ear. "What happened? Slow down, baby, I can't make out what you're saying. What do you mean Mila is gone? Where's Alexa?"

I immediately dial my woman but get sent straight to voice mail. I stare at East who is glaring back at me. "What the fuck happened?"

East punches the wall next to my head. "We're too fucking late. Grudge and Ruthie disarmed the alarm on the cabin. Took Alexa and the baby at gunpoint."

Goosebumps fan up and down both my arms. "God damn I'm going to kill them."

"Not if I get to them first," East growls.

"Prospect," I roar, and Rio comes running. "Get me Hound and Sandman now." He shoots down the hall at my order. "You go to Wylla and get as much information as you can. I'm going tracking."

"I'm coming with you."

"Best place for you is taking care of my daughter."

"They got my kid."

"That kid is my granddaughter and they have Alexa. If I don't get to her, they'll kill her without a thought. Ruthie's a fucking cunt but she won't hurt a baby."

"I shouldn't have to choose between my wife and my daughter."

"No man should." Ruthie's good at fucking forcing it. I'm going to kill the bitch. Hound and Sandman come charging back down the hall. "Sandman, you're with East. He'll fill you in. Hound, brother, let's go hunting." I grab East by the shoulder. "Don't do anything stupid. I'll bring them both home. Don't worry. Just take care of my daughter and I'll take care of yours."

He gives me a nod. I hope he doesn't go rogue, but I've got more important shit to think about it.

Like all the ways I'm going to torture Ruthie and Grudge.

First, I'm going to tear off her fingernails with pliers then dip the raw bloody appendages in salt while Grudge listens to her scream. I want her to beg. Want her to suffer. Then I'll cut out her lying tongue and traitorous heart. Fry them up and feed them to the piece of shit who betrayed me and this club. I'll force him to swallow every last fucking bite. His death will be slow. Gonna bury him and Ruthie with their beloved Lion. The three of them can rot in hell together forever.

I climb on my Harley and roar out the lot with Hound, East, and Sandman. Grudge used to spend his downtime at his grandpa's cabin. It's the first place I'm checking. Should've brought a cage because of the baby but my bike is faster. The sooner I find them the quicker I get to put a stop to Ruthie for good. The world will be a better place without her in it. I've given her one too many chances. She's made a fool of me for the last time.

Chapter Thirty-five

"I think I'm gonna lay down too." Wylla Mae lets out a yawn as she places Mila in her crib.

"Get some sleep. I'm gonna finish those dishes up I spotted in the sink and put that roast I brought over in the crockpot for you and East to enjoy later. I know the last thing either of you want to do is cook."

"Thanks, Mom." She shuffles clumsily toward her bed and falls face down.

"You rest. If the baby wakes up, I'll get her. I'll take the monitor downstairs."

Whatever she replies comes out muffled as she turns to her side and snuggles in the blankets. I switch off the light and pad down the stairs quietly. It's hard to believe my baby has a baby of her own. She's married and has her own life. I'm just grateful I get to be a part of it all. We had some rough months, but we're in a good place now. Everything is finally as it should be. I have James and Wylla Mae has her Easton Reed and Mila Rochelle.

I start in the living room picking up odds and ends that have been left out. Stuff for the baby mostly. I pack it away in one of Wylla Mae's many diaper bags. She has the one in my hand, one upstairs, one in East's truck, another in her jeep, and finally there is one in my car. Mila will never be without no matter who she is with. No one will ever be loved more than this child. She's the shining star we all need. Our hope for better days.

Setting the baby monitor on the kitchen counter, I switch it on, and give the screen a quick glance. Mila wears a sleep grin on her cute little face. I pull the crockpot from one of the cabinets and grab the roast and veggies from the fridge. With the terrible schedule they've been on since they came home from the hospital the last thing a couple with a new baby needs to worry about is what's for dinner. I planned ahead and pre-cut the veggies. I wanted to make it as easy as possible for Wylla Mae but she's exhausted. I know I wasn't always the best mom. I'm hoping to make up for it now. By being here and doing the little things I wish someone had done for me when I was a young mother trying to juggle it all. This isn't the path I would have chosen for her. East isn't exactly the man I had pictured for a son-in-law considering our past. Somehow though he turned out to be the perfect man for my daughter, and in the end that's all a mother can hope for.

The lights flicker off and on a few times. I don't think there's much wind or that we are expecting bad weather. I shrug it off and start the dishwater. Suddenly the front door blows open and Grudge struts in with Ruthie hot on his heels. "Don't fucking move," he snaps, pointing a shotgun at me.

"What the hell are you doing here?"

"We're here for the baby and you." His top lip curls and he shoots me a wink. I don't know if it's meant to make me feel better or if he's just a disgusting old pig. I'm thinking a filthy old fart. I never have liked the way he looks at me with his knowing beady little eyes and narrow nose. The man was never a looker, but he hasn't aged well at all.

"You don't want to do this. You know Murder will kill you."

"Or maybe I'll kill him and take my rightful place at the head of the club. That Prez patch shoulda been mine." He jabs a finger in his chest.

"Don't be stupid, Alexa. We both always wanted the same thing. To be the Prez's Old Lady. You may have finally gotten your hooks into James, but I got the better man," Ruthie says coming further into the house. I shudder at the thought of her and Grudge sleeping together.

"Are you stupid? James never loved you. He pitied you. Felt sorry for you. The only reason we weren't together was because of you."

"Don't piss me off, *pretty girl*," she mocks the way James talks to me. "James owes me a baby, and I'm here to collect." She picks up the diaper bag on the coffee able and slides the strap up her arm.

"Wylla Mae and Mila have nothing to do with this. You aren't taking my granddaughter."

"And what are you going to do to stop me? You make one move and Grudge will blow your head off." The prick pumps his shotgun to prove her point.

I need to stall them. If I can put them off long enough Wylla will hear and call for help or East and

James will show up. Church can't last that long can it? "I get it, Ruthie. James fucked you over. Cheated on you. Made you look and feel stupid. He did it to me too. I was a little girl playing grownup games. He's your enemy in this. Not me. Rochelle was a casualty of all our actions."

"Don't. You don't talk about Rochelle. You don't get to speak of her. I let you play the victim for years. You're nothing but a dirty little whore who ruined my family. You destroyed my marriage…you took everything from me. Now it's your turn to lose it all."

"Mom, what's going on?" Wylla Mae calls out, peeping down from the loft.

"Take care of her," Ruthie barks and Grudge shifts his direction for the stairs.

"Wylla, run!" I cry and lunge for Grudge, jumping on his back. The shotgun fires into the ceiling and the baby cries.

"Get off him." Ruthie jerks me backward by my hair, ripping a strip straight from the scalp as I land on top of her. For an old bitch she's stronger than I expected. A syringe jabs into my neck then everything is lights out for me.

**

373

"Wake up," a gruff voice booms in my ear as a slap whips across my cheek.

My eyes pop open and come into focus slowly on Grudge. "You're an ugly fuck to wake up to." I go to rub my stinging cheek, but my hands are bound tightly behind my back.

Grudge smiles, makes a hocking sound, letting his spit fly at my face, hitting me in the forehead. Bile lurches in the pit of my stomach. "You don't look so damn hot yourself, sweetheart."

"What did she promise you?"

"I don't owe you an explanation, but I'll entertain you what little time you got left." He licks his lips and plugs a cigarette between them.

"Why turn your back on the club?"

"The club." he laughs. "Bastards turned their back on me years ago. You wanna know who's had my back? It's been Ruthie. We look after one another. Have for years. She was there when Bernadette died. Checked in on me. Was my shoulder to cry on. Lion was my best friend, and I promised him I'd look after his girl and his club. Murder had his chance to do right by her and he didn't. Tossed her out on her ass after all the years she wasted trying to be a good Old Lady."

"You and I both know that's bullshit."

"All Ruthie wanted was a kid to replace the one you ripped away from her. Now she's got it."

"Is Wylla Mae okay?"

"Knocked her out but she should be fine. Ruthie would never hurt Rochelle's sister."

"You think ripping her child from her at gunpoint isn't hurting her?"

"She's young and can have more kids. Ruthie can't. If you'd had another kid, we would have put our plan into action sooner. You can thank Murder for this. She did all of it because of him. Her main purpose was to keep you apart. Now that she can no longer do that, we're on to plan B. Ruthie woulda settled for Lynn's baby, but he gave Connor to Pam and Link. Ruthie couldn't do that to her friend so here we are."

They've been planning this for years.

"Isn't she beautiful, Hank?" Ruthie rocks Mila in her arms as she paces the length of the living room of the cabin they brought us to. If I get my hands on this crazy bitch, I'm going to strangle the life out of her.

"Sure is, darlin'." He blows a ring of smoke in my face.

"Don't worry, Alexa. I'll make sure my little Ro here grows up loved," Ruthie says and kisses the top of her head.

"Her name is Mila."

"That's what I said." She continues to rock my granddaughter, and I share a look with Grudge.

"She's off her damn rocker," I mumble.

"Shut up," Grudge barks.

"What's the plan here? Why take me and not just the baby?"

"All in good time," Grudge says then looks back to Ruthie.

"Go ahead. Make the call. I'm ready to finish this and leave this hell hole."

"You're the bait to get James here." He flicks the tip of my nose and pulls his cell phone out. "Got something that belongs to you. Yeah. You know the place. Come alone. No fire."

Chapter Thirty-six

Fuckin' knew that old bastard was dirty. "He's at the cabin. He's expecting me alone."

"No way, Prez." Hound shakes his head.

"You remember the place. You'll need to park at the bottom and go up the backside of the mountain. I'll ride up alone. Gotta play this shit smart and safe."

He gives me a chin lift. I dial East to update him on the situation. "How is she? Grudge called and asked to meet." I relay the details of the phone call. Wylla Mae is shaken but trying to stay strong. East wants to meet to ride with us, but there's not enough time, and I'm not waiting. "I want this done. Let's roll."

We put our knees to the breeze. Each mile of pavement bringing me closer to Alexa. Closer to finishing this business with Ruthie once and for all. Letting her go was a mistake. Trusting Grudge to do his God damn job was an error that I'll never repeat. He's going to ground, but I'll give the honor to East. I got a score to settle with my cunt of an ex-wife.

I signal for Hound to go up the other side. Not taking any damn chances. I go through the creek and up the dirt path Grudge's old man called a driveway. At the top of the path I pull up next to Wylla Mae's jeep. Stole her kid and her car. Scummy son of a bitch. I get one foot off my bike when a gunshot fires.

"That's far enough," Grudge yells from the porch. "You alone?"

"Just me and the fucking turd I got in my pocket. The fuck you think. You see anyone else?" Stupid fuck.

"Toss your weapon out."

"Look, man, I did as you asked. I'm here. Alone. No weapon. Where's my Old Lady and grandkid?"

"You can have Alexa if you do what I want."

"What's that?"

"Ruthie and me need money for our fresh start."

"You've got to be shitting me."

"Paid my dues to the club. I think I've earned a little kickback."

"Only thing you've earned is a bullet in your skull."

"No money. No bitch."

"How much?"

"Three hundred."

"Thousand?" I have to bite back my laughter. He knows the club doesn't have that kind of cash laying around. All our shit is tied up in property and the guns we run.

"That's right. For her, me, and the kid."

Now he's really starting to piss me off. "You and I both know you won't leave this mountain alive."

"I'm ready to go to hell if that's what it takes for Ruthie to get what's hers, but are you ready to send Alexa there with me?"

Fucking hell. Where's Hound? I need to keep this fool talking. "Let me see her then we can talk money."

"Bring out the bitch," he hollers over his shoulder, right at the time I see Hound crouched at the left corner of the cabin. He gives me a nod then points to the cabin before disappearing again. He's going for the baby. Alexa's rescue is on me.

The front door opens, and Ruthie drags Alexa out by her hair, they have my pretty girl bound at the wrists and gagged. I flex my fists. I've never wanted to hit a woman, but Ruthie makes me want to pop her right in the damn mouth to knock her fuckin' teeth out.

The baby cries and Ruthie turns her back on us. Alexa shoves up off the porch using only her legs and throws her shoulder into Grudge sending him toppling down the stairs, travelling with him. He loses the shotgun as Ruthie cries, "They're taking the baby." I rush forward, planting my foot on Grudge's neck while taking possession of the shotgun. I don't give him any chances. I aim at his head and blow the motherfucker to chunks. His brain matter splatters all over Alexa's face and my pant leg.

Ruthie tries to run but trips over a rock, going down face first in the dirt. I grab her up by her hair just like she did Alexa, but I'm a lot rougher about it.

She looks up at me with dirt and tears streaking her cheeks once I get her facing me. "Please, James. I didn't want to hurt anyone. All I wanted was a baby. I'll go away. You'll never see me again." She hiccups, looking bewildered. "I'll do anything. I miss Rochelle. I want a baby. I don't have anything or anyone. Please I'll leave you and Alexa alone."

"No you won't. You'll just keep on with more of your lies and bullshit. You're done for. Turn around and get on your knees." I shove her down. I press the barrel of the shotgun against the back of her head.

"Please, James. Don't. You don't want to hurt me. I gave you Rochelle. You promised me for better or worse."

"Stop your sniveling. It's pathetic."

"At least look me in the eyes. Don't be a coward."

I look back to see Hound putting the baby in the jeep. I need to see to Alexa and blowing this bitch's head off would be too easy. "Come on." I jerk her back to her feet.

"Thank you," she whispers.

I snort. "Don't thank me, cunt. I'm still gonna fucking watch you take your last breaths. Only thing that will make me happier is finally marrying the woman I really love and starting our life together. Keep an eye on her." I shove Ruthie into Hound and tend to my woman. "Let's get you cleaned up." I remove the bandanna that's tied around her mouth, use it to wipe some of the shit off her face, then work on releasing her wrists from the rope they bound them with. I carry her inside the cabin and put her in the shower clothes and all.

Alexa says nothing and I dial East. "Got'em. Tell my girl she'll be holding Mila soon. Yeah far as I can tell. Right. See you soon." I end the call and shift my focus back on Alexa.

"Can you find me something to wear?"

"On it." I leave her to finish washing off and pilfer through the cabin. There's a suitcase of Ruthie's shit next to the bed. Bitch has been hiding here. I know Alexa don't want to wear a damn thing of Ruthie's, but she can't afford to be choosy right now. Back in the bathroom Alexa's stripping out of her wet, ruined clothing, and I hand her a towel and the jeans and t-shirt I confiscated. "Put this on. East and Wylla are coming for you and the baby."

"What are you going to do with Ruthie?"

"You really want to know?" She nods. "Setting this place up to look like a Meth house gone wrong. Ruthie will burn with it."

Alexa goes pale but makes no comment.

"C'mere." I stroke the bruise forming on her jaw and she winces. "Grudge do that?"

"Yeah. I'll be fine."

"Makes me want to blow his head off all over again."

"I'm afraid that's impossible." Her lips meet mine. I kiss her hard, deep, and fast. "Get dressed." I slap her ass and go back out to check on the baby before I grab Alexa and fuck her in the bathroom.

Hound has Ruthie tied to a tree with the rope that was used on Alexa's wrist.

"How's Mila?"

"Sleeping."

"Didn't know you were good with kids."

He shrugs. "Got nieces and nephews."

"All right, man. Need to stage the scene. Grab the prospect. You two load the van. Want it to look like a Meth lab, brother."

"You good here?"

"East'll be here soon, and I got Alexa. Come back at nightfall."

Hound gives me a chin lift and jogs back the way he originally came from. There's not much traffic out here but one never can be too careful.

"I hate you," Ruthie seethes.

I look straight through her as if she's not sitting here. She wants attention, but I'm not wasting another breath on the lousy bitch.

"You won't get away with this. You'll go down. You'll see."

Alexa walks out the cabin and goes straight to Ruthie. No words pass from her lips she straight up rears her fist and lets it fly at my ex-wife's face. Not once but three times. Ruthie cries as blood drips from her nose and split lip. "First one was for taking my grandkid. The second was from me, and that third one was for Wylla Mae." My crazy assed woman doesn't stop there. She grabs her by the hair then spits in her face. "You're nothing. After today James nor will I ever think of you. We won't speak your name. No one will. You're dead."

Ruthie laughs. "He used to fuck me before he'd come to you. Hope you liked tasting my pussy all these years."

"Maybe but whenever he was inside you, he was thinking about me. It's the only way he could get off. We'd laugh about it behind your back."

"Fuck you," Ruthie spits out.

"Yeah. My man is gonna take me home later tonight and he's gonna fuck me hard while you burn in hell." Alexa smirks and blows Ruthie a kiss.

"God damn, pretty girl, you're damn sexy when you're pissed."

"Yeah?"

"Yeah, but I need you to stop getting kidnapped when I leave you alone."

"Oh fuck off."

"Gimme' that smart mouth." I pull her in for a kiss, squeezing her ass, not giving a damn that Ruthie is watching. Let the cunt enjoy the show. "Just so you know she's full of shit. I haven't had my mouth anywhere near her pussy since I first tasted yours."

Alexa rewards me with her smile. "You sucking up to me."

"Nope. Just wanted you to know that I reserved that for you."

"Hmmm," she muses. "I don't want to talk about the past anymore. I'm ready to plan our wedding. Don't think you're getting off easy. I want the fairytale."

"Whatever you want, babe. It's yours."

"Good." She kisses me again.

East and Wylla Mae come flying up the hill in his truck. He barely has it in park before my daughter is jumping out and rushing toward us. "Where's my baby?"

"Right here." Alexa opens the back passenger side door of the jeep. "She's fine."

Wylla checks over her daughter then stares at me with tears burning in her eyes. "Thank you, Daddy." Her arms swing around my neck and her lips hit my cheek. "I love you."

"Love you too, princess." I give her a pat on the back. "You and your mom take the jeep back to the clubhouse."

"I'm not leaving till that bitch is dead," Alexa says.

"Me either," Wylla Mae digs in. "I'm tired of her hurting our family."

"Guess you do take after me more than I thought, but its best if you aren't here. Anything goes sideways I want it to land on me. None of this shit touches you." I release her. "Go on. Take Mila out of here. You too, East. Get them to safety. You got a family to think about. Your mom and me got this. Ruthie is our problem."

"You sure, Prez?"

"Isn't this sweet. Look at you one big happy fucking family," Ruthie smarts off.

My daughter storms toward her. "You're poison. You've always been toxic. I'm not a violent person but you deserve whatever you get. I would say I hope my father cuts out your heart, but you don't have one. You're hollow."

"Let's go, baby." East guides her toward the driver's side of the jeep. "You good to drive?"

"I'm fine."

"Let me know when you make it to the clubhouse," I tell him.

"Will do, man." East starts toward his truck then turns back around. He stalks toward Ruthie. "Didn't get to kill Grudge," he mutters then unsheathes the hunting

386

dagger he keeps strapped to his boot. Ripping open Ruthie's shirt, he stabs her in the chest, carving out the shape around her heart. She screams, but he caps a palm over her mouth. "Guess you have a heart after all."

Epilogue

I can still smell the fumes from the fire embedded in my nostrils days after I helped Murder and other members from the club stage the cabin like a homemade Meth lab. As for Ruthie...she got what was coming to her. Bitch passed out when East took his anger out on her. James put her in the bed of the cabin and put Grudge's body on top of hers. Both of them stripped naked. Put her fingerprints on the shotgun and placed it in the bed next to her.

Ruthie came to as we doused them in gasoline. She cried, begged, and screamed for mercy but there was none to be found. Not for her. Not after everything she had done. There was no redemption to be had. The woman was pure evil. The daughter of a true demon. She was truly her father's daughter. Everything she did was to keep us apart. She didn't want a baby. She wanted to hurt us. And now…now there is nothing left of her but charred skeletal remains. In this life you reap what you sew. I lit that match and know one day I will pay for my sins, but it won't be today.

When I close my eyes, I can hear her screams as she burned alive before the cabin exploded. The flames dance behind my eyelids and the heat of the fire licks across my skin like a forbidden lover. I shouldn't smile at the thought of anyone dying, but I fucking hated her.

James grins at me as he slides onto the bar stool next to mine. "What are you so damn happy about," I ask.

"I talked to your doctor."

"What?"

"Yeah the surgeon who handled your gunshot wound."

"Why?"

"You're full of shit. He never said you can't have any more kids."

"James…"

His finger goes to my lips to silence me. "Babe. I want to make another baby with you. I want it all. My brand inked on your skin, my ring on your finger, my baby in your belly. Gonna give you the life I promised."

My heart skips a beat. Tears burn in the backs of my eyes.

"So." He removes his finger. "You gonna save yourself the trouble and agree to it all now or do I need to take you upstairs, tie you to my bed, and take what I want?"

"Damn, can I get a vote?" Pam starts in. "Because fuck me that was hot as hell. Girl, tell him no and enjoy the punishment." She cackles.

My filthy talking biker chuckles.

I cup James's face. "I love you." I plant a kiss on his lips.

"I would too if I were you."

"Asshole." I kiss him again then lean in to whisper in his ear. "What if I want you to tie me to your bed and to say yes to negotiating this baby fever you seem to have?"

His eyes go big and he says nothing. Hoisting me out of my seat and over his shoulder, my filthy biker takes me to bed to get started on all his demands.

Keep reading for a note from the author!

Author's Note

I hope you enjoyed Tempting The Biker. Alexa and Murder's story doesn't end here. Save the date, coming February 2021 Keeping The Biker, a Royal Bastards MC, Charleston, WV wedding novella available for pre-order. And I have more books in the series on the way. Viking, Holy, Sandman, Hound, and Rio could all possibly get their own books too. More to come about them at a later time. If you want to know more about Papa you can read his story Papa Noel by Nikki Landis.

Thank you for reading,

Glenna

Playlist

Wanna know what songs I listened to while writing Tempting The Biker? Check out my playlist on Spotify

Acknowledgments

Writing Tempting The Biker was a true labor of love and about drove me insane. No joke. I love these characters so much. I lived and breathed all their heartache for the past six months. I poured all I had to give into this story and the days I wanted to give up, all my people were there to cheer me on and push me to keep going. Of course my main man, Brett is always my number one supporter. I couldn't do any of this without him by my side and picking up my slack in the real world while I exist in my fictional one.

This was a challenge, as I started writing this book amidst the Covid19 outbreak. The world changed for us all. Home schooling, trying to juggle life, and all the changes thrown at us—my oldest child beginning college and sharing my office with my youngest child. It's been an adventure I won't forget.

Nikki Landis thank you so much for allowing me to collaborate with you for Papa and Colter.

To my awesome friends. Thank you. Tina and Andi this book would have never gotten completed had you not checked in on me and gave me the push to write the ugly, raw, beautiful book that is Alexa and Murder's love story. Andi keeping me sprinting till the end. Tina talking and messaging for hours with me over the fine details. Nickie and Tempi for being part of my support team and just being there when I needed a friend on the hard days. Dawn my partner in crime kept me stocked with all my favorite snacks all summer she will never admit it, but she is one of the most caring and thoughtful people in this world. Morgan who has been with me for every single book hearing every vent and crazy idea with our much needed daily phone chats. She's the only person who can get me on the phone, ha.

To all of my fellow Royal Bastards MC authors for allowing me to be a part of such an amazing world, many thanks to you guys. The bloggers and readers who share, review, and buy my work ya'll are the best, and I am so glad to have you be an integral part of my village. Jennifer and Jessica the excitement you two had for this book made me smile so much, thank you for loving my words.

I know I have missed someone, and I promise it is not intentional. I blame my writer brain. All these places and characters take up so much space in my head I do good to remember my own name some days. But I hope you know I value you.

ROYAL BASTARDS MC SERIES
SECOND RUN

E.C. Land: *Cyclone of Chaos*

Chelle C. Craze & Eli Abbot: *Ghoul*

Scarlett Black: *Ice*

Elizabeth Knox: *Rely On Me*

J.L. Leslie: *Worth the Risk*

Deja Voss: *Lean In*

Khloe Wren: *Blaze of Honor*

Misty Walker: *Birdie's Biker*

J. Lynn Lombard: *Capone's Chaos*

Ker Dukey: *Rage*

Crimson Syn: *Scarred By Pain*

M. Merin: *Declan*

Elle Boon: *Royally F**ked*

Rae B. Lake: *Death and Paradise*

K Webster: *Copper*

Glenna Maynard: *Tempting the Biker*

K.L. Ramsey: *Whiskey Tango*

Kristine Allen: *Angel*

Nikki Landis: *Devil's Ride*

KE Osborn: *Luring Light*

CM Genovese: *Pipe Dreams*

Nicole James: *Club Princess*

Shannon Youngblood: *Leather & Chrome*

Erin Trejo: *Unbreak Me*

Winter Travers: *Six Gun*

Izzy Sweet & Sean Moriarty: *Broken Ties*

Jax Hart: *Desert Rose*

Royal Bastards MC Facebook Group -
https://www.facebook.com/groups/royalbastardsmc/

Links can be found in our Website:
www.royalbastardsmc.com

About Glenna

Glenna Maynard is a USA TODAY & Wall Street Journal Bestselling Author most known for her gritty Black Rebel Riders' MC saga.

She has a passion for writing antiheroes but occasionally takes a walk on the sweeter side. Bikers, Rockstars, the boy next door, Glenna writes them all.

When she isn't arguing with the voices in her head or drinking reader tears, she enjoys watching classic TV shows with her two children and longtime leading man. Her favorite books to read change with her mood, but she always enjoys a good historical romance.

Visit https://www.glennamaynard.com for more information.

Available Now

Black Rebel Riders' MC

Grim The Beginning

Rumor

Baby

Striker

Romeo

Heart of A Rebel

A Rebel Love

A Rebel In The Roses

Blood of A Rebel

The Devil's Rebel

Devils Rejects MC

Hades' Flame

Boogeyman's Dream

Reaper's Till Death

Cupid's Arrow

Uno's Truth

Cocky's Fight

Black Rebel Devils MC

Moonshine & Mistletoe

401

Guns & Roses

Sex & Cigarettes

BRRMC Roadhouse Tales

Devil Dick

Pecker Wrecker

Cock Blocker

Sassy Pants

Sons Of Destruction

Dark Paradise: The Apocalypse

The Cruel Love Series

Cruel Love Book 1

Cruel Love Book 2

Royal Bastards MC

The Biker's Kiss

Lady & The Biker

Tempting The Biker

Keeping The Biker

Stand Alone Titles

Beauty & The Biker

Snow White & The Biker

Born Sinner

Lil' Red & The Big Bad Biker

Making Her Mine

Dirty Love

Dirty Truth

Don't Let Me Go

Jameson's Addiction

My Best Friend's Girl

Calder & Maggie

Falling For The Bad Boy

<u>Cowritten with Dawn Martens</u>

You Wreck Me (Prospects)

You Break Me (Prospects)

You Kill Me (Prospects)

Sacking The Player